ASTER WOOD

AND THE
LOST MAPS OF ALMARA

Cover art by Ken Tan

For Evan and Zoe
My little travelers

Special thanks to:

Katharine Evans
for telling the truth

Brent Taylor
for keeping me going

and
Brian Cantwell
for always believing

CHAPTER ONE

We barreled down the dirt road to my doom.

The mud-yellow farmhouse came into view behind the tired, crumbling barn. Our car blew by the bare cornfields that lined the narrow drive. I looked over at my mom, but her gaze was set stubbornly on the road.

I had wanted an adventure. But it wasn't meant to be.

I didn't want to go. I mean I *really* didn't want to go. I had tried every trick I could think of to get out of spending the entire summer at the old lady's farm. But Mom hadn't been swayed a single millimeter by my whining, my yelling, or my threats to purposely flunk out of seventh grade next year if she didn't send me somewhere, anywhere, else.

The whole situation was colossally unfair. She was unloading me during the only time of the year I might actually be able to do something normal, or even make a genuine, real-life friend. And friends were hard to come by for a kid like me. An inept, diseased heart had resulted in near total rejection by the kids in our section of the city. I had to be careful, never knowing when the ticking bomb in my chest would decide to explode, ending my pathetic existence. I sat on the sidelines, year after

1

year, as the other kids played on the yard, made friends, ran free.

Fragile, some adults might call me. *Freak* was the word the other kids would use.

I looked out the window as the fence posts slipped by. The openness of the land took my breath away, despite all my protests about being dumped out here. Dense, gray clouds billowed far away along the horizon, threatening the empty fields below. At least it was a relief to see the sky. I always felt so closed-in in the city, with its giant buildings shooting up on every side, blocking out the sun. Here there was nothing in my way; I might even be able to see some stars, something I never saw at home. I should have been happy; it was better than being stuck in the city, which would be wickedly hot come July. But I watched my mom's eyes scrutinize the dry, cracked dashboard of the borrowed sedan as we sped along, and I was miserable instead.

I had begged her to send me to camp. They had camps, even now, even for sick kids; I had seen them on the snippets of news I pretended not to watch over her shoulder. They were in some of the last places we could go to visit nature, high up in the mountains above the acid haze. Hot sun would pink our skin during the day. And at night, an unpolluted view of the sky would reveal the cosmos winking down from above. Right now I could be paddling across a lake with some other ailing, misfit kid, all my efforts focused on trying not to tip the boat.

Instead I was strapped into the burning-hot passenger seat, all my efforts focused on not screaming in frustration. We didn't have money for camp. I knew this, but knowing it didn't help.

Grandma either heard the car coming down the drive or smelled the dust in the air, because she was standing in the doorway when we finally pulled up to the front of the house. Her belly, wrapped in a faded, flowered apron, preceded her down the porch steps as she walked out to meet us.

I didn't mind the old lady, really I didn't. But as my eyes took in the abandoned farm through my dusty window, I couldn't help but blame her for her part in my summer imprisonment.

Mom unbuckled her seatbelt and opened the door.

"You coming?" she asked, eyebrows raised.

I glared back at her.

She huffed, and then hauled herself out into the hot, sticky summer air. I could hear the loud buzzing of cicadas through the door of the car even after she slammed it shut.

Grandma waved at me as she hugged my mom. Then Mom said something under her breath and they both turned to stare. I sunk deeper into my seat, trying to burrow into the quickly warming pleather. There they stood, plotting a way to make me comply, and I fumed hotter than the fast-rising oven-temperature of the car interior.

They talked for a few minutes, giving me a chance to give in, but eventually Mom resorted to the only strategy she had left. She marched up to the car, opened the passenger door and commanded, "Out."

I climbed out of the car and stood in the spot her finger had been pointing to. She pulled out my shabby suitcase from the back seat and stood it next to me, then gave me a hug I did not return.

"Love you, kiddo," she said as her fingers knotted in my shaggy hair. "Be good."

"Bye," I groaned.

"Oh, Aster," she said, taking my face in her hands. I looked up miserably into her pleading eyes. "It won't be so bad. Maybe there are some kids around here that you can hang out with."

Kids? Out here? Was she nuts?

"It's only eight weeks," she said.

"Eight weeks," I replied blankly.

I turned to face the house. Grandma smiled. I walked up to her, dragging my suitcase behind me over the cracked dirt. Despite my efforts to grimace, I couldn't help but melt a little bit at the sight of her. She opened her arms and I relented, letting her give me a big, squishy hug.

Behind me the car sputtered back to life. I turned as Mom put it in drive and rolled out of the driveway. Once she was clear of the big, dead tree that stuck up in the middle of the flat dirt lot, she hit the gas, leaving a cloud of dust where the road had been, and raced off to the airport.

I was officially abandoned.

I unloaded my suitcase up in the guest bedroom and looked around the sad, stuffy room. Wallpaper peeled from the corners, and an old clock sat still and powerless on the bedside table. A single fly buzzed up against the window, trying helplessly to get out.

I knew Mom didn't have a choice but to work. She had spent years struggling to pay the rent, on top of the medical bills, on her own after my dad ditched us. He hadn't made it through the "hospital days," leaving around the time that all my heart problems started. Mom had stayed close with Grandma, which I guess was lucky considering that she was my dad's mother, not hers. They had sat together during the long hours in the hospital waiting room after he took off.

When I was born my heart had a tiny hole poking right through its middle. It hid, undetected by doctors, until I started having trouble breathing at school. I overheard Mom crying on the phone one afternoon, a few weeks after my first surgery, telling someone on the other end that it was common for couples with sick kids to split up. She hadn't seen me peeking around the corner until the phone call ended. She tried to reassure me, as she wiped the tears from her face, that his leaving wasn't my fault. I was five.

He moved out of our city. He sent birthday cards. At least, some years.

Mom had already stopped listening to the specialists when they got to the part of assuring her that, after treatment, I would be able to have a normal childhood. She had different ideas in mind to protect me, no matter what the doctors said. From that point forward I was pretty much held under lock and key. She was forever worried that I would fall down dead if I so much as jogged across the schoolyard. Of course, I was scared, too. Years of doctors and hospitals would be enough to make anyone think twice before joining in the athletics offered at school, but it was the difficulty I often had breathing that really kept me in line. The tightness in my chest was a constant reminder: *don't push too hard.*

I looked out the small, dirty window at the remains of the fields below. The now unused farm tools lay in piles, rusting in the mud as the earth slowly swallowed them up. Grandma had continued trying to farm, even after most other people had packed it in and left. She used to have animals on the property like horses and chickens and even a pig or two at one point, but now the barn sat abandoned. I had a vivid memory, from before I got sick, of riding the old draft horse around the place with nothing but a lead rope and a fistful of mane to keep me from the seven-foot fall to the ground. It had been thrilling and terrifying at the same time, and I had wailed when they finally tore me from the big brute's back.

All the animals were long gone now, though where, I had no idea. But Grandma had stayed on. She had said that she just couldn't stand to leave the farm, no matter what dangers the rains brought. She traveled into town once a month to pick up a box of supplies, and she grew a vegetable garden out back, covered by a clear arch of plastic sheeting. But most of us, people who didn't want to take chances with the weather, lived inside the protection of the cities.

"Hey Aster." Her rickety voice surprised me, and I whipped around. "Do you have what you need up here? I thought you might want to come on down and watch my shows with me this afternoon." She looked at me piteously.

"Thanks, Grandma," I replied. "Maybe later."

She eyed me cautiously, as if she was trying to determine how to dismantle a not-entirely-lethal bomb.

"Alright, hon," she said finally, pushing her glasses up onto her nose. "You go ahead and get settled in."

While I looked at her I secretly wondered, how old *was* she? Eighty-five? Ninety? I had never asked, and I had never really given it much thought before now. It was amazing she had survived so long out here, all alone. But something in her tired eyes told me that I could expect little excitement from her. She turned and walked unsteadily back down the staircase.

As the afternoon passed, the hot sun was slowly covered by thick thunderclouds, and the bedroom gradually darkened. After I finished unpacking I flopped down onto the squeaky, lumpy mattress.

I lay back into the musty pillows as thunder boomed in the sky above and tried to come up with something to do. The pelting of rain began to beat against the window. No going outside now. I watched the drops slide down the rippled glass and rolled over, caught up in my misery. I considered screaming into my pillow just for something to do, and I was just starting to jerk it loose from underneath my head when I heard it.

BOOM.

The walls rattled around me as the sound shuddered through the house. I sat bolt upright in my bed. Was that lightning?

BOOM. BOOM. CRASH.

I jumped off the bed, alarmed. What on earth had that been? As I walked out of my room and into the hall I could hear the sound of Grandma's quiet snore from the top step; she hadn't heard the sound. The theme song of a forgotten primetime favorite whistled out of the set. So the power was still on, then. It couldn't have been lightning on the rod fixed to the roof of the house or the power would have gone out for sure. What had it been?

I looked around the hallway, but it was empty. The noise had come from *above*.

A short, dangling string hung down from the ceiling at the end of the hall. I had never been into the attic before. I tiptoed along the creaky floorboards, grabbed at the string and yanked hard. As the door squeaked open, a ladder unfolded. I carefully placed the bottom rung on the hallway floor and started to climb.

CHAPTER TWO

The weight of my feet made the boards of the ladder bend and groan. I held my breath, trying to stifle every sound I made, but my heart thudded erratically in my chest. I could hear the uneven beat in my ears, sure that it was audible beyond my own eardrums.

At the top I stuck my head up tentatively through the opening. It was hard to see much of anything at first. A hazy beam of gray light came into the space from a single window, and the dust danced in the air in its dull glow. I climbed up further and sat down on the top rung, letting my eyes adjust to the darkness. I stayed as still as I could, listening. But no other sound came. My eyes scanned over the piles of boxes and old trinkets. Nothing moved.

There in the corner, in the area right above my bedroom, was a large wooden box. It lay on its side, half broken and lid ajar. My stomach knotted. Anything could lie hidden in the shadows behind it. Maybe it was a raccoon, I thought, or possibly a rat. A really, really big rat.

I thought about running back downstairs and sounding the alarm with Grandma, but she wouldn't be able to make it up this ladder. She'd probably have to call the cops or animal control or something. What if there was nothing there? Or, worse, what if there was no one left this far out in the country to help?

I got up from the floor and carefully picked my way over to the corner of the room. I held my hands out in front of me in the darkness, ready to defend myself if the hidden beast decided to jump out and attack.

Just a few steps in I felt a tug on my pant leg and practically leapt out of my skin. I looked down and saw a floorboard jutting up through the mess, catching the fabric near my ankle. As I stooped to untangle myself, I noticed the variety of other hazards around me. Rusty nails stuck out from forgotten scraps of wood. Huge piles of books were stacked precariously on all sides. A broken lamp lay two more steps ahead. I righted myself again and continued, creeping as silently as possible towards the box.

My breathing had started up again, but the air just barely made it in and out through my clenched chest as I got closer. Since my surgery, my chest always got this way when I was nervous. My heart would cramp up when I felt threatened, or scared, or even excited. This, of course, is the last thing you want if you're facing something that could actually be dangerous. I wondered if anyone would miss me after I was eaten alive by what was now a bear-sized rat in my mind. I reached the far edge of the room and stopped.

No sound. I stood motionless except for my eyes, which darted from side to side, up the walls, along the floor, seeking the hiding menace. I peered around the backside of the broken box. Nothing. I knelt down to look inside. Empty.

I slowly let my breath out with a long sigh of relief. All I had heard was the old place, already in the midst of decay, falling apart just a little bit more. Bolted to the wall was a long shelf piled with cardboard boxes and books. Broken on the floor was another, matching shelf. It must have finally given way under the weight of decades, sending the heavy wooden box tumbling down.

Next to the box a pile of yellowed papers littered the floor. As my breathing steadied, I cleared them away to make a spot to sit and compose myself. I slumped down on the hardwood planks, and a plume of dust flew up around me.

As I looked again at the box's interior I realized that, scared as I was, I *had* been hoping that something interesting might be inside. Hidden monsters, while terrifying, were more appealing than going back downstairs to stare at the wall some more.

I crossed my legs and put my chin in my hands. Well, that had been fun. For, like, a minute. A film of dust lay over everything in the room, and I stretched out a single finger, drawing circles on the floorboard. My nail brushed across a groove in the wood, and I cleared away the dust with the palm of my hand. There in the floorboard, carved deeply into the plank, was a marking.

I got onto my hands and knees and blew into the crevices of the carving, pushing away the cardboard box on the floor next to it that was blocking the light from the window. As the dust in the air cleared, a strange design appeared.

Two long ovals crossed over each other, and a tall, deep diamond carved out the space in the center. Completing the shape at the top and bottom were two stars, mirroring each other.

I stared at it and ran my fingers along the ovals. I had never seen anything like it before. It didn't match with any of the symbols I had learned about at school. It wasn't a Roman numeral or a symbol of the

Greek gods. What other ancient types of writing were there? Maybe it was some sort of hieroglyph. But that was ridiculous. Grandma's attic was not the sort of place that a hieroglyph made any sort of sense in. Yet still, here it was.

I couldn't shake the chills that were crawling down my spine as I looked around the room. Maybe this place wasn't everything it seemed to be. Was there something here, in the attic, in the house, on the farm, that I was missing?

"How long have you lived in this house, Grandma?" I asked an hour later, between mouthfuls of sticky spaghetti. She looked up at me and then her eyes focused on a point beyond me as she thought of the answer.

"Hmmm, let's see," she said, "I moved here with your grandfather right after we were married. We moved in with his parents, which is what most young couples did back then. So that's about sixty-five, no, sixty-seven years."

"Wow," I said. "That's a long time. When was this place built?"

"Oh," she said, "your grandfather's grandparents built it, so you do the math."

I twirled my spaghetti around and around my fork. That had to be almost two hundred years back. And it sounded like the place had been in the family that whole time. I eyed her, trying to decide if I should ask my next question.

"Did anyone in the family ever do anything… strange?" I asked.

She snorted and said, "What do you mean strange? We're just farmers, Aster, not magicians. At least, we *used* to be farmers." She smiled at me lovingly. "Though you with that blond hair, *you* might have

11

a little magic in your blood."

I snorted. It was true: everyone in my family had brown hair except for me. In the old baby pictures I had seen, most people on my dad's side had white blond hair as kids that then darkened as they got older, and Mom's side of the family was almost entirely brunette. But I had always had a light blond mop on my head, a "toe-head" as some people called it, and it had barely darkened at all since I was little.

"Hair aside," I said, "was anybody in the family *not* a farmer? You know, before? Like did anybody travel a lot or disappear or do anything strange?"

"Disappear?" she asked. She thought for a moment. "Well, your grandfather once traveled to New York City," she said, "but that's not that unusual, is it? I really wanted to go on that trip with him. I was so excited about seeing the Empire State Building. But your father was just a baby and I couldn't leave him alone here with my parents; they were getting on in their years and wouldn't have been able to manage an infant on their own." She paused. Finally she said, "I've barely made it out of this town."

I stared down at my plate. My father. His mother had cared so much for him and the people around her to not leave them when they needed her most, a trait he apparently did not inherit.

"Do you ever see him?" I asked, eyes still on my marinara.

"Who, Jack? No, not for a few years now," she said quietly. "He sent me a letter a while back. Said he was getting married. Don't expect I'll ever meet her."

We both sat in silence, the weight of the conversation hanging around us.

"Your ma doesn't know," she said. "I didn't see why I would

12

need to burden her with something like that. I'm sorry. I shouldn't have said anything to you, either."

So he really had moved on for good. I stayed silent, fuming with anger at the man I hadn't seen in seven long years.

"Aster," she finally said, "I'm so sorry...about everything."

When I looked up from my plate she had tears in her eyes. My eyes fell back to the faded tablecloth. I had set down my fork, and now my fingernails were tearing the woven fabric to shreds on the edge of where my plate sat. After a couple minutes I raised my head. She was watching me, and quickly wiped a tear from her cheek.

"You know, your ma...you know she had to go, right?" she asked.

"Yeah, I know," I said.

"I know this place isn't where most kids your age would want to be for the summer, but you know she's trying as hard as she can. You know that."

I nodded. I picked up my fork and poked at what was left of my dinner. We ate in silence for a while but with much less gusto than before. Finally, I pushed back from the table.

"Maybe you should take a trip somewhere," I said, standing. "Somewhere you've always wanted to go."

"What, you mean like New York?" She smiled at me, shaking her head. "Hon, all I really want to do these days is nap and enjoy what time I have left. Besides, I doubt that the New York I wanted to see is still there." Her eyes became serious. "Things are a lot different now, you know." She shook her head slowly from side to side. "I don't need to travel all around creation at this stage of life. Not to see that. I've done my living."

13

In spite of myself, I felt sorry for her. She'd spent her whole life working here on the farm, never going anywhere, and then had watched her home slowly being ripped apart by the elements as the planet's systems had become unpredictable. And what did she have to show for her efforts? An embarrassment of a son and a falling-down house.

I looked around the old-fashioned kitchen, at the family heirlooms hung on the walls, and thought about what her life must be like now. She was all alone out here, scraping by, surrounded on all sides by ruined earth. City life was a bit drab, but it was reliable. We knew we would eat. We knew we were safe. A framed photograph of a young family sitting outdoors at a family gathering, surrounded by brilliant green grass, caught my eye. The people around the table smiled as if they were laughing at a joke somebody just told. It was a type of life I had never known.

The photo brought me up short, and the pity I felt for her swirled uncomfortably in my chest with a different emotion. The eyes in the photo shined with something I had rarely seen in my life in the city. Maybe I had it wrong. Maybe Grandma's reasons for staying so far out were more inspired than I realized. The people at the table, they looked so…happy. But it was more than that. They looked like they knew where they belonged.

"What were you doing up there in the attic all day anyhow?" she asked, snapping me back from my thoughts. I turned and brought my plate to the sink.

"Oh," I said, over my shoulder, "I'm just digging around. There's a lot of interesting stuff up there."

"Yes," she said. "Some strange treasures are up there if memory serves. Just about anything from hundreds of years ago can look so foreign to people now. You know, your great great grandfather was a cartographer. Do you know what that is?"

I shook my head as I turned on the tap.

"A cartographer," she went on, "is somebody who makes maps. Brendan Wood was his name. He used to travel all around this area, come to think of it. People would hire him to map out their plots of land for them. Most of Adams County is probably up there in that attic."

I kept quiet and scrubbed my plate with the gray, ragged sponge. I wondered if Brendan had carved that symbol into the attic floor himself, or if, in the long years that had passed since he had built this place, it had been one of his descendants to take the knife to the wood.

The rain continued, so I spent my days exploring the attic. With each new search I found more to keep me wanting to return, and I soon forgot my irritation at having been dumped on the farm. The place was full of a century's worth of discarded treasures, and I soon realized that I could have spent a year up there digging and still not have discovered everything worth discovering. This realization came on unconsciously, but within a short space of days I started burrowing like a madman, trying to solve a riddle that didn't exist. I had a strange, tight sensation in the center of my chest, one that was unrelated to my medical condition. My brain buzzed furiously all day, and thoughts of treasure teased me all night. Something needed finding in that attic, I was sure of it.

To say the attic was a magical place would not be quite the right description. The grimy collection of prizes did not seem to go together. Curious things were mixed right in with the ordinary. A broken compass folded in with a box of old clothes. A tiny, and curiously bright, white stuffed bird perched on top of a stack of books. A perfectly round, smooth ball of some kind of stone I had never seen. An old jewelry box with an assortment of broken gold necklaces snarled into an impossible knot the size of my fist. The place was on my mind twenty-four hours a day, and I always wanted to be up there. As the days passed I forgot about the possibility of leaving the house at all. Mom would have been downright proud of my lack of adventure.

On my fourth day in the attic, I was looking through the items on the shelf next to the one that had fallen down. A pile of old papers was stacked up along one side, and propped up behind them like a plate on a wall was a large framed picture of a ship. When I moved it down from the shelf to take a closer look, a squiggly painted line emerged on the wall behind it. It was the width of my finger and ran up and down right behind where the painting had been.

The old papers, a box of used clothing and several poster tubes came down and made a pile at my feet. The more I unloaded, the more of the drawing I could see. After half an hour of relocating stacks and stacks of ancient junk, I could see the entire wall.

It was a map.

But it was a map of no place I had ever seen. It looked vaguely like a squashed combination of North America and Australia, but there were no words to clue me in about what location it showed, only lines. I knew my geography pretty well; all those hours after school and lunches on my own in the library had resulted in braniac grades in all my subjects. But this was an outline I had never studied before.

In several places on the map, golden rings were painted within the black borders. The paint the mapmaker used was some sort of metallic, because the rings had a strange flicker to them. They reminded me of sun reflecting on water. I looked around the room, trying to figure out if maybe something shiny was reflecting a sunbeam onto the wall. But then I realized it was still raining outside.

"Ouch!"

As I backed away from the wall, my hand struck the corner of a sharp piece of wood. I cradled it to my chest and spun around, looking for the offending piece of junk I had knocked into. It was the big wooden box that had fallen on my first day up here, still in the place it had landed when the old shelf had given way. I bent over, grabbed the sides of the box and heaved it upright.

I slapped my hands together and a cloud of dust filled the stale air. Poking out from between two slats of wood in the back of the box was a small corner of parchment. I hadn't seen this before; after the box fell I hadn't bothered to investigate it further.

I knelt down and gently tugged on the paper. It took a little bit of back and forth, but after a minute it gave way and I was holding an old, crumpled envelope. There was no writing, but on the backside it had a deep red wax seal, like the kinds I'd seen illustrated in history books about the middle ages. Pressed into the wax was a design, and I gulped as I recognized the now familiar oval and diamond shape, the same one that was carved into the wood beneath my feet. The seal on this envelope had never been broken. Could that be right? If so, then that meant that nobody but the person who wrote this letter had ever seen what was inside of it. Nobody.

I looked around the attic. I was a little nervous about being the first person to open it; it didn't belong to me, after all. But curiosity got the better of me, and I carefully slid my thumb under the seal. It gave way with a surprising little pop. I opened the flap of the envelope, and read the writing on its underside:

> *Dare free what lies within*
> *And see where we have been*

Huh, I thought. The writing was mysterious enough, but the ink had a strange flickery glow about it. Just like the golden rings on the wall behind me, the words on the page shimmered brightly, though this part of the attic was quite dark. What did it mean? Was some ill fate awaiting me if I opened what was inside?

I decided that I would simply *have* to open it. It was just an old letter, anyhow, I told myself. My heart did not hear my brain's logic, and it pounded in my chest with excitement. I slipped the parchment from the envelope and unfolded it, taking care not to tear the ancient document. I opened it along each crease, spreading it out on the floor in front of me.

It was blank.

I stared, feeling a little cheated. What was the point of going to all the trouble of saving a blank piece of paper for what looked like hundreds of years? I smoothed the parchment and knelt closely over it, looking for clues to its secret. Old and discolored, its edges ripped, it matched the paper that made the envelope. I pressed my nose close to every inch of the page, looking for any marking or indentation. Nothing. I sat back on my heels and blew out a long sigh of frustration.

Then I saw it. Writing was appearing on the page, as if from an invisible hand. I watched, my jaw dropping open, as the same gold ink traced the outline of the first oval.

I grabbed the paper off the floor and raced across the room, holding it up in the hazy, overcast daylight coming through the high window.

My chest slowly unclenched beneath my shirt as my shock turned to wonder. The second oval and the diamond were completed now, and the invisible pen drew the tiny stars on the top and bottom of the symbol. I stared, unblinking, at the paper, as the next set of lines appeared, letters in ornate script.

GO

The writing stopped.

"Go," I began, "What on earth does…"

But I was cut short.

A light as bright as the sun burst from the page, and I put one hand up to shield my eyes. Around me the contents of the attic moved inward. And then with a deafening BOOM they exploded away from me.

All was brightness. All was light. I spun in space. Where had the floor gone? My insides were stretched and then squashed and then stretched again. I closed my eyes to keep from getting sick.

And then, blackness. Under my cheek I felt cool, wet earth.

I was lying, face down, on grass.

CHAPTER THREE

My chest felt tight.

I opened my eyes.

My left cheek was pressed into damp ground. Little bits of silver and white twinkled in front of my face in the dim moonlight; water droplets hung off each strand of grass. I put my hands next to my shoulders and pushed myself upright, the parchment still clutched in my fist. Sitting back, I gaped at my surroundings, wiping the water vigorously from my cheek with the back of my sleeve.

Where *was* I?

In front of me swayed an ocean of deep green grass. The blades moved back and forth with the frigid breeze that blew against my back. I was surrounded on three sides by hills that rolled away into the distance. Behind me a dark grove of trees stretched out. And above, the night sky was brighter with stars than I had ever seen, even in books.

Panic filled my stomach and spread through my body, clenching every muscle it touched, until even my throat began to close up in protest.

Ninety seconds ago I had been in the dusty attic. Now... My

breathing started coming in short, panting breaths and saliva filled my mouth. I didn't want to vomit, but the panic was rising, pushing itself against my tightened throat. I turned over and rested on my hands and knees just in case I blew.

This was *not* good. Not not not good. I closed my eyes and shook my head back and forth, but when I opened them again the dark earth was still right there between my outstretched fingers.

It had been early afternoon in the attic.

The grass swirled as my stomach bucked. Everything around me seemed to be swimming. I immediately wanted to be bored again, back in the guest bedroom watching the house slowly crumble around me. Was I hallucinating? Maybe I had fallen down and hit my head or something and this was some sort of dream.

I turned around once more to scan the area. Was there some clue out there? Something I had missed? But the land was completely solitary, empty.

And *alive*.

I didn't know grass still grew like this. I had seen grass, of course, but only the short, coarse kind that grew in the park in the center of the city. This grass was wild and tall, humming with vibrance.

I stood up and ran over to the trees, immediately winded by the effort.

"Hello?" I wailed out into the forest. No answer.

I ran back into the grass, searching in the darkness, willing my eyes to find...*anything*.

There was nothing out there.

My skin broke out in a cold sweat and I began to shake. I fell back down to my knees and then slumped to the ground, pressing my cheek to the cool dirt, trying not to pass out. I waited for my breathing to slow.

Wake up, wake up, wake up.

It was cold. Much colder than back on the farm. My body was wet with the sweat of panic, and my clothes clung to my body. I shivered.

What is going on?

While my body lay there in shock my brain operated behind the scenes. I couldn't stay here, no matter where here was. Out in this wind I would freeze. And who knew what lived in those trees? I had to get moving and try to figure this out.

I must have hit my head.

But I couldn't remember falling.

I needed to decide what to do next, but I didn't know *what* to do. I was used to doing what the grown-ups told me. There were no grown-ups here. There wasn't *anyone* here.

Grandma hadn't been into the attic, so she didn't see. Had I disappeared?

Half-formed plans and panicked thoughts fought for attention in my mind. Minutes, or maybe hours, passed as I faded in and out of conscious thought. Eventually, I heaved my shaking body back up to sitting. My hand slowly unclenched around the parchment.

Parchment that was now covered with writing.

I thrust it up in front of my face. It was the same, ripped sheet I had held back in the attic, but now every inch of the thing was covered in lines and notations.

How is this happening?

It was a map. I ran my finger along the dark ink, just visible in the moonlight. Large letters blazed across the center: *Aerit Range.* Landmarks dotted the page. A grove of trees, an open plain, and what looked like foothills leading to a mountain range. In the center of the paper was a small, square outline of what was unmistakably a house. And in the center of that square a golden ring was painted in the now familiar glittering golden ink.

Then the pain struck me. Searing like a dagger through my heart, my nerves radiated misery out from my chest into my arms and legs. My throat was closing, and I slumped over again, writhing in misery. Air. Air was the elixir I needed. Cool, beautiful air needed to fill my lungs, but I couldn't find it. I couldn't breathe.

I shouldn't have run, even just over to the trees. I know better than to run.

Then I remembered what to do. I rolled onto my back, tilted my head slightly backwards, and repeated the mantra of my mother in my brain.

Breathe slow. Breathe calm. Breathe slow. Breathe calm. Breathe slow. Breathe calm.

But I was too late. Panic and exhaustion took over.

As I stared up at the bright, starry sky, the world around me went black.

I yelled out in my sleep, startling myself awake. I saw the white underside of the sheets of my bed. I was so warm, burrowed deep, and I closed my eyes again, peeking my face out for some cool air. I tucked my head back into the pillow, pulling the blankets up and settling in again. It had just been a dream.

"Mom?" I called quietly. I felt a cool washcloth pat against my forehead. Comforted by her presence, I rolled over, bringing the blankets higher to cover my ears and head, only leaving enough space for my nose and eyes to stick out from my cocoon. I breathed deeply, relishing the delicious feeling of being so snug and safe. The nightmare was over.

A snuffling noise circled around my head, and a warm breath blew against my face. A hot, wet something moved over my nose and forehead. This didn't make sense. Was she using a different washcloth? I opened my eyes and an inch from my face was the open mouth and lolling tongue of a gigantic dog.

We didn't have a dog.

A warm hand patted mine, and my head whipped around. An ancient, gray man was sitting on the other side of the bed. My eyes darted all across the room as I backed myself up against the headboard, away from the man and the dog. He stood up and peered down at me.

"It's alright, boy," he said. "I expect you just got a hit on the head is all." He walked around the bottom of the bed, the dog following at his heels.

I hadn't hit my head, but I may as well have considering the fact that this dream, or hallucination or whatever was happening to me, seemed to be continuing. I stared around the room, still so surprised that I was unable to speak. Large stones stacked precariously upon one another, making up the walls of the tiny space. Mounted to the walls were paintings; horses and flying creatures I did not recognize were represented in excruciating detail on the canvases.

Across from the bed, a fire crackled in the grate, and over it hung a large, black cooking pot. The smells of a savory meal and burning wood drifted by my nose. On the other side of the room stood a long, wooden table piled high with leather bound books and several bowls. A couple of chairs were scattered about the place, with the largest positioned in front of the fire. Through the window beyond, tree branches swayed in bright daylight.

I brought my knees up against my chest, wrapping my arms around them, and looked at the man.

I met his gaze, steely blue eyes, and asked, "Where am I?"

"What I'd like to know," he said, "is *who* are you?"

He was very, very old, but had a hardy, stout look about him. His hair was long and gray, tumbling past his shoulders, framing his face. His silver beard mirrored the hair on his head and grew so long that it almost rested in his lap where he sat. Two hands with knobby fingers and silver rings now scratched the dog under his chin. He wore gray woolen pants, suspenders and a long sleeved shirt, all stained brown by earth.

"I came here…um…by some sort of magic, I think." I couldn't think of a better explanation, and I hoped he wouldn't think I was crazy. "Where are we?"

The old man cracked a smile, his eyes twinkling.

"So you're a traveler! I thought I heard your entry last night." He poked the fire with a long, metal rod that had stood propped up next to the grate. He turned back and looked at me expectantly. "Where you headed?" The dog walked around the edge of the bed and, turning twice, settled himself into a heap, resting his head on his paws.

"Headed?" I asked

"Yes!" he boomed. "What is your destination? Your target? Where are you bound, as they say?" and he clapped his hands smartly and rubbed his palms together, waiting for my answer.

"Um," I said. "I don't really have a destination."

"Ah, just out on an adventure, are ya?" he said. "Good boy.

You're a young man, after all. That won't last forever, you know, not forever!" He stood and walked across the room to the table, gathered an armful of apples and two mugs and strode back to the fire.

"Well," I stumbled, my mouth already watering at the sight of the apples. I was suddenly starving. "I wasn't really trying to have an adventure. I mean, well, of course I wanted to have an adventure, but—" I paused, trying to make sense of my thoughts. "This sort of thing isn't really normal where I come from."

He set down the mugs on the shelf in front of the fire. "Well, you've gotten yourself into quite a pickle then, haven't you? Where did you say you were from?"

"Well, normally I live in the city with my mom, but this summer —"

"No, I mean what *planet* are you from?"

What planet was I from?

"Earth." It was an answer, but it sounded like question coming out of my mouth.

"Earth!" His eyebrows raised high on his forehead. "Well, that explains some things, don't it?"

Did it?

"What planet did you think I was from?"

"Well, you're sittin' on Aerit right now, so how do I know? Travelers come from all the planets around these parts. Don't mean I know which ones just by lookin' at 'em."

"I'm on another *planet*?" Fear and amazement wrestled for attention in my brain.

"'Course you are! Does this look like Earth to you?"

"But that's impossible!" I protested. "I can't be on another

26

planet." But as I looked over at the man, his sparkling eyes poked a hole through my certainty.

Was this really true?

"But, how—I don't understand—how did I get here?"

"Whatcha mean?" he asked. "Obviously, you took a link."

We looked at each other, and I tried to work out what was going on. Now, with him telling me I wasn't on Earth, I felt different, not quite as terrified as I had the night before. It was an explanation, if nothing else. As for the matter of how I had managed to get here, that I couldn't comprehend at all.

He took a big bite of one of the apples. I was distracted by his crunching despite my efforts to stay focused. My stomach rumbled loudly.

"Um, sir?" I asked.

"Sir?" he laughed. "Don't call me sir! I have names! Call me Kiron. It's just one my seven. Kiron's always been my favorite. Better than Rupert, at least."

"Uh, ok then," I said. "Kiron, can I have one? I haven't really eaten since early yesterday and—"

Before I could finish he picked up an apple and tossed it across the room to me. My hands whipped out and caught it with an ease that surprised me. But I was too hungry to question this temporary increase in my coordination. I greedily bit into it, the sweet juice running down my chin.

"Hungry, eh?" he asked. I nodded. He took a bowl from the shelf and, drawing out a long ladle from the cooking pot, spooned some of the contents into it. He plunked a spoon into the bowl and set it on the small table next to the bed.

"Thank you," I said, between enormous bites of apple. My crunching had alerted the dog, and he now stood at the side of the bed, his long, pink tongue hanging out the side of his mouth. Tiny bits of drool dropped to the wood floor as he watched me eat with ferocious concentration.

"You know my name now," he said as I ate. "What might yours be?"

"Aster," I said. "Aster Wood."

His jaw dropped open, and it was a few long moments before he was able to close it again. I was too distracted by the delicious smell coming from the bowl to pay this much attention. I picked it up and started spooning a thick meat stew into my mouth.

"Huh," he said, as he leaned forward, tugging on his beard with his gnarled fingers. Then he stood up and started pacing around the small room.

"Your say your name is 'Aster Wood'?" he asked.

I nodded again, mouth too full to speak.

"Not 'Brendan Wood'? You sure?"

I stopped eating. "How do you know that name?" I asked. Grandma had told me about Brendan Wood just yesterday.

He peered down at me with a look that indicated he couldn't decide whether I was being earnest or playing a game.

"It's Brendan I've been waiting for all these years, must be a century or more," he said.

I gaped at him, my stew forgotten. "How old *are* you?"

"HA!" he boomed. "Older than you can count, boy!" Then he stared into space as he thought. "You was supposed to be Brendan Wood. And now you're finally here and you're Aster Wood. Don't make no sense."

"Brendan Wood was the name of my great, great grandfather," I said.

"But then, you *know* Brendan Wood?" he asked.

"No," I said slowly, wondering if maybe he was a bit mad. "He died way before I was ever born."

His face fell.

"Brendan Wood is *dead*?"

"Well, yeah," I said. "He was ancient. I mean, he lived a *really* long time ago." I considered this shaggy man, who was claiming to be well over a century old, and I wondered if a hundred years counted as a long time in this place.

"And you are descended from Brendan Wood, you say," he was mumbling more to himself than me now. "I got the wrong damn Wood." He studied my face, peering into my eyes.

"What do you know about Almara?" he said.

"What's…Almara?" I asked.

He looked at me in shocked, almost offended, disbelief.

"Why, he's a great seer, ain't he? How can you be a Wood and not know about Almara? Your own kin? Most powerful of the wizards that left for the Fire Mountains hundreds and hundreds of years back."

A wizard? My own *kin*?

"Is he a…friend of yours?" I asked.

"Naw, naw," he said, waving his hand. "My folks knew him, though, when they were real young."

"And you think that I'm *related* to this Almara person?"

"How do you not know this already?" he asked in return. "I thought there wasn't another soul left alive that hadn't heard the story of

Almara. And here you are, descendant of Brendan Wood and all, and clearly you jumped here, and you're telling me you don't know any of it? Why, he's a great—" he paused, studying me yet again. "You really don't know?" he finally asked.

"No," I said, staring.

His eyes slowly fell to the floor and he grimaced. It was a look I often saw on the faces of my classmates during difficult exams.

"But how can you not know?" He spoke more to himself than to me and shook his head slowly from side to side. Finally, he looked up at me again, studying my face. "You're not foolin' me, are ya? This isn't one of Larissa's tricks? Cause if I find out that old bat sent you here, I swear I'll—"

I shook my head.

His shoulders sagged as he gave in. He couldn't find the lie he sought in my face.

"Alright, let me think," he started, and stared into space. "I take it you ain't never traveled before, eh?"

"Traveled?" I asked, thinking of the images of camp on the TV news. "No, not really."

"Alright. This place," he gestured at the room around us, "this place where we're sittin' is a planet in the Maylin Fold, Aerit. Our closest neighbors here are Aeso and Aria. The three together are called the Triaden cause they're so close, easy to travel between. How you hopped a link to Aerit all the way from Earth I ain't got no idea. Earth is so far out, I ain't heard of anyone traveling to or from there in a long, long time. Not since Brendan."

What?

He continued. "Aerit and all the planets in our part of the

universe are tied together like a string of pearls."

"Like a solar system?" I asked, grasping for a piece of knowledge I understood. I had known about solar systems since the first grade.

"No," he said. "It's nothing like a solar system. Every planet in the Maylin Fold orbits around a different star."

I frowned. "I don't get it."

"Here, lemme show you." He stood up and snatched a piece of blank paper from the wood table, crumpling it into a tight ball as he returned to his seat by the fire. Then he took the metal fire skewer and stabbed through the center of the ball. When he removed the stick, he uncrumpled the paper and held it up for me to see. Several holes were pierced through the page in various locations.

"This paper represents space, the holes, planets. To most minds, traveling from one area to the next means you go in a straight line from place to place." His forefinger drew a line from a hole on one side of the page to a different hole on the other. "But travel like that takes a ton of energy, and more importantly, time. Time that none of us have, not even the most talented wizard."

He set the paper down at the foot of the bed and slowly began to crumple it back into a ball.

"As luck would have it, space isn't flat like the page of a book. It's dented, crumpled, folded together in ways more complicated than you can imagine. But you see," he squashed the wad of paper tightly in his gnarled fist, "now those holes are together again just as close as can be. That is the Fold."

"And you can travel between the planets as long as they're in the Fold?" I asked.

"Well, you should know since you just did it yourself. But yeah, you're gettin' it."

I picked up the ball of paper and opened it back into a square, amazed. "How many are there? In the Fold, I mean."

"Planets? Dunno. Least a thousand. But only fifty or so you or I could walk on." He paused, twirling his beard around his fingers.

"Now, here in the Triaden, a few hundred years back things were looking pretty bleak. The plants were all dyin', people were hungry. The weather started doing some pretty strange things. We'd have hot sunny days during the winter months and snow during the summers. Right as the farmers would sit back to watch the baby sprouts start to raise up out of the ground, the snows would come and kill all the new growth. Some places had horrible droughts that lasted decades and drove the people from the lands. Some had torrential rains that turned the land to mush and drowned whole towns while they slept. People were scared."

I gulped and forced a large mouthful of stew down my throat. I had heard a story just like this before, but it was back in history class. That story, of course, had been about Earth.

"But the problem went much deeper than just the weather," he went on. "The sickness was affecting the people, too. Not all common folk know this, but the people were gettin' as sick as the planets."

I stared at him, transfixed. The dog whined at my half-eaten bowl of stew.

"Some died. Some of 'em went mad. Some turned real nasty almost overnight. There was a sort of a shift in the feeling of the place. People went from being good neighbors to shuttering themselves inside every night. Ya just didn't know what to expect."

"Did everyone get sick?" I breathed.

"No, that was the thing. The sickness didn't kill or change everyone, but everyone felt the effects of it just the same. That's why Almara and the eight were so spooked. He was the high seer, ruled over the council of eight. They all kept court at Riverstone, the great castle in the far western lands on Aria. They were Sorcerers, all of 'em, the biggest congregation of magical blood in a thousand years. But none of 'em knew where to start. It wasn't like they could just shout up at the sky and make it stop snowing. Nobody even understood what was happening. That was their quest, to discover the truth about why everything had gone haywire. And then figure out how to fix it. After a time, word got back to my folks that they were heading for the Fire Mountains. But no word ever came again. A few years after that, things started changing. The snows stopped coming so often. The suns in the winter clouded over like they should. The fruit started falling from the trees again."

"What about the people?" I asked. "Did they get better, too?"

"A bit, I suppose." He sipped at his tea, thinking. "Nobody knows what happened to Almara and the eight. Some say they died. Some say they found the magic they were looking for and set everything right. And it's true; things *are* better now. But they never returned."

"But of course they must have died," I argued, "if they lived hundreds of years ago."

"Not likely," he answered. "A man with power as great as Almara, I wouldn't be surprised if he's still trekkin' about. A talented wizard can live hundreds, if not thousands, of years."

He set down his mug and prodded the fire with the metal stick. "It makes me wonder, though, why *you're* chasing Almara. Especially since nobody's trained you up. And all the way from Earth, too."

"I'm not chasing anyone. I found this, well, this map in my

Grandmother's house. And I looked at it and read it out loud. And next thing I knew I was lying in grass, which is odd because on Earth there isn't—"

He choked on a sip of tea and stood up abruptly from his chair, his eyes wide.

"Boy!" he exclaimed. "You must have found Almara's first link!"

"What?"

"The map!" he bellowed. "I figured you found some old link of Brendan's or something, came here by accident, but what you're describing ain't no ordinary link, and it ain't no ordinary map. It was one of *Almara's*. So you really are meant to follow him!" His face broke into a wide, relieved smile. "I was beginning to think that the maps were lost forever."

"Wait, what's a 'link'?"

"It's the connection between planets. It's how you got here. And before Almara set out, he made a set of links for his son Brendan to follow. But these weren't just links, they were maps, too. Whoever used 'em could jump from place to place and follow the quest. The maps didn't have nothin' on 'em when Almara left, but as he traveled they filled themselves in, keeping a record of where he went. Not just anyone could get their hands on the first one, it's locked by a powerful magic, but *you did*."

"His *son* Brendan?" This conversation was quickly spiraling out of control, and a note of panic crept into my voice, the temporary comfort of the warm bed forgotten. "Look, I've never heard of Almara. He's not part of my family, and I'm not looking for him. This is just a mistake. I think I should just go back home and—"

"Listen, whether you know it or not, Almara is your ancestor. I guess, then, that whatever power Brendan had must have been passed down to you. It ain't no mistake, believe me. You finding Almara's map means that you're destined to follow him. Though it doesn't explain why Brendan didn't come back, himself..."

His eyes scanned the room and fell on the parchment I had found in the attic.

"Ah!" he said and, crossing the floor, picked up the crumpled page from the chair next to the bed. "This was next to ya on the ground last night when I found ya. It's the map, you say? Here, I'll show you what I mean." Then he stopped and stood still as a statue, his mouth wide with surprise.

"*Gold*," he breathed. He ran his fingers across the symbol at the top of the page.

"Yeah, so what?" I said, too irritated to care about the look of wonder on his face. His wide eyes looked into mine, but only briefly before they were drawn back down to the page like a magnet.

"Ain't never seen gold," he said.

"You've never seen *gold*?" Gold was valuable on Earth, but still relatively common. I remembered the tangled ball of necklaces from back in the attic, carelessly tossed into a box.

"Heard of it, of course," he said. "Can't make an interplanetary link without it." He tore his gaze from the page and held it out to me. "This is *here*."

"It is?" I asked, reaching for the paper.

"Look!" He brought the map over to the other side of the bed.

He was right. On the parchment a detailed representation of the very room we were in had appeared, erasing the marks from the night

35

before. And right in the center was that single, glowing ring of gold.

"I can't believe this is finally happening," he murmured.

I had had enough. Sickening twists of my stomach, magical inking maps, relatives from other planets. I slumped back into the bed and put the pillow over my head. This *couldn't* be real.

He was tugging at the ends of the pillow, but I fought to keep it over my face.

"Boy, you'd better come to terms with this. Whether you like it or not, you'll be questing to find Almara." But I won the pillow battle and he stopped trying to take it. I felt him sit on the edge of the bed, and I could hear his muffled voice through the feathers.

"When I was a boy, my father taught me all about Almara. About the quest, about the eight, everything I just told you. But when I got older he shared our family secret with me, the reason why we lived out here in the fields, waiting. It was the duty of my family to wait for Brendan Wood to return, and to help him along his way to get back to his father."

I peeked out from behind the pillow.

"Now," he continued, "you're tellin' me that Brendan Wood is long dead, that you're his descendant, and that *this map* is the thing that brought you here. That means that *you* are the one meant to find Almara. *You* are the one who needs to find the other links and catch up with him. *You* are the one I've been waiting for all these years."

"That's impossible," I said stubbornly. "I'm from *Earth*, not Aerit. My great great grandfather Brendan Wood was from *Earth*."

Wake up. Wake up. Wake up.

He shook his head sadly, and the look on his face filled my stomach with lead. I didn't know if this was real, everything that was happening to me, but if it was, who was to say that he wasn't telling me the truth? Was I really descended from this other world I was now walking around in?

While I thought about this possibility, he stood up and began shuffling around the room, rummaging through papers and trinkets. From the shelf above the counter in the corner he took down several glass jars. They reminded me of Mom's spice rack back in our apartment, but these held leaves and twigs that looked nothing like her basil.

I sat up and swung my legs around the side of the bed. My socked feet found the wood floor and I walked over to the table.

"What are you doing?" I asked.

"Gotta get you ready to go," he said.

"I can't go anywhere," I argued miserably. "I'm sick."

He stopped his shuffling and looked me up and down.

"You don't look sick." He retrieved a large, battered book from underneath the bed and heaved it onto the table.

"Well," I argued, "I *am* sick. Too sick to be following the trail of some lost sorcerer on some other planet. I need a doctor."

"Ha! You ain't gonna find a doctor around here." He began leafing through the tissue thin pages. "Anyways, you look fine to me." He wasn't even looking at me.

"But," I argued, "if I keep going like this I could have another cardiac episode and die. I can't go on some quest. I can't do anything." I slumped back onto the edge of the bed.

"Well, that's the dumbest thing I ever heard! You have to go! Ain't no one else gonna be able to find 'em. It's your job and your birthright." A glint of mischief crossed his eyes, just for a moment. Then he looked back down at the book and said, "Besides, I don't expect you have much of a choice. How were you planning to get home, anyways?"

I studied the dark grooves in the floorboards. "Can't you send me back? If you know so much about this traveling stuff, then you should be able—"

"HA!" he laughed. "I can plot links, kid, but not links so far as Earth. If I tried to send you back you'd end up in deep, dark space more likely than not. Earth is unstable, out on the far reaches of the Fold. It's constantly moving. No, you need a master cartographer to get you home. I mean, well, I done a spell or two in my day, and I'm a talent to be reckoned with when it comes to growing food and, you know, some other…essentials. But I ain't got power like that." He continued to read, his attention flitting between me and the book.

"Well, how am I supposed to get back home then?"

"The only way you're gettin' home is to find Almara. Sounds like you ain't got a choice but to move on, don't it? And it's my job to get you closer to him."

"But I can't move on, don't you get it?" I said. "Even if I were related to Almara, I can't keep running around like this. I'll fall down dead before I ever find him."

"Hogwash!" he boomed. "Besides," he peered down at me, "that stew wasn't just plain stew. I knew you were in trouble when I dragged you in here last night. Worked a bit of my own magic over the pot before I let you slurp any of it up."

"You…drugged me?"

"What? Nah! I gave you the medicine you needed to recover. And now you're just fine, ain't ya?"

I stood there, partly angry, and partly curious. I did feel better, loads better, than I had yesterday. Here I was, standing, arguing with the old man. My heart rate had stabilized, and my chest didn't feel tight with the panic of the previous day.

"Well," I said, "I guess I feel alright. But, you know, I really shouldn't be going anywhere until I've—"

"You'll be goin' whether you think you should or not," he said. "If you want my help to get you to the next link, then you gotta do your part. You sure do argue a lot for a Wood."

He turned his back on me and rummaged around a bit more. Then his hunting stopped. "Yeah," he said, "I ain't got the acorns."

"What do you mean?" I asked.

Ignoring my question, he grabbed a piece of parchment from under a stack of books on the table, retrieved a long feather quill and began to scribble on the paper. "You need to go…here." He had drawn a rough map on the page, and pointed his finger now at a large X off to one side.

I looked over his shoulder at the drawing.

"What's there?"

"The largest oak in spittin' distance. You need to go get me as many acorns as you can carry."

"What are you going to do?" I asked.

"I got real work to do, boy. You'll see when you get back."

He finished writing, then walked to the door and picked up a large, woven basket that was fashioned to be slung on a man's back.

"Here," he said, "put this on."

I hesitated to do as he said. My eyes peered through the small window that looked out over the garden. The afternoon sun shone on the vegetables out front.

"I don't know," I began.

"Kid," he said, "do you want me to help you or not?"

I did want him to help me. But I also wanted to stay alive.

"Yes, but—"

"Get over here, then."

I trudged over and he roughly strapped the enormous basket to my back. It was lighter than it looked, but awkward to wear, and I stumbled to the side as the back end of the thing stuck out, throwing me off balance. Then he stuffed the parchment in my hand. "This'll get ya around the place, I expect."

I looked at the paper skeptically.

"Gather every acorn you see or can get to; we need just the right one. When the basket's full, you come on back. I got things need tending to around here before you can get movin' on the next jump."

"But, wait, you know where I'm supposed to go next?" I asked.

"You just worry about what I tell ya to, and I'll worry about gettin' ya on the trail. Alright?" He stood back and put his hands on his hips, clearly not interested in any answer but the one he wanted.

I nodded, feeling dejected.

"You're sure I'll be ok?" I asked. My hands folded over my chest protectively.

I swear he practically threw me out the front door as he said, "Be back my sundown. Got it?" And he slammed the door in my face.

CHAPTER FOUR

I stared at the front door, trying to decide what to do. A little window was set at eye level on the wood. As I studied it in a daze, the door to the peephole opened and Kiron shouted through it.

"Get out of here, boy!" He closed it with a snap, and I could hear him mumbling in irritation on the other side of the entry.

This guy was crazy, no doubt about it. Here I was on some alien world, a world Kiron thought had produced my ancestor. Crazy. But as I looked up at the sky, a strange teal-blue, a tiny finger of doubt scratched at my brain. What if I was the one who was crazy? Or, at least, what if I was wrong?

I turned and walked down the front steps, where I found my boots. Sitting, I laced them up and stared around at the tiny homestead.

A large vegetable garden grew directly in front of the house. Surrounding it was a tall, mesh fence, but no plastic like at Grandma's. The rains must be safe here, then. I remembered Kiron's story about how the weather had returned to normal after Almara set out. But a lifetime of avoiding toxic rain had me looking skyward, and I was relieved that not a single cloud floated in the sky above.

To the side of the house was a chicken coop made from an assortment of leftover pieces of wood. Five fat hens clucked their way around the yard, scratching and digging, and one enormous rooster kept watch over his girls. I had never seen a chicken up close before; farmed chicken and fish were the only foods that were grown outside the city and trucked in. I took a couple of curious steps in their direction. The rooster immediately puffed up his feathers and ran straight for me. Surprised, I simply stood there and watched him bear down upon me. He squawked and bit at the leather of my boots, the toughness of which I was quite thankful for at the moment. It would have been funny, but he wouldn't stop coming for me, and I felt strangely alarmed at this small, vicious animal. I flailed my legs as he attacked, trying to get him to let go of my pant leg, but in the end he successfully chased me from the place outright.

I swear I heard muffled laughing from inside the house.

Once the rooster was convinced that I was far enough away from his brood, he stood and regarded me, blocking the path as I turned to look back. He allowed me scant moments to take in the little dwelling. The building was made entirely of stone save for a thatched roof. A wisp of white smoke curled up out of the chimney. Behind it a thick pine forest stretched out for miles. The adults back in the cities would long to see a place like this, to stay here, away from the cement forests at home. They would remember the feeling of green all around, of living things shooting up from the ground. But to me, this was the stuff of fantasy, a lost history never to be witnessed again.

How was this happening?

Quick as a flash, the rooster lost his patience with my delay. He screeched and thrashed at my clothing and fingertips until I was well down the path away from the little farm.

My heartbeat slowed from the flight down the trail as I walked. Usually when I overexerted myself, the squeezing in my chest would linger for days, sometimes from something as simple as walking up a flight of stairs. But here, the pain had all but vanished.

The technical term for my illness was Ventricular Septal Defect. Oxygen had trouble making it to the parts of my body where it was needed, leaving me weak and short of breath a lot of the time. The surgery I had to close the hole when I was five was partially successful, partially not. The hole had closed for a time and it looked like I might be home free, but then gradually it began to open again. Mom and I had talked about more surgery with the doctors back in fifth grade, but they were concerned that my heart might be so weak that I wouldn't survive the stress of anesthesia.

I wondered if Kiron was right, and if I really was well enough to be hiking along this strange countryside. I would take it slow, I told myself, just in case.

I studied the map carefully as I walked. The paper showed a rough outline of the surrounding area. I kept a lookout for the landmarks, but mostly I trekked along absently, too distracted by everything I had just learned.

The stories Kiron told were bizarre. If he was telling me the truth, he must be hundreds of years old. And a man named Brendan Wood had once lived here, that was certain. Could I believe that this person was really my relative?

No, I thought. *It's not possible.*

But then my eyes focused again on the unusual terrain that surrounded me.

It shouldn't be possible that I'm here at all. Why is it not possible that the Brendan Wood from Aria and the Brendan Wood from Earth are the same man?

None of this mattered, of course, because whatever the truth was, I seemed pretty stuck here. Sure, I could decide that Kiron was nothing more than a crazed old man and go along on my way. But where would I go? Looking out over the rolling hills, I saw no other signs of life. Well, not human life. Birds flew overhead, squirrels and rabbits crossed my path more than once. But it didn't look like there was anybody else around apart from Kiron who might be able to steer me towards the answers to my questions, much less home.

I decided to trust him. True, I had little choice, but the decision came easily because he seemed, mostly, to be a kind man. He was gruff and old and cranky, yes. But he had fed me and comforted me and given me a direction where there was previously none.

I stared at my feet as they crunched through thousands of tiny, fallen branches and leaves, not looking up as I crossed over into the shade of a grove of trees. The greenest of the leaves stuck to the sides of the leather, making my boots look like they were being eaten by the forest.

An hour passed. Then another. I began to get frustrated with my lack of progress. I had only seen one landmark so far, the petrified remains of a long dead tree sticking out from the hard earth. I trudged onward down the trail until I came to a small grove of apple trees. Fat, round fruits littered the ground all around where I stood. I gathered up an armful and found a place to sit, resting my back up against one of the thick trunks.

As the sweet, tart juice of the apple dribbled down my chin, I wondered what my mom was doing right that minute. She must have abandoned her summer trip by now, gone back to the farmhouse to Grandma to search for me. Guilt seeped into me as I thought about the job she had been called away for, the opportunity now lost. Had she called my dad? I didn't know if she would, but I wondered what he would think, learning that his first son had vanished into thin air.

He wasn't normal, my father. His reaction would never be able to be predicted.

"What was he like?" I had asked my mom years ago, hungry for details about this man I was tied to, but who seemed so ambivalent about me. Her fingers paused on the lamp switch on my bedside table at the question. She looked at me, hurt shadowing her face. I was instantly sorry I had brought it up.

But then she smiled, the outline on her lips conflicting with the pain in her eyes.

"He was a very nice man when we met," she said. "He loved to sing. Everywhere he went he was singing or whistling or humming. I could never get him to shut up." She laughed in earnest at the memory. Then her face gradually fell. "But some people aren't built to handle the stresses of life. Some people…get lost."

"Is that why he left?" I asked, flinching a little as I waited for her answer. She sighed and put her warm hand against my cheek.

"Your daddy got sick, hon," she said. "We tried to help him but he just wouldn't let us. By the time he left he couldn't see logic at all anymore."

I remembered this. Over time he had become a frightening man. Some mornings when I was very little, I'd look out the window and see him tromping through the street in nothing but his undershorts, ranting at the top of his voice. Once, my mom went out to try to talk to him, to get him to come inside out of the cold fall air. He had hit her with the back of his hand. She fell to the ground, her hands raised in front of her face in defense. But he just walked away, talking to the people only he could see.

"Maybe he could get better," I said, my hopeful tone betraying my resolve to sound like a grown-up.

"Maybe," she said, stroking my cheek with her fingertips. "But I don't think so, hon. Some people just...can't."

Maybe. Maybe the disappearance of his only son would be enough to call him back from the edge of...of what? Insanity?

No, I thought, it was better to not expect a response at all. He was gone, my dad, and he was never coming back. Now I had to stay focused on staying alive and getting back to the people who *did* care about me. My mom. Grandma.

As I sat, a strange tingling sensation started to move across my skin. It felt itchy, and I shook both of my arms out, trying to release the unfamiliar tension. Soon the feeling began to penetrate deep into the muscles of my legs, and my heart beat hard and strong in my chest, willing me to my feet after only resting a few minutes. The feeling was unusual, something I didn't often feel: energy. Bottled up inside my motionless body, it had suddenly come to the surface, demanding to be released. I tossed the rest of the apples into the basket and walked out of the grove to the hard dirt path.

Suddenly, a long, slim hare leapt right into my path, stopping directly in front of me. I froze five feet away from him, surprised out of my thoughts by his arrival. We each stood completely still, mid-stride on the path, and looked at each other. He didn't seem scared of me, just curious, so I knelt down and put out my hand to see if he would let me touch him. His twitching nose tested the air around us.

His coat looked like a soft, puffy cloud, and my fingers ached to touch the silky fur. My eyes held his gaze, but he didn't come forward to my outstretched hand. I had always had an affinity for animals, though I rarely saw any at home. Pets were a luxury for the rich. I murmured to him softly, "Come here, little guy." But the sound of my voice startled him and sent him scampering into the bushes on the side of the trail.

"Awwww," I complained. "Come on, little guy."

I walked over to the bushes, but he was long gone. Remembering the rich stew from earlier today, it occurred to me that I was probably lucky to have seen him at all. It would appear that rabbits around these parts might frequently be in danger of a quick death followed by a long simmer in Kiron's cook pot.

The sun was starting to sink behind the trees and the light in the sky was shimmering gold by the time I reached the acorns. The oak wasn't with the other trees that were near the trail; it was way out in the middle of a field, standing alone amidst wild grasses and shrubs. I made my way down a gentle hill and started through the grass.

The tree was enormous. Or maybe it wasn't. My experience with trees was, admittedly, nonexistent. I picked up an acorn and twirled it around in my fingers. I wondered why he wanted acorns, of all things. Native Americans had harvested acorns and ground them into flour. Were these for us to eat? I tentatively placed my teeth against the hard skin of the nut and tried to bite it, quickly spitting it out when the bitter taste touched my tongue. I hoped Kiron had some other plan in mind for my foraging.

A brigade of squirrels battled me for the tiny treasures, which were spread out all along the base of the tree. The fluff-tailed creatures came down the trunk in pairs, stuffing the hard seeds into their mouths and darting back up, disappearing into the dark folds of the trunk. I moved over the ground and collected as many as I could as the night began to descend. I filled and filled the basket until I could no longer discern the acorns from rocks on the ground in the gathering darkness. I hoped I would have enough as I started back towards the house.

I was downright proud of myself. This morning I had been sure that I wouldn't be able to make it the whole day out in the wilderness on my own. But here I was, a heavy basket half full of the requested nuts, and I was barely even tired.

That was when I heard the first call.

Through the twilight came a single, lone cry. I stopped in my tracks and listened. At first I was entranced by the sound, and more excited than nervous. Was it a coyote? A wolf? The closest I ever got to nature was the reptile room at the science museum, an inadequate dose of our lost world. I imagined a sleek fox getting ready to hunt in the night. He would catch the scent of a squirrel, or a rabbit, maybe, and burst forth on its trail. The picture in my mind was almost beautiful as I imagined nature taking its course, the hare devoured, outwitted and outrun by his opponent.

But as I walked out of the field and up towards the apple grove, the first voice was joined by another. And another. Soon a chorus of howls seemed to fill the air on all sides. Too many of them were out there to fit in neatly with my serene nature story.

My skin began crawling with energy again, but this was of an entirely different sort. Without even giving thought to the internal injury I could sustain, I bolted.

Immediately, the howling increased. The yipping of what sounded like dozens of animals echoed through the night, and I pushed my legs to run faster, faster than they had ever moved in my life. I blew through the field and up the small incline to the apple grove. There I paused, looking back for just a moment to get a glimpse of my pursuers.

I should not have done this.

There, bounding through the grass at top speed and headed straight for me, was an enormous pack of...what were they? Wolves? Hyenas? I had never seen, in a lifetime of browsing nature books, an animal that resembled these. Two feet tall, four legs, and the snarling snout of a dog combined with the tusks of a wild pig. Their silvery, wired hair stuck up haphazardly from their bodies in stiff tufts. There had to be at least fifteen of the beasts, and with each stride they took they released more howls, calling more and more to the hunt.

I turned and ran as the first of the animals was making the hill below me. In seconds the leader was snapping at my feet. I pushed myself harder and broke away from him, the huge, awkward basket bouncing violently against my back. Around me the woods came alive with sound. Squirrels scampered up, snakes slithered down, and all the while the pack pursued me. I wasn't yet tired, but as the threat increased I moved faster. And faster. Soon I left the pack behind, but I did not stop. My breathing was even, my heartbeat impossibly steady.

I focused intently on the trail, barely visible now with only the moon lighting the path. At first my feet slammed into the packed dirt, but as the minutes passed they seemed to barely touch the earth at all. Fifteen minutes passed like this as I flew across the countryside.

When I finally did stop near the giant petrified tree, the land around me was silent. I was ok. My heart beat hard, but strong, and my chest was unclenched and open. The cold night air felt refreshing against my hot cheeks.

My breath slowly quieted as I listened for sounds of pursuit. I heard nothing. Not even the howls of the hunt could reach my ears here. Where had they gone? Had they given up?

I leaned against the ancient, solid trunk and suddenly realized that it had taken me many hours to make the distance between it and the oak tree. How had I gotten back here so fast?

Then the truth hit me so hard it almost knocked me down.

I had outrun the pack.

I had outrun the pack?

CHAPTER FIVE

It wasn't possible. I hadn't hit the ground at even a jog since I was five. The beasts must have fallen back, maybe distracted by a different source of dinner. But the proof was all around me. The wolf-pigs were nowhere to be seen, and I had already reached the ancient, towering tree, which should have taken at least two hours. I stood listening, still trying to make sense of the fact that I was alone.

"ASTER?" I heard the distant call of Kiron and turned towards the sound. Barely visible in the faint moonlight, a curl of smoke rose from the cottage. I moved away from the trees and towards the homestead at a quiet walk, surprised to still be alive, and with a mind full of questions.

The chickens had already been locked in their coop for the night. Through the two windows in the house a faint, warm light flickered. As I approached the door, I was unsure about whether to knock or just open it. But right as I made the top step it flew open in front of me. Kiron's hand dashed out of the opening, grabbed onto the shoulder straps of the basket I was tied to, and pulled me inside.

"My boy!" he bellowed. "Where have you been? I thought I had lost you for sure."

"You almost did," I said.

"I told you to be back by sunset, did I not? There's reason to stay inside after dark around these parts."

"I met some of those reasons while I was out," I said, dropping the awkward pack to the floor.

Inside the room it was stifling hot. The enormous dog was sprawled out next to the fire, clearly exhausted from following Kiron around with whatever he had been up to all afternoon.

"You did, did ya?" Kiron asked. "Still alive, I see."

"Yeah," I said, pulling out one of the heavy wood chairs at the table. "They chased me. A big pack of wolves or pigs or…I don't know what they were, but they chased me back from the oak tree."

"Ah, that would be faylons. They chased you, eh?" He crossed to the other side of the room and began stirring an enormous cauldron that was perched precariously over the fire. "All the way back from the tree? I thought you were sick…" He glanced up at me, smirking.

"Yes, they *did*," I replied, annoyed. I poured a cup of water from the jug on the table and gulped it down. "You might have told me what was out there."

"Well, you mighta listened to me in the first place and been back before sundown. Anyways, you made it back in one piece, didn't you?"

That was the weird part, I *was* still in one piece. And I felt better, healthier, than I could ever remember feeling in my life.

"I don't get it," I said. "I feel, well, I feel pretty good."

"That don't surprise me none," he said. "You're Triadesh, I told ya. You belong here." He picked up my pack and dumped its contents onto the table.

I stared at the pile of acorns. I belonged here? In a place where the ill can outrun monsters in the night?

Kiron studied each acorn carefully, his face hovering just an inch off the tabletop.

"Ah, here we are," he said after a few minutes, selecting a clean, fat nut. He held it up to the light and turned it around and around, inspecting it from all sides. Then he turned back to his pot. "Come look at this." He walked to the fire and plunked the acorn into the brew unceremoniously. The contents of the pot sizzled and spat.

I looked down at the large pile of remaining acorns, abandoned. Not good enough, apparently. Then I pushed back the chair and stepped over to the edge of the fire. Now that I was closer, I could see that the pot was lidded with a strange dome, almost like a huge soap bubble. Inside the pot a clear liquid boiled, dissolving the acorn almost instantly. The liquid looked like melted glass, clear as a diamond. Next to the fire was a raggedy canvas backpack, stiff an cracked. Kiron motioned to me to look into the cauldron, as he was doing.

"That was it," he said, "the last ingredient."

"What is it?"

"This," he said, "is a brew of *veiled truth*."

I peered in at the liquid. "Um," I said, "what's it for? Do we drink it?"

"No! No!" he exclaimed. "Never drink a brew of veiled truth! Once taken, you will be invisible for life. There is no going back!"

"Alright, ok!" I said, taking a step backwards. Invisible for life? "But what's it for?"

"The brew," he said, "is for this." He picked up the backpack and, spearing the handle onto a long branch of wood, slowly dipped it into the pot. As the fabric touched the liquid it gurgled and fizzed. When he raised the stick out of the pot again, half of it was gone and the backpack had vanished. I looked into the pot and saw nothing but the clear, shining liquid.

The dog growled. My jaw dropped. Kiron looked at me expectantly. It took me a minute before I could finally speak.

"How did you do *that?"* I asked.

"Years of practice, my boy, years of practice. There are all sorts of treasures around this farm that ain't visible to the naked eye." He moved the stick away from the cauldron and the brew dripped off the bottom of the invisible pack onto the floor, where it hissed on the wood planks. He held the stick out to me.

"Touch it," he said. "Go on!"

I held out my hand and felt around in the empty air where the pack had been moments before. Hot, wet canvas met my fingers, though I could see nothing. I pulled my hands back abruptly and inspected my fingers, half expecting them to disappear, too.

"It will only vanish what's within the dome," he said, inclining his head towards the pot.

I grabbed with both hands and slid the pack off the stick, amazed.

"And the best part," Kiron said, "is this!" Setting down the stick, he picked up two apples from the hearth, took the bag from my hands and proceeded to drop them into it. They instantly vanished. I gasped. The dog was on his feet and gave two warning barks, alarmed.

"Oh, shut it, you!" he said to the animal. The dog whined and growled, and finally retreated back to his napping spot, groaning as he settled himself back down on a heap of blankets.

"Now," Kiron said, "it ain't limitless. You can only carry what you can fit into the bag. But whatever goes inside it'll become invisible, and the pack will never weigh you down while you travel, not even with the heaviest ore in the land packed to bursting within it."

"What happens if I take it off?" I asked. "What if I lose it? How am I supposed to find it again if it's invisible?" I felt a little panicky being entrusted with such a prize.

"Calm down! You ain't gonna lose it. You can't. I've tied the pack to your aspect." His eyes sparkled; he was clearly proud of himself. "A tricky bit of enchantment, if I do say so myself. There are two commands that only you can give to make the pack disappear and reappear. Speaking the command *obscure* makes the pack invisible, and *reveal* is the command to, well, to reveal it. Go on!"

My heart was still racing when I said, "Uh, ok. *Reveal.*"

The now familiar diamond and star symbol appeared, floating above Kiron's hand, and came to life. The symbol didn't just glow, it positively burst with light. The pack then materialized all at once with a "pop."

"Obscure!" I said, smiling and eager now.

The pack rotated in midair and then collapsed inward on itself, like the spiral of a tornado. It disappeared again.

I gaped. This was *insane.*

"But why didn't it appear and disappear when you said the commands?" I asked.

"I told you, I've joined it with your aspect," he answered.

I looked at him blankly.

"Your aspect! The energy force that surrounds you. I used a piece of the bed linens you slept in last night to tie it to you. It held your vestige."

"Right," I said slowly, trying to hide that I had no idea what he was talking about. "Well, that's great! It's amazing." And it was, whether I understood it or not.

Seeming satisfied by my response, he hung the pack over the mantle to dry and poured us both mugs of tea. I accepted the one he held out to me, but when I took the first sip I almost spit it out, it was so bitter.

"Ugh!" I couldn't help but exclaim. "What is that?"

"Mulberry tea. Here, put some honey in; it helps with the flavor." He handed me a jar with a spoon stuck fast in golden sugar. "Keeps me young!" His eyes had a manic glint that shone in the firelight.

I'll bet, I thought. But I didn't argue. Whatever this guy was feeding me was at least partially responsible for my surviving this day. I stirred two large spoonfuls of honey in the mug and took another tentative sip.

He brought out the now cold pot of stew from this morning. The dog was up again, wagging and drooling, as we dug into our meal. The temperature didn't much matter; I was ravenous, and the stew was still delicious. My body felt oddly empty as I dug in, like I hadn't eaten in several days.

"So what's the plan?" I asked between mouthfuls. I was still feeling exhilarated by my escape from the faylons, and worries about my heart were getting further and further from my mind.

"You ain't ready yet. Tomorrow I'll start teachin' ya what I know. Depends on you, I guess. We'll see what you can do."

"Where am I going? I mean, after that?"

"How am I supposed to know?" he answered gruffly. "I ain't never followed no maps of Almara. Nobody has! That's the whole point, ain't it? You're the first."

I stared hard at the bowl as I scraped up the last bits of meat. Why me? Why hadn't it been Brendan? I wondered what my life might have been like if Brendan had made it back home to Aria, if Brendan had followed the path I was now on. Would I have ever even existed? And if so, would my body have been so weak and sick, like it had been on Earth? Or would I have felt, from birth, this strange strength that was now coursing through me? I felt better now, trapped in a world that I didn't understand, than I had ever felt back home.

I shook my head as these thoughts swirled around inside it. I needed to stay focused and get home. The fact was that Brendan had stayed on Earth, and that I was born on Earth, not here. My mom was back there, probably worried beyond belief that I had disappeared. And Grandma, too. I couldn't just leave them there, alone and frightened, while I stayed here on Aerit. My dad would be no comfort to them. He probably wouldn't even care if he found out I was gone. I grimaced at the thought of him. No, he would be no comfort to my mother.

I had to go back.

I contemplated the task in front of me: to either find Almara using the maps he had left behind, or find someone else powerful enough to send me home.

I tried to stifle it, but a large yawn escaped from my throat. Kiron put the remains of his stew on the floor for the dog. "Time for you to sleep," he said.

I looked around. Yesterday he had let me sleep in the bed. Would I be on the floor tonight? I couldn't help looking at the thick blankets longingly.

"Go on," he said. "I'm a night owl anyways. Don't often sleep much at all anymore, come to it."

I handed him my bowl and removed my boots, gratefully climbing into the big bed. Peering over the top of the covers, I watched the fire crackle and pop. The dog jumped up onto the bed beside me, and tucked his wet nose underneath my hand. I scratched his ears.

"You're a good boy," I crooned at the mutt. "What's your name, anyways, boy? What a good dog." The dog sighed loudly through his large, wet nostrils.

"Crane," Kiron said, watching the fire. "Dog's Crane."

"Crane," I said softly in his fuzzy face. I continued to scratch him, but my eyes drifted to the images hung on the walls.

"What are those pictures of?" I asked.

"Ah," he said. "They're just an old man's musings. Memories. Bit prettier than the real thing was in a lot of ways. And also not, not so wonderful as it was to actually see it. You can change a memory all you want, pretty it up in your head after the fact. But you ain't never gonna get to experience it for real again."

"So those are places you went? Animals you saw?"

"Mostly, yeah," he answered. "The horses, yeah. The winged horse and the dragon I seen for real. Some of the others I just heard tale of."

The dragon peered down haughtily from the canvas, terrible and menacing. It was no storybook creature, that was for sure. Tales of boys riding on sleek, sparkling beasts did not compare to this, the account of what Kiron had seen with his own eyes.

I rolled over and rested my cheek against the cool pillow. Kiron was astounding, at least by my standards. Traveling between worlds, tracking dragons and who knows what else. Making backpacks invisible and impossibly light. If I told tales like his back on Earth they'd all think I was crazy. And these weren't just stories he'd made up.

Dragons. As my eyelids drooped the thought occurred to me; to witness a real, live dragon, however horrible, would be quite a memory to have, indeed.

CHAPTER SIX

I was running.

My feet slammed hard into the cobblestones that lined the village paths. The small book was clutched in my left hand, the backpack in my right. I could hear them behind me. Shouting and panting, the men pursued me through the square. I dared look back only once; they were too close! In the front of the pack, the angry face of the dark-eyed man made me gasp in panic. His strides were huge as he barreled down on me, his black clothing whipping in the wind he made as he ran. I would need to get farther out. I sprinted between two of the dwellings, turning my body as I ran to avoid scraping my shoulders along the sides. I hoped that the men were too broad in the chest to make it through this way.

I broke through to the outer barrier of the city, breathing hard. I made for the main gate; the guard stationed at the entrance hadn't yet figured out what was going on and he fumbled and stuttered as I approached and then blew by him. He would soon join the others on my trail. It would have to be now.

I made it to the top of the first small hill outside the gate and turned around. My eyes caught the looming shape of the horde of villagers bearing down upon me. I thrust my hands up, both hands gripping the book, and...

"Hey," Kiron said, shaking me by the shoulders. I was back in his little cottage, the bedsheets tangled around my legs. The light from the rising sun was barely starting to creep into the black night sky.

"Come on, boy, you can't sleep the entire day away."

I blinked in the dim light, trying to keep my eyes from closing again, but breathing hard from the force of the dream. He walked to the remains of last night's fire. I looked at his back as he worked over it, coaxing the flames back to life. He must have slept a little, then, to have let the fire go out. He pulled his suspenders up one at a time, and dropped them into place on each shoulder with a snap. When he turned back around to face me, the fire burned brightly behind him.

"So, what's the plan?" I asked him blearily.

"Eat," he commanded, pointing at the table. "Then we train."

I dragged myself out of the bed and hobbled over to the long wood table. The bowl was full of some sort of cooked grain. I peered into it and examined the mush skeptically.

"How will we get the next link?" I asked, picking up a spoon..

"I got the link already," he said. "I had it my whole life, but you ain't ready to go yet. You may be feelin' better, but you're gonna have to learn a lot more if you want to survive a quest to find Almara."

"Wait a minute," I protested. "You already have the link?"

"Of course I do. My pa left it for me before he died." He looked up at me from his mug of tea. "Course, now it's you I gotta look out for instead of Brendan. Bit more complicated than we planned. You don't know nothin' about Maylin or Almara. You'll be lucky to survive the quest to find him."

"What do you mean, I'll be lucky to survive?" I asked.

He fiddled with the business end of a heavy looking ax that rested on the table, picking at the blade with his fingernail.

"Not everyone's gonna be agreeable to your journey. More likely than not you'll be runnin' into trouble before it's over."

"But why would anyone be against my finding Almara? He's supposed to be the good guy, right?" I swallowed a mouthful of the mush, which had a neutral flavor, but a texture akin to a raw egg, slimy and viscous. *I could always just run away*, I thought. If I was so fast here, how fast would others be?

He stood and crossed the room, opening the front door to the cottage. A thick beam of sunlight played with the dust on the floor, and Crane the dog took off running into the garden, the outdoors more appetizing to him than the contents of my bowl. I swallowed the same mouthful again, the first having not quite made it all the way down.

"Yeah, well, not everybody is a good guy," he said. "I expect you'll meet a fair number of good and bad before this is over."

He hoisted the ax from the table and looked at me pointedly, raising it above his head and thrusting it downward through the air.

"Now, I ain't no warrior," he said, "but I do have some experience with an ax. I can throw, I can chop. This is where we'll start."

"Where we'll start?" I asked, gulping another spoonful. Despite my aversion to the goop, I still felt hollow from the previous day's exertions.

"First axes, then knives, and then practice with a sword for good measure," he said, stepping out onto the front door stoop. He raised his head up to the sun and closed his eyes for a moment. The bright, clear rays lit his cheeks.

My natural inclination was to argue with him, to remind him again that I was feeble. That ax looked heavy, and three days ago I wouldn't have even attempted lifting it. But as I absently smacked at my porridge, I could not deny the energy I now felt flowing beneath my skin. The arguments faded on my lips as I looked at the long, silver sword that rested against the wall, glinting in the stream of sunlight from the window.

I managed to force down several more spoonfuls of my breakfast, but gave up once I could no longer swallow it all the way. I picked up a mug of tea and washed down the fat, slimy grains that still stuck in my throat, and followed Kiron out into the morning. As I laced my boots I, too, raised my face to the sun. The warmth it gave contrasted with the crisp cold of the morning. Kiron moved across the yard, and started scattering chicken feed over the grass. The hens clucked and pecked, the rooster cautiously following them around.

I stood up and carefully approached, pressing my luck with the bird. I pressed too hard, and he was on me in an instant, biting at my legs and screeching so loud you'd think I was trying to murder him. What was it with this stupid bird? I finally got a clear shot and kicked him full force across the yard. He stood up, ruffling his feathers in indignation, and then came at me again.

"Alright, that'll be enough," Kiron boomed. Suddenly the old man was between us, and he shooed the bird back over to his flock. Surprisingly, the rooster did not come for me again once Kiron intervened. I guess he knew who was boss around this place.

Kiron led me behind the chicken coop, where the pines fanned out beyond the homestead. The smell back here was delicious, like the scented candle we lit every Christmas in our apartment, only way better.

As we moved into the trees we soon came to a large clearing. In the center several stumps stuck up from the forest floor, and off to one side a large pile of uncut firewood was stacked neatly next to one three feet across.

Kiron stopped in the middle of the clearing, raised his ax, and threw it hard. The ax soared through the empty space easily, and found its target, a tree. It stuck firmly into the wood.

"The goal," he said, turning, "is to learn how to use weapons. But also to learn how to use everyday things as weapons, things people won't think to keep from you."

From his pocket he pulled a thin piece of twine, perhaps a foot long. He dangled it out in front of him and slowly approached me.

"If you can use a rope, a twig, a pin in your defense, you will soon find that you will be able to travel freely and without fear."

He moved so fast that for a moment I couldn't figure out where he had gone. But as I felt the rope around my neck and his beard scratch my ear I realized what he had done. My hands moved to claw at the twine, but before they even made it to my throat he had already released me.

I rounded on him, alarmed and angry.

"What was that for?" I yelled.

He smirked. "That was to get your attention."

I backed up several steps, but he turned away and walked to the tree where the ax had stuck. Freeing it from the bark, he turned and approached me once more.

"The ax is the easiest of the weapons to master. Some will recognize it as a threat, some will not, but in any case the handling and throwing of an ax lends itself to many other types of defense." He turned the ax backward and held out its handle to me.

I stared at him skeptically for a moment, waiting for him to attack me again, but when he didn't I reached out and took the wood. It was warm in my hand, and heavy, but not as heavy as I had expected. Still, the blade of the ax fell towards the ground as he released it, and I needed two hands to hoist it back upright.

"Now," he said, "throw."

He did not offer any further instruction, so I tried to mimic what he had done when he had thrown the ax into the tree. I raised it above my head with both hands and threw it. The tool tumbled head over tail three times before landing harmlessly in the dirt at the base of the tree.

Well, at least it landed in front of the tree I was *aiming* for.

"So, not quite, then," he said.

He motioned for me to follow him and we both approached the tree. He picked up the ax and handed it back to me.

"Now, try from here."

We were only three feet from the tree, but I did as he said. As I raised both of my arms he stopped me.

"One arm."

I released my left hand from the wood and brought the ax down towards the tree trunk, hard. To my great relief and excitement, the blade stuck in the wood. A thin sweat broke out over my forehead as Kiron commanded, "Again."

I did it again. And again. I threw that ax so many times over the next several days that my arm began to feel like lead. As I learned the balance of the ax, Kiron had me back farther and farther from the tree, until I could hit it from fifteen feet away. I didn't stick the target every time, but any success was better than where I had started from.

When he finally brought out the knife for me to practice with, I had become so accustomed to the weight of the ax that I could barely handle the tiny blade. It would fly like a hummingbird from my outstretched hand to the trunk I targeted, but then bounce off the bark harmlessly with a ping. I tried for hours and hours, but wielding the little knife was something I was hopeless at.

Each day consisted of learning the ways of the new weapons, and each night I spent learning to pick locks with a short pin I could hide in my pants. Kiron's other skills, like strangling people in their sleep with nothing more than the shoelace of a boot, I was less enthusiastic about. I simply refused to believe that I could wind up in a situation where murder became necessary. I was alarmed at the violence of it all. From what he was teaching me, it really did seem that he thought I would be fighting for my life the moment I left this place.

But the satisfaction I felt at learning such difficult and unusual skills kept my fears at bay. I chewed through each new task like a starving dog chewing on a difficult bone. It was just so…different… being able to *do* things. My heart had remained constant since that night with the faylons, and my chest hadn't tightened again. I flopped exhausted into bed after the end of each day, and awoke each morning eager for more practice.

Finally, after about a week of working with the ax and the knife, the day of sword training came. Kiron had only one sword, so he had me work with a long, heavy stick to mimic the silver blade he held. He proceeded to slash at me with the sword, first on the left, then the right. Back and forth, back and forth, until I finally got the hang of watching not only his weapon, but his eyes, for clues about where he would strike me next.

After four days of this I was not only able to deflect his blade, but could thrust it from his hands entirely with a swoop of the stick.

"You're ready," he said, panting, as my stick touched the edge of his neck. He was sweating from the exertion of trying to keep me off him, but I had become more aggressive as the days passed, and had managed to get him into this precarious position for what was now the third time.

I stepped away and lowered the branch. I was both exhilarated and unsure.

"How do you know?" the old me asked, worried. "Maybe I should stay here longer, practice longer, before I head out."

"No," he said, regaining his balance. "I can teach you no more. Another week's worth of practice will only serve to increase your worry. You must go now, while it is fresh in your mind and your muscles, and before you have a chance to think on it too hard."

Well, it was too late for that. I had been thinking hard on it already. But as much as I wanted to wimp out, to stay put at Kiron's and hope for some impossible rescue, my mother's face kept floating into my head. I couldn't leave her there alone forever.

That night we feasted. Kiron had spent the afternoon slaughtering and butchering the chickens, and the carcasses were now drying into packable fare over the fire. I had been anxious to be rid of the horrible rooster, but when it came down to it, and his head was pressed down on the block, a deep pang of sadness sank into my chest like the blade of the ax into his neck.

We settled in for the night, both of us quiet as the thoughts of tomorrow stirred in our minds. Kiron sat back in his chair by the fire, and pulled from under his shirt a small piece of folded parchment. He held it out to me.

"What's this?" I asked.

"It's your link," he said. "Tomorrow, we'll make the jump."

"You're coming with me then?" It was a question I had been afraid to ask.

"Don't see as I have much of a choice."

I breathed a silent sigh of relief. I unfolded the paper and recognized the now familiar symbol of Almara at the top of the otherwise blank page. I looked up at him skeptically, but smiled when I said, "You sure this is the right piece of blank paper?"

"Yes, you brat," he shot back, but the skin around his eyes crinkled in amusement.

My fingers traced the ovals on the golden symbol.

What sort of place awaited me on the other side of this link?

CHAPTER SEVEN

The next morning the sun did not make an appearance. Low, gray clouds covered the hillsides like a lid on a pot. We woke in the dim light and started getting ready.

Kiron was at the table, rummaging through piles, finishing the packing of the bag. "First, we'll clear out," he said. "You ain't leavin' from here. Last time that happened, the cottage was nearly wrecked from the force of the thing."

"And good morning to *you*," I said sarcastically. But he wasn't having any humor today. He had a concerned look on his face as he readied the pack.

The same sort of explosion must have happened when Almara had jumped from here two hundred years ago. I thought about what the attic back home must have looked like after my departure. I wondered if police were swarming over the farm, looking for me.

I sat up and stretched with a loud groan. Crane stretched, too, but made no move to get up. He yawned and each of his four paws extended, his toes reaching deeper into the blankets. I rested my hand on his furry stomach for a moment while I grappled to break free from the haze of sleep. I hadn't thought about the dog. The chickens were gone now, but what fate awaited the hound?

"What are we going to do with Crane?" I asked. "Is he coming?"

The dog's ears perked up at the sound of his name.

"Nope. We're gonna drop him with my sister. Only one of my kin still alive."

"You have a sister? Why didn't you tell me?"

"Ain't your business," he said. "Anyways, we'll only be with the old witch for a few minutes."

My mind buzzed as I tried to imagine a female version of Kiron.

On the table, he lay out our breakfast; four boiled eggs on two plates and a slab of cheese for each of us. I was thankful for the lack of slimy mush. I shuffled to the table and slumped into one of the chairs just as he was pouring out two mugs of sweet tea. It was hot and spicy, and it cleared my head as I sipped it. Crane waited for us to rise from the table before bothering to get down from the bed to search for fallen crumbs.

"Where will we go?" I asked.

"Empty field just down the hill," he said. "Nothin' to destroy out there but dry grass and wildflowers. We'll jump to Larissa's first and then take Almara's link from there."

"Larissa, is that your sister?"

"Hmph."

I retrieved my boots from just outside the front door. As I pulled them on I took a long look at the cozy farm and wondered if I would ever see it again. I realized with a certain amount of sadness that the silence of the farm had meant the slaughtering of the birds.

"You ready?"

Kiron helped me with the bulky backpack, which was awkward

70

at first, but quite light. He nestled the knife I had used in practice into the side pocket, even though I was useless with it. As soon as the pack was on my back, I commanded it, *"Obscure!"* and it collapsed and disappeared, though I could still feel the straps resting on my shoulders.

"Got the link?" he asked.

I pulled it out of my pocket and showed it to him.

He hoisted the ax from the table by the door and handed it to me. He had fashioned a sort of sling for it, and he helped me secure it around my waist. The ax hung heavy and secure at my side.

"I think the sword would call too much attention," he said. "But this will do. If anyone asks you about it, just tell 'em you're a woodcutter's son. You're better with it than the other weapons anyways."

It was true. Days and days of practice with the heavy weapon left me feeling confident when it was in my hands. Its weight comforted me.

We walked away from the little house, and then Kiron stopped and turned. He regarded it for a long moment. It was only then that I realized the sadness on his face.

"Aren't you coming back?" I asked.

"Doubt it," he said gruffly, turning away from his home. He walked resolutely away, and he didn't look back again. I felt like I should say something, but I couldn't think of anything that wouldn't sound trite. The truth was that I was very, very thankful he was coming with me. I followed in his wake.

The morning air was cold, and a stiff wind blew across us. Crane bounded down the path up ahead.

As we walked, Kiron started rattling off instructions. "The plan was that Almara was to leave links in each place he and the eight traveled through. If we can find 'em in each place, I expect, they'll lead us to him, eventually."

The gravelly rocks crunched under our feet as we made our way to the top edge of a hill. Below, a big basin of empty field rolled out in front of us. Kiron started down the slope without a backward glance. His footsteps were sure and strong, well versed along this precarious path. I stumbled down behind him, trying to keep from kicking the rocks I loosened with my clumsy steps. After a few minutes, he began to speak.

"When I was a boy, I wanted more than anything to see a Pegasus, a winged horse. I was just fifteen when I set out, not a whole lot older than you. My Ma and Pa weren't too happy about it, so I snuck out on a moonless night and made my way towards the edge of this land, to a place I knew I'd be able to jump to the other side of the ocean."

We were at the base of the hill now. He reached out his hand to me to help me down from the last big rock, and continued.

"It took a few days before I started to regret my decision to leave home, but by that point I was already two jumps away from here and well on my way. I figured I could give up and go back home, or I could suck it up and continue on. I ain't no quitter, but the draw of home comforts swam through my mind plenty as I went along. Even though I figured Pa's belt would be meeting with my backside on my return." He smiled to himself. I wondered why such a horrible thought would make him do anything of the sort.

"Two weeks in, I was getting closer to the valleys where the Pegasus fly. I was cold, hungry, and covered in the dirt of travelin' from head to foot. But as I stepped down into the first of the valleys, I sped up despite bein' so tired. I knew they were close. And they were. Two days later I stepped round a corner of rock and there they stood!" He beamed. "Four of 'em grazin' in the green grass between two steep cliffs of rock.

As they saw me round the turn, they raised their heads, and their great wings rose, too."

"What were they like?" I asked.

He paused as he remembered, and then he stopped walking and faced me.

"They were like nothin', nothin' I'd ever seen, nor seen since. Best thing I ever done." His eyes stared out across the grass over my head as he saw the memories in his mind. Then he looked at me severely. "Don't you give up cause you're cold or hungry or miss your mama. Seems to me you're here for a reason. Could be that you'll find somethin' you're lookin' for, too. Sometimes, you just gotta take what you're handed."

"But I'm not looking for anything," I said.

"Ain't ya? Everybody's lookin' for something. Think on it, boy."

As I followed along, I tried to think of something to look for, some reason for continuing on this quest other than a desire to get back home. Adventure? I had wanted adventure, but I hadn't needed to look for it. It had simply landed in my lap. A Pegasus? A Dragon? Sure, seeing fantastical beasts would be wonderful and terrifying, but since I had only known of their existence for a couple weeks, I didn't really have a lifelong desire to fuel an entire journey to find them.

A thought popped into my head then, and it pulled me up short. My eyes glazed over as I stared into space, trying to pinpoint what I was feeling. There was a difference between my world and this one. Aside from the obvious, vibrant nature springing up all around, monsters and magical creatures, disappearing backpacks, there was a difference in the way I *felt*. I remembered the pounding of my heart as I had run from the faylons. The steady, *strong* pounding of my heart. In all the days since that one, hadn't I worked my body to the limits of its endurance? I had not only remained healthy, but I'd enjoyed every minute of it. I still hadn't told Kiron about just how fast I had run that night. Maybe I hadn't even really believed it myself until this moment.

I made the decision quickly, and before Kiron had a chance to even open his mouth to call out to me, I was blowing past him, well on my way to being out of earshot. I ran as fast as I could across the field in the direction we were already traveling. Crane's alarmed barking soon fell behind me. My feet, unlike their descent down the slope of the hill, found their footing easily here. Each step crunched the dry grass and pushed me faster to take the next and the next. I breathed deeply and pushed harder. The grass began to blur past my vision as I rocketed forward. The blood poured through my veins, pumped by what I recognized now as a continually strengthening heart. Then I gradually slowed as I reached the center of the field, gasping for breath.

This was my reason to continue along my current path, to continue with this quest. As Kiron trudged towards me from a thousand yards away, I rose my face to the sky, sucking in air. I would follow Almara's breadcrumbs and fly through these worlds. I might not get another chance, not ever in my life, to be so free and strong as I was here. My newfound health didn't give me something to look for, but it gave me something to *stay* for.

I would enjoy it while I could. And when the time came to return home, I would go.

As Kiron came within shouting distance, I could hear him mumbling between hoarse breaths. "Stupid," huff, "boy," huff, "kids," huff, "don't," huff, "listen," he growled. Crane reached me first, still barking in protest, and jumped up on me, putting one paw on each of my shoulders. I prepared for a cranky lecture as Kiron neared, but when he got close he simply stopped and put his hands on his hips, breathing hard. He stared at me for several moments.

"You've got some things up your sleeve, boy," he said finally after catching his breath. I smiled. "Alright," he said, "this is as good a place as any."

He released the first two buttons of his shirt and opened it. Beneath the rough fabric a long chain necklace rested against his chest. It reminded me of the charm bracelets some of the girls wore at school, only instead of the little beads and trinkets that hung from theirs, this had a variety of stones fastened around its edges.

"What is that?" I asked.

"Our transportation."

"Is it a link?"

"*They* are links. Each one will take you a different distance in the direction you point it. Most ain't interplanetary, like Almara's, but handy. I told ya I ain't never seen gold, and I ain't. But deep within this one," he fingered a slim, black rock fastened to the chain, "a tiny piece of gold lives. Pa made this one for me before he died, so I could always get back here to the farm. Back home. But when he forged it, the gold disappeared inside." He held the rock up to the sun, trying to see through the opaque stone to the secret power it held within it. But it revealed nothing.

"No matter," he said. "Now, listen." He paused and looked me in the eye. "About Larissa. She's a slippery one. Don't believe what she tells ya. You follow my lead and keep your mouth shut. She fancies herself as powerful as Almara or any of the eight, and if you press her she'll claim to be able to send you back to Earth. But there ain't no way. She's a trickster, and there's nothing more amusing to her than pretending she can do things she can't…just long enough to get what she wants from folks. Truth is, the only way you're getting home is to find Almara. You understand?"

"Yeah, ok."

He reached behind his neck and unfastened the necklace. He chose a thin, black stone and gripped it tightly in one hand, the rest of the links dangling from the chain.

"Now get over here and grab onto Crane." I did as he said and reached for a tuft of hair behind Crane's head as Kiron wrapped his free hand around my arm. "This'll be awkward with the two of us and a stinkin' mutt to boot," he grumbled.

"Crane doesn't stink," I protested. He ignored me and thrust his hand out in front of us, pointing the link in his intended direction. Kiron spoke softly at first and then more loudly as his arm made tiny adjustments in the cool breeze.

"Karashasho," he commanded in a low, humming voice.

The dry grass around where we stood flattened to the ground, and at the same time my insides squeezed tightly. This was a different feeling than Almara's link. I wriggled in pain as the ground disappeared and we spun into the jump. Kiron's hand tightened around my arm, a warning to stop squirming, but I couldn't breathe and fought his grip. A second later we all slammed into the ground in a great, yelping pile of dog and human.

I lay on my back until I caught my breath, and then sat up and looked around. We were high in the mountains, splayed out on a large, flat precipice of rock. I gaped at the precision of our landing and wondered how Kiron had directed us to this exact location. We easily could have landed on the side of the mountain, or in the valley below. I was just opening my mouth to ask when I saw her.

On the far side of the plateau I could make out an ancient woman angrily slamming the door to a tiny wooden house, yelling furiously in our direction as she stomped across the rock. The brisk wind seemed to follow her as she closed the gap between us, and I felt goose bumps rise on the flesh of my arms.

"I thought I told you never to show your stinking face here again!" she shouted over what was quickly becoming a gale. As she approached us she bent to pick up rocks from the mountaintop. A moment later they were raining down on us as she heaved them at Kiron.

One of them, about the size of a golf ball, met with the side of his head and he shouted, "Quit it, you old witch!" He was on his feet now and approaching her. Crane disentangled himself with my legs and quickly ran to his master's defense, barking and snarling at the shriveled woman.

Kiron closed the space between the two swiftly, before another rock could make contact with his skull, and held her arms down at her sides. She struggled and shouted, "Let go of me, you dirty louse!" With her arms held she used the only weapon she had left and kicked him hard in the shin.

"Argh! You stupid bat! Just listen, Larissa! I brought the book!"

She stopped struggling and looked up at him.

"Is this a trick?" she spat.

"No," he said, "no trick. I need your help, and I brought you the book. You can keep it this time." She seemed to relax slightly at his words and he released her arms. She took the opportunity and landed a kick to his other shin before she turned to walk away.

"Argh!"

"If you came here for help then you came to the wrong place," she shouted over her shoulder.

"Larissa, wait!" Kiron hobbled after her, Crane circling the two on their way to the shack. Kiron managed to catch the door before she was able to slam it in his face, and followed her into the small dwelling.

I sat, left alone, on the mountaintop.

CHAPTER EIGHT

I waited for the shouting to stop before I approached the front door of the little house. The wind had died down, but my goose bumps remained from the cold mountain air.

The vista was spectacular. As far as I could see in every direction mountain peaks kissed the sky. I could understand why Larissa would want to live here, but as I looked around at the barren precipice, I wondered what she ate. Unlike Kiron's farm, no animals or garden surrounded her home to support her.

I knocked softly on the door and heard the smart clicking of boots on a wood floor. She wrenched the door open and glared down at me.

"So you're him, are ya?" she demanded.

"Um, what?"

"Yeah," she said sarcastically, "he sure does seem like destiny's choice for such a quest. You've only been waitin' a hundred years and *this* is the one you choose?" She shot Kiron a superior look and walked away from the open doorway. I stood there for a moment, unsure of whether or not that meant I was invited to come in, but the cold outside made me shiver involuntarily, and I stepped into the tiny space and shut the door behind me.

The house was almost a perfect square, and just large enough to fit a small wood table and two chairs. I didn't see a bed, but a crackling fire flickered in the grate. Crane whined and circled the small room, unnerved by the conflict between the two. I stood still by the door and soaked up the warmth from the fire.

"I told you," Kiron said, "I didn't choose him. I couldn't possibly choose the one meant to follow the links. He's Brendan's descendant." Kiron sat in one of the chairs, his back to the fire, his hands on the table. Larissa bustled around the room, now packed to bursting where it had been all hers just minutes before.

"Well, I ain't taking that stinking dog," she snarled.

"You gotta take the dog, Lissa. What am I supposed to do with him? I can't bring him with us. Not with what might be out there."

Her eyes softened slightly at these words, but then quickly hardened again.

"Not my problem," she grunted. She flopped down into the other chair and stared at me.

"Well, sit," she commanded. Before I could open my mouth to remind her that there were only two chairs, a third caught my eye in the corner of the room. I shook my head. Had I just missed it when I walked in?

She glared across the table at Kiron. Their resemblance was remarkable. Like him, Larissa had silver, kinked hair, that grew almost to her knees. Though she lacked the full beard of her brother, a few stubborn whiskers poked out from her chin. Her knobby fingers drummed against the tabletop as she glowered at him.

"You can have the book, Lissa," he pleaded. "No tricks this time." Kiron dug through the pack he had placed at his feet and unearthed the large book I had seen him studying back at the cottage. Despite her anger, her eyes poured over the cover hungrily. He pushed it across the table to her. She opened the cover and leafed through the thin pages, then slammed it shut.

"Why should I?" she said.

Kiron sighed. "Because you're my sister and I need your help. Besides, you've always wanted this and now I'm giving it to you. Isn't that payment enough for a few months of making sure he doesn't starve?" Crane had seated himself the floor, and his head turned back and forth between the two as they talked. Larissa looked down at the dog, and he licked his lips submissively.

After several long moments of looking back and forth between the book, and then the dog, and then the book again, she finally closed her eyes and nodded.

Kiron sat back in his chair and smiled. "Good girl."

"It's mine, anyways," she said.

He couldn't resist the bait.

"That's a lie and you know it," he said.

"Pa left it to me," she said.

"He left it to *me*," he said. "Why would he leave the book to you? First, you don't need it, and second I was the one he set to wait for Brendan, not you."

"Oh, I've needed that book plenty," she argued. "A poor old lady living up here all on her own with barely a magic spell to keep her safe."

Kiron snorted.

"Sister, you got so much magic in you that you talkin' of wanting more is just mad. Seems like you might consider helping those of us who've needed it to get along instead of trying to steal it."

"I never stole that book from you!" Her eyes flashed angrily.

"That's just cause you tried and failed so many times," he said.

She scowled, and then turned to me.

"You. You know what you're gettin' into?" she asked.

"Well, I guess so," I said. But I was starting to wonder if I did.

"HA!" she boomed in characteristic Kiron fashion. "Very convincing. Well, I better feed you up then." She rose from the table and swiped the book, quickly hiding it in a cupboard in the corner of the room.

"We ate not so long ago," Kiron said.

"Tea then?" she asked.

"Yes, please, dear sister."

She grimaced, then glanced my way.

"What's your name, son?"

"Aster Wood," I said.

"Well, Aster Wood," she gathered three mugs from a shelf and they clinked together in her hands, "seems you're about to set out on quite an adventure with my brother, here. You think you're up for it, do ya?"

"I hope so, ma'am. I've been feeling a lot better since I met Kiron."

"Yeah," Kiron said. "And this one came along with a few unexpected...quirks." The corner of his mouth raised up in a secret grin. I smiled.

"What do you mean, 'feeling better'?"

I told her about my heart and my unexplained recovery since

arriving at Kiron's homestead and eating his food.

"Rubbish!" she boomed. "You think this old fraud is healing you with some sort of magic potion?"

I didn't know what to say. Kiron looked very uncomfortable.

"I'm not a fraud, Lissa," he began. "I been givin' him Mother's old brew mixed in with his soup for over a week and he's—"

"That old crone couldn't have healed a paper cut with all the salve in the cosmos and you know it," she said. Then she turned back to me and handed me a mug of hot tea. I hadn't seen a kettle anywhere. "Reason you're gettin' better is you're getttin' closer to the center."

"The center?"

"Center of the Fold." She blew on her tea and sat back in her chair looking at me. I looked at Kiron.

"You know that's just a legend," Kiron said to her.

"What is?" I asked. She smirked.

"You're from Earth, that right?" she asked. I nodded. "That explains it then. The closer you get to the center of the Fold, the healthier you become. It's always been that way."

"It hasn't always been that way," Kiron protested.

"What do you know, brother?" she shot back. "You never made it farther than Aerit. Pa and I traveled all the way to Genopa and back, and I felt the power myself."

Kiron flushed a deep, angry crimson.

"You mean, you're a traveler, too?" I asked.

"If Genopa was so grand, why didn't you *stay*?" Kiron snarled.

She ignored him. "Of course I'm a traveler. Our whole family was travelers. And the flying beasts of *Genopa*," she glared at Kiron, "weren't happy with a couple of humans trekkin' about, I can tell you that. But my dear brother here has held the secret of interplanetary link creation since our Pa died eighty years ago, tucked deep away in the pages of that book. *My* book."

"You can make all the links you want here on Aerit," Kiron spat. "One planet is enough for anyone, even you. Pa left that book to *me*, and he didn't leave no instructions about sharing it. Besides, where you gonna get the gold to make a long link, anyways?"

"You're sharing it with me now, ain't ya?" she boomed. "Anyways, Pa was mad as a hen by the time he died, wasn't he? Anyone in their right mind would've known that I was the one who should've been waitin' for Brendan." She turned to me. "My pa and I traveled all around the Fold for ten years or more before this fool got involved. Thanks to *him* I haven't left Aerit in eighty years. He's kept that book close to his chest all that time, and without it I'd be hopeless to plot a long link on my own. He says Pa wanted it all kept a secret. But he don't know. He don't know what Pa and I had." She looked at him. "And you *don't* know what gold I do or don't have. Pa made me promises, too. We talked about the trouble that was takin' over the planets, the sickness in the fields."

"And the people? You know about them?" I asked. Kiron shot me a warning look. *Don't,* it said. She didn't pick up on my misstep.

"Well, the people were upset, of course, but there wasn't much a common man could do to fight what was happening to their lands. Good thing Almara set out when he did or everyone would've starved. You gotta live where you can stay alive, after all."

"But if you can't make links, how do you get around on Aerit?" I asked. I couldn't help but continue to question her despite Kiron's discomfort. "I mean, we're in the middle of nowhere up here. Where do you get your food?"

"Oh, I can make links. Just not *long* links, links to other planets. Aerit, in all its mundane glory, is mine to travel. And I have other ways of getting what I need. You know, a woman needs a sliver of entertainment, too. Gotta keep life interesting."

"What do you mean?"

"Larissa here is a sailer," Kiron said gruffly.

"You mean, like on a boat?"

They both looked at me, surprised, and then burst out laughing. Their humor irritated me. It had been a perfectly fair question.

"No, no," Kiron said, snorting. After a few moments he composed himself. "Larissa can fly."

"You can *fly*? How?"

"Like this." She pushed back from the table and stood up.

"Lissa, not here," Kiron protested, pushing his own chair back, suddenly alarmed. "Stop showing off. You'll burn the place to the ground."

The air began to boil around her boots, and a moment later she hovered two feet off the floor. My jaw dropped.

"Now, now, big brother," she sang, "don't you worry. Things have changed a little bit since we were young." Kiron pressed his body to the wall, staying as far from her as he could in the tiny room. "The fire of my youth has waned somewhat, but the power is still strong." She gently floated back to the ground and took her seat again.

"How did you do *that*?" I asked.

"Oh, it's just a matter of a little bending around my edges. Anyone close to the fold can do it if they practice for long enough. But even I'll admit that I have somewhat of a gift for it." She smoothed out her long, wool skirt with mock modesty.

"Hogwash, Lissa," Kiron said. "Don't make the boy think anyone can fly. You know it ain't true." He took a long draw from his mug.

"That's all *you* know," she said. "Flying can come in awful handy, you know. If you ever get yourself into a spot of trouble, say, with a villager when a spell goes awry... Awful handy." She produced a large plate of muffins from next to the fire and set it onto the table. It had seemed to appear from nowhere; I was almost certain it hadn't been there a moment ago. Crane's mouth dropped open and drool began to pool at the end of his tongue. She tore off a large chunk of one and fed it to him under the table.

"Can you take people with you?" I asked.

Kiron said "No," and Larissa said, "Sure," at the same time.

"Wanna go out for a sail?" she asked.

"*No*, he *doesn't*," Kiron said pointedly, as much to me as to her. "Seems to me I recall hearing of a little problem with a flight of yours from the folks down in Larshur Village. Something about you dropping that poor blacksmith as you flew over Round Pond."

"I didn't *drop* him. The idiot let go."

"You still took the payment from him though, didn't you? Broken leg from what I heard," he said. "And lucky he didn't drown."

"Of course I took the payment, fool!" she barked, her good humor evaporating.

"Um," I said. "Maybe next time. Seeing as how we're just starting out today and everything, I should probably keep my feet on the ground."

"Suit yourself," she said. "Anyways, looks like my days ahead will be filled with jumping now, not flying. The spell has been hidden away in that book for almost a century. Imagine if Pa knew that you finally gave it up…for a *dog*." Kiron kept his eyes on his mug.

"Where will you go?" I asked. "Back to Genopa?"

"Nah, I wanna go farther in than that. Towards the center." Her eyes gleamed with excitement and unmistakable greed. "Been planning it my whole life. Just been waiting for you to finally croak so I could claim my birthright." She nodded at Kiron.

"Charming," he said.

"What's in the center?" I asked.

"No one knows," she said. "But I'm gonna find out."

"There ain't no center," Kiron said. "Space don't have a center. It's impossible."

"But the Fold does," she snarked at him. Then she looked at me conspiratorially and leaned closer. "And in the center, power like none of us can even imagine. You wanna fly? You find the center and you'll do it and more. You wanna eat? A never ending feast awaits you. Knowledge? You'll learn everything there ever was to learn about on any world and beyond. Health? Find the center and you'll be reborn, clean and strong."

I was entranced by her words and couldn't tear my eyes away from hers. I imagined my frail body, newly made and pulsing with energy, not unlike it was now. Only forever, with no lingering worry about when my luck might run out.

But Kiron wasn't impressed. "Oh, sure," he said. "Find the center, which doesn't exist, by the way, and you'll be all powerful. Ain't that right, Lissa?"

"You don't know squat," she said, sitting back in her chair. I shook my head, breaking her spell. "Where are *you* headed, then?" she asked.

"How would I know, Lissa?" he said. "It's Almara's link, not mine. I don't know where it'll take us."

"Not yours and a good thing, too," she said. "How'd it feel, Aster, traveling by link made by my brother's clumsy hand?"

"That's enough," he spat. "We're going." He pushed back from the table and raised his traveling pack. "I wouldn't leave him with you if I had any other choice. Just promise me you won't cook him up. Or turn him into one of your experiments." He looked at Crane, who had risen to follow him.

"Nah," she said, and she seemed to melt a little. She reached down and scratched Crane behind the ears. He licked his lips and sniffed in her direction, looking for another mouthful of muffin. "Gets lonely up here anyhow. If it wasn't for Reynold I'd go crazy for sure."

"Who's Reynold?" I asked.

A loud squawk came from a bird in the corner of the room that *definitely* hadn't been there a minute ago.

Kiron looked at her and his face softened, too. "Thanks, sister."

"No big trouble," she said and then turned to me. "Keep your wits about you, kid. I expect you'll be seein' some things you ain't never seen before. Just remember, where there's smoke, flame follows close behind. You smell smoke, you run the other direction. Yeah?"

"Yeah, ok," I said automatically as I eyed the bird. His beak was large and yellow, and I shuddered to think of how it would feel sinking into my flesh.

We walked to the door and Kiron stooped down to pat Crane. He didn't speak to him, but looked him deep in the eyes before he turned and left the house. Crane whined, but did not follow. I gave him a scratch under his chin before heading out the door.

"Aster," Larissa called after me and I turned. Her face had slackened and the folds of her skin knit together over the bridge of her nose with worry. "Take care of my brother, eh?" I nodded, and then followed Kiron out onto the rocky bluff.

He was already several paces away from the house, walking swiftly towards the spot we had landed. I jogged to catch up with him.

"Come on," he panted, "before she notices."

"Notices what?" But no sooner was the question out of my mouth than Larissa's shrieking was audible from inside the house.

"Get the link!" Kiron boomed. "Now!"

I scrambled for the map, stuffed deep into my pants pocket. Kiron gripped my arms with both of his hands and looked me in the eyes.

"You better get on with it before she gets out here," he said impatiently.

"Kiron, you stinking goat of a human being—" she yelled over the wind, which had picked up again. She was barreling towards us over the rock, Crane barking at her feet.

"Now's the time!" Kiron yelled, "unless *you* want to be one of her experiments, too!"

I didn't need to be told twice. I thrust the map up above my head and hollered, "Go!"

The force of the jump knocked both Larissa and Crane to the ground, and Kiron and I escaped into the black of space.

CHAPTER NINE

As we spun away from the mountaintop, flashes of light blinked behind my tightly closed eyelids. I tried to pry my eyes open against the whirlpool of air that twirled me like a child's toy, but a wave of nausea forced me to squeeze them shut again. I hunched over, clutching at my stomach. The jump was unpleasant, but Almara's link wasn't painful like Kiron's had been.

When we landed, it was on hard cobblestone. I stayed crouched down, and my hands pressed into the cold, dirty stone of the street. I was gasping, and a sweat broke out all over my body as I tried to force down the large lump that threatened in my throat. I sat down on the stone, and found the air was cool, helping me regain my head. Whatever there was to see during the jumps, I wasn't sure if it was worth it trying to look again.

Kiron sat back against a stone wall opposite me. We were in a long, narrow alleyway.

"What happened?" I asked. "What did you do?"

He smiled between gasps, his eyes closed as he rested his head back against the stone. From beneath his coat he produced a thin, crumpled page. It was from the book.

"You took the spell," I said slowly. "Why?" No wonder she had come after us.

"Lissa was never meant to continue past Aerit," he panted. "Pa was clear as crystal on that fact."

"You tricked her." I was impressed despite my concern.

"Lissa has more power than me, that's for sure. But she's arrogant. Arrogance breeds ignorance. I've always been the brains of the family."

After we both caught our breath, I asked, "What about Crane? She's sure to do something horrible, isn't she?"

"Nah," he said, getting to his feet and brushing the dirt from his clothes. "Lissa's soft spot has always been animals. No matter how much she hates me, she'd never hurt Crane. Though, after this, I suspect he won't be mine anymore. She'll keep him from me, just outta spite. No matter. That mutt will have a great life with her. She adores dogs."

"But why do we need the spell?" I asked. "Aren't we supposed to use Almara's links? We won't need to be making more, will we?" My stomach squirmed at the painful memory of the jump from Kiron's farm to the mountaintop.

"I needed something to convince her to take Crane. Without an offering, and a good one, she woulda said no, just to punish me. The book was the only way. But I couldn't let her have the spell. We have it now, in case we ever need it. Here." He handed it out to me.

I stared blankly at the paper and then at him. "But— why are you giving it to me?"

"It was always meant for you," he said. "You're the one meant to be on this quest, not me. I'm just along for the ride." He shook his outstretched hand impatiently.

I took the thin paper and folded it carefully, putting it in my pocket. Then I took his hand and heaved myself upright.

As my breathing slowed, distant sounds found their way to my brain through the ringing in my ears. I was thankful for the cover of a deserted passage. We must have been far enough away from the people of this place that they hadn't heard us land. Beyond the shadows, the sounds of men and horses, wagons and commerce came to me. I steadied myself against a stone wall, and held up this most recent link. We both peered at the page.

The outline of a city had appeared. A perfect square was outlined into the center with several streets lining the perimeter. From each corner a wide lane cut through the streets diagonally to the square. In the center a golden ring twinkled at me.

"Where are we?" I asked, handing him the map.

Kiron studied the map. "Aeso, I believe." He looked at the buildings on either side of us and ran his free hand over the stone walls. "Probably in the city of Stonemore."

I looked down the alley towards the street beyond.

"But how do you know?"

"I don't," he said. "But I've seen a schematic like this before. It is likely." He held the page close to his face, examining each line. "That's where the next link hides," he said, pointing at the circle.

I began to brush the dirt from my own clothes, but he stopped me.

"No, stay dirty. Your clothes are already unusual. You'll blend in better with a little dirt on 'em. Ready?"

I folded the map, tucking it into my pocket next to the spell page, and we began to cautiously make our way out to the city beyond. We stayed back, hidden in the shadows, just close enough to observe the bustling lane before joining the foot traffic. This was a busy place. Women walked past the alley carrying bushels of wheat and fruit, children skipping along in their wake. The hooves of enormous horses clacked against the stone; some drew smart coaches, some open carriages carrying items for trade. It looked like a town on Earth from a thousand years ago.

Aside from the nerves I felt at being in a strange place, again, I was mostly relieved at what I saw. These people were busy going about the daily chores of life. Women chased small children that went astray, scooping them up out of harm's way whenever a horse passed by. Men and women alike hauled provisions through the streets, some headed for the market, some for home. Shopkeepers with empty shops stood in their doorways watching the crowds amble by, waiting for business. Hopefully nobody would notice our presence here at all. We might be able to slip right through this place, none being the wiser.

Kiron lead me out into the lane and I resisted the impulse to keep my hand on the blade of the ax. I was a stranger, yes, but would they notice? As I walked I found that, for the most part, they seemed not to. Kiron pretended he knew exactly where he was going, so all I really had to do was keep up and try not to draw attention to myself. I tried to keep my pace at the same time casual and purposeful. If I ran, they would see me. If I gawked, they would see me. If I kept the pace, as they did, I would be, hopefully, invisible.

Well, almost invisible. The occasional child stopped and pointed in my direction, tugging at the skirt of his mother to look. What was it? I looked down at myself, and back up at the passersby. My clothes? My boots? My hair? That had to be it. Most of the people here had dark hair; the lightest I saw was a medium brown. And here I was with a mop of white-blond, bursting through like a flashlight in the dark. The adults didn't seem to notice or care, though, so I continued forward and made a note to rub some dirt into it at the earliest opportunity.

People and horses traveled every which way on the lane, but the majority of them were headed in a single direction. We followed the crowd silently, towards what I didn't know. I studied the city around me. Aside from the roofs of the dwellings and shops, all the buildings here were made entirely of the same mottled, gray stone. Decoration, or color of any sort, was sparse on the storefronts. Either they didn't care for such embellishment or they didn't have the means for such things; the grimy, gray dress of the citizens around me made me suspect the latter. These people weren't living in squalor, though, and aside from the occasional child with muddy cheeks, most faces were scrubbed clean.

My eyes scanned the facades as I walked for any sign of Almara, but I found nothing. On one side of the street in front of a small shop, a butcher was cutting fish on a long table. Perched on his shoulder, a small gray tabby cat watched the scene with interest, waiting for the right moment to make his move. A small group of children were gathered around the man, absorbed as he chopped off head after head of the day's catch.

Thwack, went the knife.

"Eeeeek!" squealed the children as the fish's head jumped away from its body. The adults nearby smiled despite themselves, as did I. Three other smaller cats scampered about at the butcher's feet, searching for fallen morsels.

Farther down we passed a boy about my age, maybe twelve or

thirteen, following behind an important looking man dressed in finer clothes than the rest of the crowd. The boy carried a satchel and a scroll of paper, which he was scribbling onto with a large, ornately decorated pen. The man spoke with authority to a shopkeeper, who wore a solemn look, and the boy paid me no notice as I passed by.

As I continued on, the street got more crowded. I could see up ahead that the narrow passage became suddenly wide, and as we passed under the archway that marked the end of the road, I was deposited into a large, open square. Booth after booth of fruit, meat, linens, and trinkets were scattered about the place. People walked in every direction, large packages underneath their arms or strapped to their backs, as they went about their shopping. Kiron pulled me off to the side and spoke quietly in my ear.

"This is the square shown on the map," he said. "Whatever we're looking for, it should be here. We'll start in the middle and work our way out from there. We'll search separately, it will call less attention to us, but stay close. I've heard of this place." He looked warily around. "We're unlikely to find friends here."

"Ok," I said. "What if we get separated? Shouldn't we have a place to meet or something?" I was getting nervous. I tried not to imagine what might happen to me here if my guide suddenly went missing.

Kiron looked all around, and then up at the arch that hung over the entrance to the square.

"Right here," he said, gesturing to it. Carved into the enormous stones that made up the arch were the words *Stonemore East.* Behind where we stood was the door to a tailor's shop. "We'll meet at the tailor's if anything happens, ok?"

I nodded.

"Remember, stay in sight. Stay close."

Together we dove into the market. I focused my attention on the merchants who sold the smaller items, trinkets and books, searching for anything bearing Almara's mark. Kiron followed my lead and looked at the stalls opposite the ones I searched along the row. He had explained that not every link would be a paper map, even though the first three had been. He had instructed me to focus my attention on finding the symbol, no matter what it was drawn onto.

The tables were stacked with pottery, little wooden boxes, the occasional silver pendant, cutlery, and every other mismatched item imaginable. I was lost in a sea of possibilities. I tried to stay focused on reaching the precise center of the square. The sellers watched me closely, but it was my hands they paid attention to. Of course, I was no thief, but in a busy place like this there must be plenty of kids looking to snatch treasures off of tables when nobody was looking. I kept my hands open and where the merchants could see them, and doing this I was able to work my way through the square without arousing suspicion.

Patrolling the square were official looking men who rode gigantic black horses. They steered them up and down the rows two by two, their eyes constantly scanning for trouble. They were impressive and intimidating, dressed entirely in black, spears attached to the sides of their mounts. The people in the market moved out of their way as they passed, clearly not wanting to tangle with them. I steered clear as well. Mixing with what appeared to be the law was not something I was keen to do.

I made it to what appeared to be the center of the square and turned on the spot, trying to measure the distance between myself and each of the four sides of the center. Kiron paused and nonchalantly inspected a table of pottery while he waited for me to move. This was as good a place to start as any. I stopped at a table that was piled high with small, metal cups. Their elaborate carvings caught my attention, and my eyes moved greedily over them, searching. The man behind the table stood up to his full height and peered down at me.

"What's your business here, son?" he asked. "What does a sprout like you need with wine cups?"

I looked up into his face, my mouth falling open despite my best efforts to keep it shut. The man was huge.

"Uh," I stammered, taking in his wide stance and, unmistakably, the handle of a dagger that jutted out from underneath his coat. "I thought they looked very pretty. I'm, uh, looking for a gift," I finally got out.

"A gift?" he replied suspiciously, his eyes narrowing.

"Yes, sir," I said, trying desperately to recover a little of my courage. "I'm looking for a gift for my mother." I may not be a thief, but in this case I had little choice but to lie.

He rested his hands on the table, the tips of his fingers tense.

"You have silver?" he asked.

"I'm saving up, sir. May I…may I touch one?"

"What's your name, boy?"

"My name?" I asked stupidly. My mind raced to come up with a false name. I didn't know why, but I felt that it would not be wise to tell the people here my true one. I grasped at the first one that came to mind, my father's. "I'm Jack," I looked about wildly, trying to think of an appropriate last name. The walls of the square, the cobblestone streets, the dress of the people, all led me to conclude, "Jack Gray."

The man stared at me for a moment, seeming to try to decide whether or not to believe me. I didn't dare try to look to Kiron for help.

"Well, Jack Gray, the answer is no, you may not touch one. But I will show them to you, one at a time. Which one would you like to see?"

I let out a breath of relief, hoping that he didn't notice, and pointed to a cup that had swirled etching all around the base.

"That one there, please, sir."

He picked up the cup and held it out, turning it slowly in his hand to show off the detailing. The filigree wrapped all the way around, but no sacred symbol was there to be found. I asked him to show me another, and another, but it was the same with each. He must have seen the disappointment in my face.

"Not fancy enough for your ma, eh?"

"No, sir," I replied. "These are very nice cups. But they're not quite right."

"On your way then, Jack Gray." He placed the last delicate cup back in its spot among the others. There was no mistaking his tone. I was dismissed.

"Thank you, sir," I said as I began to back away from the table.

Suddenly his eyes widened in surprise, but I had no clue why. A moment later, I was struck with the force of one of the enormous, patrolling horses, and was knocked backwards off my feet onto the hard street. The horse's hooves pranced next to my head in agitation. The backpack, unseen by everyone, had thankfully cushioned my fall. I was unhurt but for my two scraped palms.

My palms didn't worry me, though. What worried me was the face of the angry man coming down from his horse. He hovered over me.

I don't know why I hadn't put it together before now, but

suddenly my blood was liquid ice. I knew this man. Why hadn't I seen the similarities? The dress of the soldiers who patrolled, the cobblestone streets, the ancient buildings on every side. This man, this man with dark eyes, came closer and closer.

I shrunk from him. I feared him. He grabbed my shoulders to lift me to my feet with the force of a giant. He set me down hard with an angry shove and released my me, his dark, terrifying eyes boring into mine. They seemed to be without pupils. From the center of each eye to the edges of his irises was nothing but solid black.

It was the face of the man from my dream, the face of the man who had chased me from this very place in my nightmare many nights ago.

He opened his mouth, to say what, I never heard. I forgot Kiron, standing five feet away, mouth agape in shock. I forgot our quest. I forgot about getting back home to Earth. All that remained in my head was me and this man, and his proximity shook my very bones. I took advantage of the split second between his terrifying grip releasing me and the beginning of his tirade, ducked underneath his still outstretched arm, and ran.

CHAPTER TEN

I must have surprised them all, because nobody came after me at first. As soon as I rounded the first corner of tables set up in the square I ducked down as low as I could, sprinting for the closest exit. It wasn't until I was already through and barreling down a side street that I heard them begin their pursuit.

The cool air coursed through my lungs, and my light feet raced over the stone. My slightness was just the ticket. I took great care not to bump and jostle the people in the streets, a task made easier since this side of the city was less populated than the lane I had followed to the square. I wanted them to be so unconcerned with this boy running past that they forgot me almost as soon as I passed.

As soon as I possibly could I darted into a narrow alleyway, not unlike the one I had arrived in, and continued to make turn after turn until I lost track of where I was. It didn't matter. Escape mattered. After several changes in direction, I finally came upon an alcove that protected a forgotten back door. I huddled in the shadows, catching my breath and listening intently for any sign that my pursuers were closing in.

I heard very little. It was quiet here, in the depths of the maze I had run into. Perhaps people occasionally came to this place, but mostly it looked unused. After several minutes I decided it was relatively safe, and I sat down to rest against the wall.

What a mess. Twenty minutes in this place and I had already lost Kiron and called an enormous amount of attention to myself. How was I supposed to find the link to get back out of this place with an angry group of guards chasing me? Despite these considerable problems, I couldn't help but feel elated at my easy escape. I had legs that moved so fast I felt certain that they must look blurred to anybody who happened to be watching. I put my hand over my chest, and I could feel the steady thumping of my heart underneath it.

Would Kiron be found? Would someone figure out that he was associated with me? I didn't know. My hair had set me apart from the city people, but he looked just like everybody else. Maybe no one had noticed that we had been traveling together. Maybe he would be ok.

I rested for over an hour, too scared to do anything but hide. I wanted the dark man to forget all about me. Night quickly began descending, and I pulled out the map to look for new clues. There were none. The same maddening circle of gold glinted up at me, but no further instruction had emerged. So far I had seen nothing even close to resembling Almara's symbol. I supposed that it could have been worse. What if we had arrived and everything had had the mark on it? How would we have chosen then? I made a plan to wait for the cover of darkness, and then set out to find Kiron back at our meeting spot.

While I waited for night to fall in earnest I revealed the pack and had a lunch of sorts. Kiron had packed a variety of apples, nuts, bread and, of course, smoked chicken meat. I avoided the loudly crunching apples but chewed on the tough, dry meat. All the time I moved with extreme caution and listened for any disturbance on the tiny paths that had led me to this place, but no threat seemed to have followed me this far into the depths of the city.

Once I could no longer see the sun hitting the top edges of the buildings around me, and the light in the alleyways became blue and murky, I stood up and considered which direction to head in. I couldn't sit in this hiding spot forever.

No sooner had I struck back out in my attempt to rejoin Kiron than I discovered I was completely lost. I had half expected him to come around the corner while I waited, but now I understood why I hadn't seen him. No wonder nobody had found me. The little side alleys were weaved together into a labyrinth of possibilities. I had no idea which direction I had come from, and now I didn't even have the light of the sun on the rooftops to keep me on a steady course. I walked along for what seemed like hours, though it could have been only minutes, but seemed to make no progress at all. Every time I tried to stay headed in a single direction I was greeted with a dead end, or an unexpected turn I had to take. Left, right, straight, left again, left, straight, right. I had no idea where I was going, only that my need to get out was increasing with each minute that ticked by.

The tall walls seemed to push in on me from all sides. I could feel my breathing coming in shorter and increasingly panicked gasps. *Breathe,* I thought. *You're okay. It'll be okay.* Without realizing it my pace slowed and I came to a stop, leaning my back against a wall and lifting my chin to let the air into my constricting throat. Through the crowded rooftops above I could see a star poking through the deepening twilight, then another. Why had I waited so long? Why hadn't I started moving when I had at least the shadows from the sun on the buildings to guide me? I was going to be stuck back here for the night, maybe longer, I was sure of it. Where would I sleep? Where would I hide? How would I ever find my way out and avoid capture at the same time?

I slid down to the ground. The cold hard stone against my back kept me from toppling over from the dizziness that crept up the back of my neck and sent my head swimming. My chest clenched for the first time in many days. I dug my fingernails into the stone walkway, holding on to the earth as my breathing increased and the world began to turn upside down.

But it wasn't enough. The fog of unconsciousness settled over me, and I felt my forehead knock softly against the ground as my body slumped over.

I woke many hours later in the same position. My body was stiff with cold. This frigid air had not settled on the city until deep into the night, and I my breath floated out in front of my face in small plumes of steam.

I slowly sat upright, rubbing my head and trying to remember what had happened. The memory of panic came back to me, but the feeling of it was gone now. I crossed my arms over my chest and shivered, looking up to the starlit dome above. I had to get moving. My teeth began to chatter violently behind my numb lips.

I hoisted myself upright, bracing against the wall again, but my feet were steady now. I chose a direction and set off, taking care to keep my tread quiet.

I walked. And walked. For hours I simply kept on, grateful for the small warmth the easy action of walking brought to my body. The alleyways were dark, but not completely black. Somewhere in the sky, beyond the edge of the tall structures above me, a moon shone down.

I had been an idiot. To think that ten hours ago I had actually felt a desire to stay in this deeper part of the Maylin Fold, to continue to gain strength, even though I was away from the people I cared about. My mom. Grandma. Now I was hunted, lost, and freezing.

They must still be at the farm looking for me. What would they think about my disappearance? My stomach knotted as I imagined Mom's face, fearful and guilty. She would think I had run away. She would think I had been so angry about being stuck at the farm that I had taken off. And later, when they didn't find me, she would think I was dead, my body hiding somewhere in the countryside, lost forever.

And Grandma; would she be blamed? Would she get into some kind of trouble for not watching me more closely? I had been right under her nose, but now I was so far away that none of them would have been able to bring me home, not even if they knew where I was.

I couldn't think about that now. I had to stay focused, to stay on Almara's trail. They might not be able to bring me home to Earth, but somewhere deeper in the Fold was the man who could send me.

A dim light slowly began to creep into the alleyway, and suddenly my next turn to the left released me from the labyrinth in the buildings. I restrained myself from running right out into the lane ahead. My brain tried to cling to reason, and I stopped moving. I forced myself to wait, to listen.

The night was very late, as I had guessed. Not a single person crossed on the narrow street in front of me as I hid in the shadows. A lit torch in the street cast a greenish glow on the storefronts, but nobody was out. I put my hand on my ax and cautiously stepped out into the open, breathing deeply, my chest relaxing for the first time in hours.

I was ecstatic to be out of that maze behind the buildings. I was so relieved that I dropped my hand from the ax and barely bothered to keep an eye out for possible pursuers. It was luck alone that kept me from being caught at this time, for the cover of darkness also covered my own stupidity at letting my guard down so easily. But I couldn't help my carelessness. The joy that came from being lost, and then suddenly not, was overwhelming. I chose a direction and walked briskly along in the dark shadows of the empty buildings.

Soon I came to the entrance to the main square I had run from earlier. I peered around the edge of one side of the opening, but no one patrolled. It seemed that even those enormous black-clad guards had need of rest.

I didn't dare call out to Kiron, but my eyes searched for him in every shadow. He had to be here.

I cautiously moved out into the square. The memory of my escape from the man with the dark eyes was still fresh, and I kept a sharp eye out for anyone that looked like they might be associated with him.

I scurried from shadow to shadow along the outer perimeter of the square, slowly making my way to the arch Kiron had indicated, *Stonemore South.* I finally dared to open my mouth.

"Kiron," I whispered into the darkness.

No response.

I waited and watched, searching for any movement, any sign that Kiron had made it out of the square alright. But no glint of his silver beard or swish of his coat greeted me. No irritated response came to my inquiries.

I didn't want to stay put. First of all, I was scared of being caught. But secondly, I felt a need to search for the link with or without Kiron. He would be angry if he found me just standing here doing nothing, the opportunity to search in the dead of night wasted. Under the cover of the black morning, I crept low to the center of the square. All of the tables had been removed and the entire space was now empty. When I reached the center I turned around and around, searching for some indication of where to find the link. The map had pointed me here. Right here. I knelt to the ground and ran my hands along the roughly hewn cobblestones. No patterns betrayed the secret.

Across the square two men began arguing. They had stumbled into the street moments ago, drunk, and were now throwing punches at each other. I wished hopelessly that I could disappear as effectively as my backpack. *Don't run. Don't run,* I thought. *Stay calm.* I walked as quickly as I could to the shadows at the edge of the square.

Soon one of the men passed out on the cold ground, and the other stumbled away into the night. I released my breath slowly and closed my eyes with relief at not being seen.

His hand gripped my shoulder suddenly, and I almost cried out in surprise. Kiron spun me around before I could make a sound and pressed his index finger to his lips. I nodded, gasping, as he pulled me deep into the shadows. When we were completely hidden he turned around.

"Where did you go?" he whispered.

"The alleyways," I said. "I'm sorry. I got lost once I was clear of them. What happened after I ran?"

"The dark one was furious. He ordered his entire guard after you. They didn't notice me, but I saw them searching for you for the rest of the day. They've been questioning the towns people. You stick out with that glowing mop on your head."

I absently ran my hand through my hair. I had been targeted, and now it wouldn't just be the children of this place interested in my appearance.

"What am I going to do?" I asked nervously.

"Don't worry about it yet. It's still black out and there's no one around. But we'll need to come up with a plan before dawn."

"Did you find anything?" I asked.

"No," he said. "I searched high and low through the market, but I didn't find nothin'. And the stones in the square reveal no secrets. We'll search now, while the guards sleep. You take the north side of the square, I'll take the south. We'll meet in the middle."

I didn't like the idea of splitting up again so soon after reuniting, but I was feeling lucky I had avoided a lecture about my flight earlier. And relieved at having located my companion again. I nodded, and we set off in opposite directions.

The edges of the square were lined with little shops and offices, vacant and dark. I stepped quietly past each of them, peering into the small windows, searching for any sign of Almara. I ran my hands along the walls of the shops, trying to keep from running into them in the darkness. After passing several of the facades, my hands slipped from the rough stone of the buildings to something smooth and round and cold. Several of these unusual rocks were placed side by side, at least twenty. I took a step back from them, trying to determine what sort of stone the pavers were hewn from. Maybe it was a clue.

Suddenly, I understood. I covered my scream with both of my hands as I realized I was facing a long row of human skulls in varying states of decay. Then, realizing that I had just been touching them, I frantically wiped my hands on my pants. I furiously rubbed my mouth with the edges of my shirt, trying hard not to let a single sound escape me. I moved quickly to the end of the row until I found the ragged stone again. I walked quickly past the next few facades, trying to put distance between myself and the carnage.

I rested my back against a wall when I was far enough away to be able to breathe again. What was this place? Chills ran down my spine when I remembered the children I had seen earlier today. They lived out their lives with trophies like this to look at every single day. It was disgusting. And terrifying.

When I caught my breath, I moved on, this time taking the chance of a knock on the head and keeping my hands down. I had rounded the first side of the square, and was just turning to investigate the next when a flash of light caught my eye.

The representation of the symbol was brief, and I almost missed it entirely. Sitting in the window of a small shop was a slim, silver device, lit only by a single oil lamp deep in the interior. The several parts to it moved constantly. Two circles entwined with each other and spun around a center diamond. From the front it was unrecognizable, merely a trinket on sale in a shop. But when viewed from the side, the circles changed shape, elongating into ovals. Every tenth rotation, the top and bottom star of the symbol would be visible for just a fraction of a second.

It was a trick. Nobody looking at this device from the main square would see what I could see now. It would take viewing it from the side, at just the right angle, for the circles to appear elongated, and only every couple of minutes did the two stars become visible. They flashed so briefly that any onlooker would think it was simply a trick of the light, and after regarding it for another moment would look away.

I, however, knew better.

I approached the window and looked inside. A man sat behind a desk amidst mountains of trinkets. What was he doing up so late? I moved closer and tapped softly on the glass. He looked up at me over his spectacles for a quick moment, then waved me away with his hand and bent down again to his work. I tapped again. He glared up at me once more, and impatiently waved me away again.

I thought about my options. I could wait until morning, when the cover of darkness would no longer be my ally, until he opened his shop. I could pound on the door right now, hoping that he would let me in with minimal fuss and that I wouldn't call the attention of any guards. Or I could somehow, silently, convince him to allow me entry.

I continued walking around the square towards the next corner where Kiron and I would meet. I could just make out his shadow as he darted in and out of hiding, making his way towards me. He was taking forever, but I didn't dare come out from where I hid, nestled into the doorway of a tailor shop.

When he finally arrived he breathed, "Anythin'?"

"Yes. Follow me."

I led him to a dark corner a couple doors down from where I had seen the symbol.

"Watch." I pointed to the window.

After a couple of minutes the rotating pieces aligned and Kiron gasped. He started to walk towards the window, grabbing my arm to pull him along, but I planted my feet. He turned, not understanding.

"I already tried twice," I whispered. "There's a man inside but he won't come to the door."

He looked towards the window, and then back to me, his eyes darting around as he thought.

"Show him the pack," he finally said.

"Why?" The pack was a treasure, and I was wary of showing

anyone I met what it could do. "It'll probably just scare him."

"No, the *symbol* on the pack."

"Oh!" Yes, of course. If he saw Almara's symbol on the pack, he would know I was someone he could trust.

We both moved towards the window. I removed the canvas from my back and revealed it as we closed the distance. Then, when we reached the glass, I held it up, showing the symbol clearly. I tapped again.

The man was clearly irritated, and he ignored my tapping. I persisted, and with the third round of insistent taps he threw his pen down on the table and stood up from his chair, glaring at us through the glass. For a moment his eyes only saw my face, then Kiron's, but then they moved over to the pack and his snarl faded. Upon seeing the symbol, his mouth dropped open and his eyes grew round. He quickly made his way around the desk and shuffled to the door, unlocking several bolts. The door flew open and he pulled us both through it, furiously bolting it back up behind him as if expecting the devil himself to arrive on our heels.

CHAPTER ELEVEN

He looked like he'd seen a ghost.

"Come, both of you, hurry back here," he said nervously, and he pulled us towards the back of the shop. He was a short, round man, and I watched the back of his shiny, bald head as we moved through the mountains of merchandise. Every table was piled high with trinkets of all sorts; dishes, goblets, jewelry, chairs piled on top of one another, little boxes for keeping treasures, and books, everywhere books. One might call it an antique shop…or a junk shop, depending on your perspective.

He thrust us through the doorway at the back of the place into a tiny room. Once inside, he retreated back into the shop and returned a moment later with the candle. He closed the door behind him and set the candle down before he spoke again. He seemed to be having a harder and harder time doing so the more he looked at us.

"What—" he began, and then, "Who—" He seemed incapable of speaking a full sentence. I put my bag down on the floor and slumped into one of the two chairs that were wedged into the space, waiting for him to compose himself. This was the first time I had felt at all safe since leaving Kiron's farm.

"Where did you...come from?" he got out finally, pushing up his thick spectacles onto the bridge of his nose. "Who are you?"

Kiron looked at him skeptically from where he leaned against the wall, and I was the first to speak. "My name is Aster," I said. "Aster Wood. This is Kiron." I motioned to my ancient traveling companion.

He seemed to not recognize my name. He continued to splutter for a moment and then finally collected himself.

"I am Chapman," he got out at last. "You must forgive me, but I have never met another. All of these years I have followed, alone and unsure. And now two of you arrive at my door in the dead of night! Quite surprising."

"What do you mean you've never met 'another'? Another what?" I asked.

"Another Almarian," he replied.

Kiron huffed.

"Almarian? What's that?" I asked.

"What do you mean?" he said. "An Almarian. Surely you understand. Are you trying to trick me?" His eyes widened once more and darted back and forth between Kiron and I. He stepped back from the table. "Did...did the Shield send you? To...to..."

"An Almarian is a sort of follower," Kiron said to me, ignoring him. "They see Almara as more of a god than a man. They worship him and what little of the frillier bits of history they are aware of, stories made pretty by the telling." He turned back to the man. "I didn't know that Almarians still existed among the planets in the Fold, I hear mention of him so seldom. Nobody sent us."

Chapman looked terrified. He sure was anxious. "We came here on our own" I said, trying to calm him.

His face relaxed somewhat, not catching Kiron's slight, but he went on more cautiously.

"Well, this is unheard of! Imagine, two servants of Almara in Stonemore!" His emotions seemed to be bobbing back and forth between fear and excitement.

"Well, we're not really *servants* of Almara. It's more like we're sort of…following him."

"We are the *Corretage*," Kiron said, raising his head high and peering down his nose at Chapman.

Chapman's face broke into a tentative smile.

"But, surely you must be joking," he said, and looked at each of us in turn, waiting for us to laugh. Then, when we didn't, he furrowed his brows in confusion. "But that is impossible!" he said.

I turned to Kiron. "What's is 'Corretage'?"

"It is the name of the group at the center of Almara's original purpose," he said. "Almara, the eight, my family, Brendan, and now you. There may be others, but I don't know of 'em. Truth be told, I'm surprised that a simple Almarian knows of it at all."

Chapman picked up on the insult this time, and bristled.

"You are quick to judge the Almarians, friend, if you are who you say you are," he said. "In any case, you'd best hide that mark you showed through the window. Just you flashing his symbol will mark you as a servant, and a traitor, here. Such…support is considered a crime in Stonemore. I'm surprised you weren't discovered already. You're lucky you didn't find yourself tied to a whipping post before now."

"A…whipping post?" A heavy weight dropped into the pit of my stomach, and I was reminded again of the skulls in the square. What had I gotten myself into?

"Oh, yes," he replied. "Any mention of Almara is not tolerated in Stonemore."

"But why?" I asked. It was my turn to be nervous.

He snorted. "In Stonemore, the great battle between Almara and Zarich cemented his status as an untouchable. Contact with, or even mention of, Almara results in imprisonment here."

"Imprisonment? But isn't Almara trying to help everyone in the Fold?" I asked.

"Yes, of course," he said. "But there are those who are threatened by his immense power. And they remain in Stonemore where they are in control." He pulled back a chair and motioned to a short stool hidden under the table for Kiron to take. A look passed between Kiron and I. His told me to keep my wits about me. Mine told him to not be so rude. When he sat, Chapman began to speak.

"Many hundreds of years ago, when Almara and the eight made their way through Stonemore, Zarich the Great had issue with their intentions. At every turn he strove to trip them up, and yet they were able to continue in their quest here in the city, seemingly unharmed by Zarich's meddling. Finally, infuriated by his inability to halt their explorations, Zarich and the Shield waged a great assault on Almara and the eight as they slept, and fighting ensued." He smiled. "It is said that the center of Stonemore was lit up as if all the stars in the cosmos had descended here to participate, such a defense did Almara and the eight put forth."

I had taken one bite of cheese from a plate Chapman had laid in the center of the table, but as I listened to him I had forgotten to chew it. I swallowed the hard lump so that I could speak again. "What happened next?"

"Zarich lost," he answered, a note of triumph in his voice. "Those who followed Almara escaped Stonemore with him as the sun began to shine over the eastern hills. However, a great treasure to was taken from him that night. Legend tells that Zarich had won the Stone of Borna in the battle, and that Almara was forced to continue on his quest without it."

I was completely entranced now. "What is the Stone of Borna?"

"It is said to be a magical jade stone of great healing power, a treasure in any land. As big as my fist and ten times as heavy, the great green rock can keep the holder youthful far longer than the natural ways of our world allows."

Kiron couldn't help himself. "Hogwash." Chapman glared at him.

"What happened to the rock after Zarich took it?"

"Nobody rightly knows," Chapman answered, sitting back in his chair and folding his stubby hands over his round belly. "After that battle, both Zarich and the stone disappeared from public view."

I looked at Kiron. "Well, most of it falls in line with what I know," he said. "Though the Stone is just a story, nothin' more than a myth made up by those who wish for magic rather than practice it." He looked at Chapman condescendingly.

Chapman spluttered with indignation. "No one holds all of the pieces to Almara's puzzle. I, myself, have studied the lore of the Stone of Borna for many years. You may choose to believe as you wish, but it is unwise to discount every piece of information that others present to you. Especially those who let you into their shops in the dead of night." He let the vague threat hang in the air.

"I'm sorry," I said, trying to recover the friendly mood. "My friend here is very old…and *cranky*," I glared at Kiron. "We are very appreciative of the shelter you've given us. Thank you."

"I figured we'd end up in Stonemore at some point," Kiron said, ignoring both of us, "but I didn't think it would be so soon in our journey that Almara would bring us to a place so full of hostility." He turned to Chapman. "How do you get by here, and with your head still attached to your body?"

Chapman gave an involuntary shudder. "Most of the true believers of Almara fled with him after the battle, but a few remained in secret. My ancestors were among them, and they passed the story down generation after generation so that someone here in Stonemore would always know what had really happened. The silver scope in the window is many hundreds of years old. It has never, not once, called attention to itself until tonight. I am the last in the line, and I know of no other in Stonemore who serves Almara."

"Who rules Stonemore now?" I asked.

His eyes immediately filled with fear, and he leaned in close, whispering quickly. "The Shield runs the city now. They are led by Cadoc, the general of the army."

"And the Shield…they are the men in black? The ones on horses?"

"Yes," he answered, his face falling into a grimace of dislike. "But Cadoc, he is not who he claims to be. Zarich disappeared, and Cadoc appeared to take his place." He was talking faster and faster. "But there are…similarities between the two men…if you know what to look for. The crook of a nose, the manner of the way he holds his sword. His eyes. I believe they are the same dark eyes that Zarich once looked out from behind."

"You mean they're the same person?" I whispered, looking back and forth between the two men. Kiron sat quietly, silently nodding his head.

"I do not know for certain," Chapman said. "It certainly sounds mad. The fight was hundreds of years ago. But the similarities between them are too great for any Almarian to ignore. He shows no mercy to those who oppose him. He is known, among the few who whisper, as the Dark King."

I had a feeling I knew exactly who this Cadoc was.

"Why did Zarich hate Almara so much?"

"Oh," said Chapman, relaxing a bit, "men of power seem to always hate other men of power, don't they? Like little boys they always want more and more. I suppose Almara flaunted his power somewhat, and it was just too tempting for Zarich to resist trying to wrest it from him." He peered at us over his narrow glasses. "But tell me now, how did you come to be in Stonemore?"

It was our turn to talk, but neither of us did. Clearly, Stonemore was a dangerous place for us to be. Was the mark in the window enough for us to trust this Chapman?

"I'll tell the story," Kiron said, answering my silent pleas for help. It would be a delicate task, telling this man only what was necessary for him to know.

"We thank you, friend, for takin' us in at such peril to yourself," Kiron began formally. "But we can't tell you all you might desire to hear. We come to Stonemore to find one of Almara's maps. Do you know of these?"

Chapman laughed. "Why, yes of course I know of the maps. But straight off you are telling me that you wish to accomplish the impossible. The maps are lost, as you, yourself must know."

"It's our purpose to find 'em," Kiron said. "We've charted a course to the link already, but searchin' for it for the day and night has led us nowhere but to you. Tell me, what lies beneath the square?"

It was as if Kiron had smacked Chapman on the top of his bald head. Chapman's eyes bugged.

"Why do you ask this, man?" he said, his breaths immediately quickening. He looked terrified.

Kiron held out his hand to me. "The link, please."

I reached into my pocket and pulled out the map of the city, handing it to Kiron.

"I ask," he said, "because we hold one of the lost maps. I'm its keeper and its guard, and have been for most of my life." He unfolded the map and spread it out on the table between us and Chapman. Chapman stared at the page in stunned silence. Kiron pointed to the shimmering golden ring at the center of the square. "This is where our treasure lies," he said. "But cobblestones are all that greet us out there. I ask you again. What lies beneath the square?"

Chapman continued to stare at the map, and then sat back in his chair, eyes still wide.

"The dungeons."

"Then that's where we're headed," Kiron said.

"But, you're mad!" Chapman said. "Anyone who has ever been known to descend below Stonemore has never resurfaced alive. It is said that a treasure hold lies beneath the city. Within the dungeons lie the silver and gems of Stonemore. But, of course, once there you would have no hope of escape. Others have tried before you to gain the treasure. Their heads have been displayed in the square for all to see."

I shuddered.

"It is the safest place for both criminals and treasure alike. There, the guards patrol in constant motion, and there is no hope for breaking either in or out. If any artifacts from Almara remain, that's where they'll be. But it would be suicide to attempt breaking in."

"How do you know this?" Kiron asked.

"Everyone knows it. Fear and desire govern this place."

I sunk back into my chair.

"What is the matter, son?" he asked. "Why do you need this map so badly? I mean, aside from the obvious reasons? You'll never get to it, I'm afraid. It's too well guarded."

"That map," I said slowly, "is my only hope of ever making it back home." His face fell with concern and I put mine into my hands. It was true. Now that I had been face to face with Cadoc, the man from my dream, I felt sure that the item I was looking for was a book. And without it, I would be stuck here in Stonemore. And Cadoc already knew my face. I would have to live out the rest of my days within the walls of this city, in hiding. Or on the run, forever trapped in Maylin. Maybe Kiron would take me in. I could be a sort of helper on his farm.

"We'll get to the link, boy," Kiron growled. "I ain't no master, but I have a few tricks that even this Cadoc won't expect. I didn't wait my entire life to be thwarted by the small issue of a locked door."

The three of us sat in silence for a time. Kiron finally relented and sampled the cheese from the plate, smacking his lips appreciatively, as if all this had been normal dinner conversation.

I couldn't stay here, that was certain. Whether I ever made it home or not, I would have to get out of Stonemore. I thought about all Chapman had told us, the Shield, the fear that the citizens here had to constantly endure. And for what? So that Cadoc could enjoy the feeling of power while everyone else suffered? It wasn't right. It was sick. And because of this man, or whatever he was, I was stuck here in the middle of it, under his thumb.

Well, I wasn't going to tolerate it. I wasn't going to just sit here and hide like a little kid. If I needed to break into the vault then that's what I would do.

I was going *home.*

Courage began to rise in my core until it filled me like a balloon and I stood from my chair.

Two things became clear to me in that moment.

First, somebody needed to make things right.

And second, I was about to become a thief.

CHAPTER TWELVE

That night, after Chapman had propped his eyes open for as long as he could, I lay awake and listened to the little man snore. The small apartment where he lived, tucked into the back of the shop, was more like a furnished closet than it was a real home. But I suppose he spent the majority of his time out on the floor of the mercantile. He clearly wasn't prepared for visitors.

Kiron rested silently in his corner of the room, awake or asleep, I didn't know. We had all stayed awake long into the night, occasionally nibbling on whatever scraps Chapman could find in the single, sad cabinet. It wasn't a noble's life, he'd told us, running a little shop here in the square. With no wife to care and cook for him, he would often take his meals down at the local pub and didn't keep much in the way of food in the place. He wasn't poor, exactly, but the city life left him with only what he could buy from the money his trinkets earned him. Sometimes he would get lucky, he said, making a deal that would keep him in bread and ale for weeks. Other times were lean. But he patted his round belly and told us, "I've had a good run of late."

As we talked and traded bits of information, we discussed the possibility, or rather the impossibility, of stealing Almara's book from the hold below the square. He took easily to my story of travel; apparently such things were, while not the norm, not unheard of in this place. After all, Almara himself had been such a traveler. But when I showed him the powers the Kiron had brought forth and instilled in my backpack, his mouth dropped open and stayed that way for some time.

"Never, in all my years, have I seen such a work," he finally said.

This seemed to soften Kiron's edge.

"You've never seen magic before?" I asked.

"Baubles, yes," he replied. "Things that shine and twinkle, a potion that brings peace to the ill of heart. But an object like this," he gingerly touched the edges of the pack and lifted it, light as a feather despite its ample contents, "this is extraordinary." He laughed as he raised it up and down with a single finger.

"But the battle between Zarich and Almara..." I replied. "Certainly you've had experience with magical spells in the past."

His eyes widened as they fell on my face. "No, child!" he exclaimed. "I wasn't even a twinkle in my great-great-grandfather's eye when that battle took place. And in the days since, magic has been a dangerous trade in Stonemore. No," he looked back at the pack, "this is something the likes of which I, and probably anyone in this city, have never seen." He turned to Kiron. "How did you manage this?"

Kiron's eyes betrayed the pride he was trying to conceal.

"My pa," he said. "He passed down knowledge of the spell to me when I was still a boy."

Chapman marveled at the pack for a while, but eventually his eyelids began to droop. Finally, when he could barely manage intelligible speech any longer, he set out mats and blankets for us and then shuffled over to his own bed. He muttered himself into sleep, and Kiron stayed silent, leaving me to contemplate the task ahead on my own.

The last thing I wanted was to end up in some sort of jail or, my stomach knotted at the thought, a dungeon. How in the world were we supposed to get down there, much less back out again in one piece? I was no idiot, but I was still just a boy. Hatching such complicated and dangerous plans was surely the realm of some genius, not a kid. And what if the book wasn't even there? Or worse, what if I had it wrong and it wasn't a book I was supposed to be looking for at all?

Another threat floated into my mind as I chewed on these problems: Cadoc. I had seen Cadoc in my dream and here he was, alive and real. Could I be sure that the book I ran with in that dream was the very same I must seek now? I was going to have to trust that it was; the similarities between the dream and what had happened yesterday were just too great. It's not every day that your dreams literally become reality, and I would just have to accept that the other parts of my dream were becoming real now, too.

I rolled over and tried to find sleep. But I couldn't erase Cadoc's dark eyes from my mind. That man, he wasn't right. No light of kindness or humanity lay behind that black glare, and when I closed my eyes all I could see was his stare looking back at me. Every inch of my body was tensed, ready to fight him, but now, at the wrong time. I needed to sleep now, not prepare to battle. I rolled over again and again on the hard mat. Eventually, I tried an old trick my mother had taught me: counting sheep. She had described it to me one night in the hospital where I lay, scared and agitated, waiting for surgery.

"Just imagine them," she had said, "one by one. Close your eyes.

Can you see their white fuzzy coats? Are they jumping the fence, one by one? Watch the sheep, love, and count them as they each take their turn." Her cool hand rested on my forehead as I watched the imaginary sheep behind my eyelids.

My chest hurt with the memory of her, but in a different way than when I overexerted myself. I turned over again and tried to see the sheep in my head. I imagined each individual sheep readying himself, and then clumsily jumping the fence, pushed forward by the flock behind him. I could start to feel my body relax, distracted by keeping count of the silly creatures. Slowly they made their way across the rickety fence, one by one, until I lost count.

As my thoughts changed to dreams, the sheep morphed into other animals. First, a buck with a full rack of antlers. Then a horse who whinnied and jumped without hesitation, his long tail fluttering out behind him. The last beast I saw before I finally faded away was a slight, white wolf, very unlike they vicious faylons that had chased me. He gazed at me for a long moment, as if we were old friends, and finally leaped the barrier to follow the other animals into the darkness. I stared over the fence into the black forest all of the animals had disappeared into and watched the glow of the wolf fade away. I saw no more creatures that night.

When I woke the next morning I was alone. Dusty light filtered in through the tiny window of the room, and I lay for a time watching the little bits of it dance around in the beam, happy to be safe and hidden. On the other side of the door I could hear Chapman milling around in the shop. I sat up and took a look around the tiny space in the light of day.

The walls were lined with shelves from waist height to ceiling.

Though the majority of Chapman's collection was displayed in the front of the store, it looked like back here was where he kept his treasures. Silver twinkled down at me from the shelves and glinted off the shined leather bindings of ornately decorated books. As I stood up I saw a small plate of cheese and bread was laid out on the table. He must have gone out for more food while I slept, but where was Kiron? I took a slice of cheese and nibbled it as I made my way over to the door into the shop.

I opened the door a tiny crack and peeked through the opening. Chapman paced back and forth, his eyes frequently scanning the square through the large windows of the shop. Nobody else was in the room with him, though judging by the light falling on the square beyond the windows, it was already midday.

"Chapman!" I whispered through the crack in the door. He started and looked up, his eyes darting over to where I stood, and then to the front door. Before I could make another sound he waddled towards me, his hands outstretched and waving, hissing at me to get back into the room. I quietly closed the door. A moment later I could hear the faint tinkling of the chime at the top of the front door to the shop. The chirping of Chapman and the deep murmurs of whoever had entered filtered through the back door. I had hoped that I would be safe in the shop, but now I wasn't so sure.

I carefully made my way back to the table and took a piece of bread, chewing it silently as my eyes drifted along the walls, searching for ideas. Several minutes later I heard the chime once more and then a distinctive "click" of a lock. Chapman opened the door and slipped inside the tiny room.

"You must be quiet, child!" he hissed at me. "The Shield is looking for you!"

I started choking on the last bite of bread in my mouth.

"What?" I said through a thick mouthful, pounding my fist on my chest to try to clear it. "But how? Why?" Why were they still after me? All I had done was run away.

"This morning they were in while you and Kiron slept and asked me if I had seen a boy of your size and description. I said no, of course, but we were lucky that you were still sound asleep and they didn't notice the door back here!" He slumped against the wall and clutched his hands to his chest. "Oh, my," he sighed through deep breaths. Beads of sweat were popping up all over his bald head. "This is not what I was expecting. It will complicate things."

"But why am I so special that the Shield has any interest in me?" I asked, still alarmed. "I'm just a kid that ran from them in the square. They don't know who I am or what I'm after, so why bother?"

"I don't know," he replied, "but does it really matter? Somehow or another they've figured out that you *are* someone to bother with. And they're dead serious. I've rarely seen the men look so threatening as they did this morning."

My heart sank. They were hunting me. How could they possibly know that I was worth the trouble of pursuing?

"I think," said Chapman, "that you had better stay back here for a few days. I'm sure that after a time of searching for you their interest will ebb. You are just a child, and to them it must appear that you've vanished entirely. Maybe their searching will lead them elsewhere, or to the conclusion that you've fled."

"But what about Kiron? Where is he?" I asked.

He rested his back against the door, dropping his hands to rest on the wood by his sides, as if his will alone could keep the hunters out.

"Kiron does not attract the same attention as you," he said. "He is out in the market, seeking information. I daresay he doesn't trust what I have to offer him. However..." A sly smile played on his lips as he pulled out from his overcoat a folded piece of heavy parchment. As he pushed the now empty plate aside, he opened it and spread it onto the table. It was a map.

By this point I was starting to get sick of maps. Maps had gotten me into this mess. Now I had to rely on them to get me out of it again. But as I looked at the paper, a smile started dancing on my lips as well. Chapman had been quite busy this morning, it seemed. This wasn't just any map. It was a map of the dungeons, and there, right in the center, was the treasure hold.

Over the next several days I read and drew and noted every possible idea and crazy plan I could think of to get us down into that space. Kiron was often gone during my brainstorming sessions. He made a habit of leaving early in the morning, not returning until late in the afternoon, and he mostly avoided talking to Chapman at all. My questions regarding his whereabouts were greeted with a lot of huffing, and I was starting to wonder what he was up to. Curious as I was, though, I was also getting irritated. Weren't we supposed to be doing this together?

Chapman, while blundering and easily flustered, turned out to be quite a brilliant guide in Kiron's absence. He was a genius of sorts when it came to Stonemore, and from book after book on his shelves he found details to help me. The Shield guards did not reappear in the shop, and we both hoped that the time was drawing near that I would be ready to commence with the plan.

The barman down at the tavern had disclosed that The Shield had been questioning all around the city about me, but that the questioning had begun to wane. Nobody seemed to have any details about who I was or why The Shield was so obsessed with finding me, and this remained the one piece of information that we absolutely could not get our hands on. We couldn't seem to find a way around this roadblock, however, and we had plenty else to focus our attentions on as we planned the raid on the hold.

On our sixth night hiding in the back of the shop, Kiron woke me well before dawn. Chapman's rattling snores were loud in the cramped room, and I was surprised they hadn't woken me before now.

Kiron gently shook my shoulder. "Come with me now," he whispered, so softly that barely heard him. I rose from my mat on the floor, and Kiron collected my shoes and pack from next to the door. He crept out into the dark shop and I followed quietly.

"What's going on?" I whispered to his back. He turned and pressed a single finger to his lips. Then, at the front door, he reached up and disconnected the tinkling bell. We slipped out into the night, unheard by the sleeping Chapman.

We slunk a few doors down to an empty vestibule, and he passed me my boots.

"Kiron," I tried again. Again his finger went to his lips. When my boots were tied in place he set off along the outskirts of the square. I strapped the invisible pack to my back as we walked. He led me down one of the side streets that fed into the square, and soon turned a corner, diving into the alleyways that snaked behind the streets of the city.

Finally, after making so many turns that my head spun with trying to remember the way back out, he stopped at a wooden doorway and pushed it open, stepping inside. I followed him in, and a moment later a single candle flame pierced the darkness of the room. He closed and bolted the door behind me.

The room was a mess and layered with a thick film of dust. A single chair sat against one of the stone walls, and the floor was littered with the decaying remnants of whatever had transpired here in the past. It looked like it had been years since anyone had set foot in this place. Kiron removed his own pack from his back with a groan, rubbing the base of his neck with his withered hands.

"Kiron, *what* is going on?"

"We're done with that old fool," he grumbled.

"What do you mean? Chapman's done nothing but help us since we got here." I looked around the room hopelessly, suddenly feeling grateful for the comfort that Chapman's floor had provided.

"We can't trust him. His story doesn't add up. That, or he's just an idiot. Either way…"

"His story adds up just fine," I argued.

"I saw him at the tavern two days back. I'd been watchin' him. Something about him didn't sit right with me. So I took a corner table deep in the back and kept an eye out. He's been meetin' with those guards, The Shield, as he calls them. Almost every day I've seen him sittin' side by side with one or more of them at the bar."

I thought about this. "But…that doesn't necessarily mean anything. I mean, if a guard of the Shield came and sat by you at the bar, and then you got up and left right away, wouldn't that make the guard suspicious?" My stomach twisted with worry and confusion at this new information. Was it possible that Chapman was a spy?

"Hmph," Kiron replied. He sat down on the dusty floorboards. I stayed standing, unsure of what to do next.

"Well, what are we supposed to do now?" I finally asked.

"I've worked out how to get you down under the city. Tomorrow night we meet the boy and make the trade for the information."

I dropped my pack to the floor. "How to get *me* down under the city? What about you? I thought we were doing this together!"

"Naw, that's impossible. You'll be posing as a servant. We'd never be able to get in together."

My breath caught in my chest.

"But—I can't go down to the dungeons on my own—" I began.

He raised both of his hands up. "Just hold on," he said. "I got a plan." I stopped sputtering and he continued. "Use your brain, boy. The two of us, we make sort of an odd pair. If we were to try to break in together, we'd be caught for certain. But just one of us can maybe pull it off. There ain't no reason for an old geyser like me to be wanting access to the dungeons, but there is reason for a kid like you."

"And that is?"

"A job," he said. "You'll dress as one of the child servants who clean. We meet the kid tomorrow at the tavern on the other side of the city. Chapman won't know to find us there."

All the breath seemed to leave my lungs and I sunk down to the floor, defeated. My brain wrestled with the impossible task in front of me: breaking into the dungeons on my own.

"You're wrong about him, you know." I had grown to really like Chapman over the past week. He had a lighter personality than Kiron, though he did seem to be very frightened most of the time. But that didn't mean that he was waiting for a chance to betray us.

"Whether I'm right or wrong, it's not wise for us to give away all of our information for free. Chapman gave us some of what he had, and we him. But he doesn't need to know every single detail of our plans." He paused, considering me in the dim flicker of the candle. "It'd be good if you'd learn to not trust everyone you meet. It's common wisdom that those who should be trusted the least often appear the most trustworthy to unwary eyes."

"Well, who am I supposed to trust, then?" I shot back.

Kiron sat silent for a long moment as he thought of his response. Finally, he spoke.

"Trust no one."

CHAPTER THIRTEEN

Through his research and carefully worded questions to outsiders, it was determined that the dungeons were, in fact, inhabited. Kiron had gathered the tidbit, about the children working in them, from the woman who sold potatoes in the market. Apparently her sister's son had worked for a time underground, and with some digging around Kiron was able to discover the entrance to the place. I was horrified at the thought of interacting with the prisoners, or whatever possible vermin might also reside in those chambers. But I was also starting to feel shut in, always hiding in tiny, stuffy rooms, and my newfound energy was making me fidgety and nervous without an outlet.

I felt bad about leaving Chapman behind. I was sure he was alright, and that Kiron was wrong about him. He had taken us in, risking his own neck in the process. But, on the balance, it was Kiron I needed to stick with; he knew the most about Almara and how to find him. Though I was going to need to talk to him at some point about his trust issues.

The next day we spent indoors. Kiron didn't go out a single time. Maybe he was worried that I would run back to Chapman's, but I wouldn't have. I was too busy panicking about facing down an underground holding pen of prisoners all by myself.

"The boy intends to run," he said as the sun began to sink behind the buildings. "The abuse his family has undergone at the hands of Cadoc and his army have brought him to the edge. He's agreed to tell us how to gain entry in return for a link for his family."

"A link?" I asked. "One of yours?" He nodded. "But, where are you going to send them?" I remembered the pain of traveling by Kiron's links, and the mirth Larissa had shown of his linkmaking skills.

"It ain't interplanetary," he said. "But this'll get 'em to the other side of Aeso." He removed the long chain from his neck and chose a fat blue stone. He twisted the metal it hung from until it broke free from the chain.

"But, Kiron," I said, "how do you know where that will take them? I mean, didn't you make it back on Aerit?" He looked up quizzically. "How do you know it will work on Aeso?" His eyes widened as he realized I was right. He hadn't considered this unknown outcome, had forgotten that the link was an *Aerit* planetary link.

He stared down at the stone, studying it, trying to decide what to do.

"Well," he finally said, "I don't see that we have much choice."

"You mean you're going to give it to the kid? But you have no idea where he'll end up!"

"I got a good idea," he said. "And that'll need to be good enough."

"Nice bargain," I said sarcastically.

"Look, do you wanna find Almara or not? This is the only way to get you down there. Our only other option will be to use it ourselves and hope that *we* can get free of Stonemore and then back to my farm. But I didn't leave my whole life behind to help you and then have you back out on me."

"It's not right," I argued, shaking my head. "You have to tell him the risk."

"I ain't tellin' him squat."

"Well then *I* ain't going," I said.

We stood glaring at each other, but I wasn't backing down. He was calling all the shots here, and I was starting to think that he was only right part of the time. If I was going to risk being locked up in a dungeon, I at least wanted to have a clear conscience before they threw away the key.

"Fine," he said. "I'll tell him. But *after* we get the information. You mess this up, boy, and it'll be years before we find another way down there. You understand me? *Years.*"

"Fine," I said. "But if you don't tell him, I will."

"Hmph."

It was settled.

As night began to fall, we made our way through the alleyways out to the lane. Kiron turned in the opposite direction of Chapman's, and together we walked for a time through the waning crowd. Kiron had found some charcoal and rubbed it into my hair, effectively disguising me from The Shield. I looked like a dirty, brown-haired kid, like any of the other kids around. I found great relief and being able to walk with relative freedom through the city. The cold air was refreshing as it bit at my cheeks.

After fifteen minutes of walking, we reached a shabby, dimly lit building. Kiron opened the front door to the place and we went inside. A long bar dominated the space, and a few odd tables were scattered about.

A large hearth at the far end of the room housed a crackling fire. Kiron nodded brusquely to the barman, who nodded in return, and made his way to the back of the room, where a dirty, thin boy sat huddled next to the fire. We both pulled out chairs and sat at the table across from him. Kiron held up three fingers to the barman, who nodded again, and then turned to the boy.

He looked sick, as if he had been malnourished over a long span of time. He looked up at Kiron with the distrust of one who had long since quit believing in kindness.

"Calder," said Kiron, "this is Aster. Aster, Calder." We nodded at each other.

"Did you bring it?" Calder asked.

Kiron produced the small blue stone and placed it on the table. Calder's eyes widened and his bony fingers shot out to take the stone, but not before Kiron's hand had grasped it again and pulled it away.

"Not so fast, boy," he said. "You have something for us as well, I think."

The barman approached the table, arms loaded with plates, and set our dinner in front of us: stew and a large slab of bread for each. Calder immediately turned his attention to the meal, dropping his attitude entirely at the sight of food, and began to eat as if he were starving. He scooped up the stew with the bread and his dirty hands. His spoon lay on the table, forgotten. I watched him, horrified, thinking of the hunger that must make someone inhale their food like that, as if it would disappear at any moment. I picked up my own spoon and took a tentative bite, but my eyes stayed on the boy, and the viewing made me lose my appetite. Kiron was not so moved as I, and slurped up his stew noisily.

After several minutes, Calder finished his meal, all but licking the bowl clean. As he ran his fingers along the edges of the bowl to get each last drop of stew, he sat back in his chair and looked at me.

"So, what do you want to know?" he asked.

I looked at Kiron expectantly, but he was still eating and motioned for me to speak.

"Uh, well," I said, "I need to know how to get into the dungeons."

"Why?" he asked.

"There's something I need down there."

His face cracked into a wicked smile, and suddenly I felt less sorry for him.

"Like treasure?" he asked.

"Um, of a sort," I said.

"You gonna eat that?" he asked, pointing at my mostly untouched dinner.

"No."

His hand shot out and gripped the edge of the bowl, sliding it across the table towards him.

"Well, getting in is easy enough," he said through a large mouthful of stew. "It's getting out that's the trick."

"And how do I get in?"

"There's a house," he said thickly, "just off the square on the south side. It looks like people live there but nobody does. They keep a single candle burning in the window every night; that's how you'll know it. The dungeons begin underneath the building. They keep the door unlocked. Don't need a lock, since a sentry is posted behind the entrance twenty four hours a day."

I gulped.

"Don't worry," he smiled at me as if I were much younger than he was. "Just tell the sentry that you're taking my place. Then, go to the back of the building and down the spiral staircase. Yell out for the keeper when you get to the bottom. You might have to yell for a while. He's usually passed out drunk most of the mornings I've gone."

I took a deep breath. "Ok, so then what?"

"Then you clean," Calder said simply, and winked at me. He bit off an enormous chunk of bread. "He'll show you the mop and pail," he continued over the mouthful of bread. "The keeper of the dungeons hates me. Tell him...tell him I broke my leg or something like that." He smirked. "He'll love to hear about me getting hurt. Explain to him that you're the new boy sent to clean up the mess that I left before I fell down some stairs or something. Watch out for the keeper. He's a mean old mule, and he won't tolerate any lip. None at all. And watch your ears."

"My ears?" I asked.

"He's an ear grabber, the keeper. More than one kid has cried like a baby after a run-in with him."

My hands went up to my ears involuntarily, a gesture of protection from an unknown hurt.

"So, how do I get out once I've...cleaned?" I asked.

Calder's smirk turned into a full blown smile. It made me nervous.

"You actually *do* clean," he said. "Be prepared for a long day, or days, of work before that guy will let you see the sun again. And a word of advice: do it right the first time. Once he kept me down there for four days because he didn't think the floors were clean enough. I was almost starved by the time he finally let me out, and even then I think he let me go just cause he was sick of looking at me."

"So, I can't just leave?" I asked.

Calder looked at me with a mocking smile. "Kid," he said, "it's a dungeon. Everything is locked up, and the only one with the keys is the keeper."

My curiosity got the better of me, and I whispered, "What's down there?"

He leaned in and murmured conspiratorially. "Ghouls." His eyebrows danced on his forehead like he was telling a ghost story to a frightened group of campers. "Men so old their souls have long since withered away. Keep back from the bars."

I couldn't tell if he was serious or just trying to mess with me. He took the last bite of my stew and pushed the bowl away from him, rubbing his full stomach appreciatively.

"Now, I believe it's your turn," he said to us both, his mocking, mysterious tone fading away.

Kiron placed the blue stone on the table again, and Calder grabbed for it. Kiron's hand landed on Calder's before he could snatch the link away.

"This ain't no cheap trinket, boy," he growled. "You gotta be careful how you use it."

"Ok," he said, taking his hand back. "How does it work?"

"Make sure you and your family, or whoever you're takin' along, are gripping each other tight. Then you point the link and give it the command. *Horasha*."

"And it will take us out of here?"

"Yep."

"But there's something you should know," I said, eyeing Kiron. I didn't like this kid, but it wasn't fair not to warn him. "This is a link that was made on Aerit for travel on that planet. We're not entirely sure it will work the same way here."

"What do you mean?" he asked.

"Well, there's a possibility it could take you back to Aerit. Or even somewhere else. Somewhere we can't predict."

His demeanor changed, and his eyes, filled with arrogance a moment before, became soft and frightened.

"It doesn't matter," he said, looking down at the stone. "I don't care where it takes us. As long as it's as far away from here as possible. As far away from him as we can get is all I want."

"From Cadoc?" I asked.

He looked up and seemed surprised that I had guessed correctly. Then he nodded and lowered his head.

"It's yours, boy," Kiron said. He stood up from the table, and I did the same. As we turned to leave the tavern, Calder called after us.

"I don't know what business you have down under the city," he said, "but if I were you, I'd forget it. You've got the power to escape Stonemore."

We stopped and turned back to him.

"You should use it while you still can."

CHAPTER FOURTEEN

Late that night I lay on my back staring into space, trying to mentally prepare myself for the task that lay ahead. We had determined that I would head down to the dungeons the very next morning; it would look suspicious if nobody at all came to clean, and it seemed clear that Calder would be leaving Stonemore as soon as possible. Maybe he already had.

Kiron and I had talked late into the night, going over and over the plan. He had found a set of dirty, worn clothing for me to wear: my uniform. Ratty as the shirt and pants were I was glad to note that they did not smell as bad as they looked. A moth-bitten coat would protect me against the cold down below.

He had taken another link from the chain around his neck and given it to me.

"What's this for?" I asked.

"In case you can't get out," he said. "Only if all hope is lost."

"What about you? Then we'll be separated."

"It doesn't matter so much what happens to me. What matters is that you get your hands on the next link. Here, take it." He dropped a thick, gray stone into my hand. "Command is *Forasha*. This is a short distance link. It'll take you out of the city, but not too far beyond. Then there'll be a hope of us finding each other."

I accepted the link, hoping that I wouldn't need to use it, and concerned about what would happen if I did. Would it send me back to Aerit? What if I ended up floating in empty space?

I was to give Kiron my backpack and ax before I set out. The close quarters of the dungeon, and the keeper's reputation for brawling with the children who worked there, would make carrying anything with me far too dangerous. Kiron would leave my things behind the spot where the soup lady stood in the square, and he would watch the area to make sure they were not discovered before I was able to return. We would meet there after I found a way out of the dungeons and then continue on together.

I dressed in the old clothing and packed my own clothes into the pack. Kiron had taken a file to my boots to make them look less noticeable; they weren't of the sort that a poor boy would wear in Stonemore, where the kids were lucky if they had shoes at all. I lay on the shabby floor of the forgotten room and stared up at the ceiling. Only a thin sliver of moonlight crept in through a thick crack in the stone wall. My fingers studied the grooves in the stone link in my pocket.

I was buzzing with nerves. The silence that came from Kiron's side of the room told me he was also awake, but we didn't speak. I don't know how many hours we both lay there with our eyes wide, and I'm not sure if I ever slept, but after an eternity of running the plan over and over in my mind, he finally rose. It was time.

No light came into the room any longer. The moon had set hours ago and it was too early for the sun to make an appearance. We both put on our boots, and I handed him the backpack before vanishing it. Then we crept through the alleyways into the city beyond. Kiron peered out into the deserted street. Then, satisfied that it was empty, we slipped out into the night of Stonemore.

Nobody was out. I was shaking with nerves, but the cold air was invigorating. I breathed deeply, trying to stay calm, and my hopes rose that what I was about to attempt might be possible.

We silently made our way through the square, sticking to the shadowy edges, to the closest avenue. I looked across the space towards Chapman's little shop, hoping to see the flickering candle, but the windows were dark. We slinked around the corner, leaving the square, and found with relief that it was also deserted. Kiron walked with me only the distance of a few of the buildings before he stopped and pulled me into the alcove of a butcher shop. Large hides of beef hung looming in the dark window as he turned to me and quietly spoke.

He placed one hand on each of my shoulders and looked me square in the eye. "Be careful. I'll watch for ya, help ya if I can."

This was it.

I nodded, breaking the gaze he held with me and looking over towards the door.

"I'll see you when I'm out," I said, my heart pounding.

My eyes met his once more. I nodded again, and then turned. As I stepped out of the cover of the butcher shop, he whispered behind me

"Good luck."

I dashed across the street to the single door that had light flickering behind it. When I turned back, he had disappeared, hidden well in the shadows. I reached for the handle and, just as expected, it turned easily. The door was easily eight feet high and six inches thick, and would have been impossible to open had the hinges not been so well oiled. Crossing the threshold I carefully closed the enormous door behind me, which thudded shut with an awful sound of finality. Perhaps those breaths I had taken outside just now would be the last fresh air I would taste.

A man sat slumped in a chair, and he jolted awake at the thump of the door. He looked me up and down, grumbling, and then waved his hand toward the back of the room. A torch lit staircase spiraled downward. His eyes were already closed again, so I snuck past, trying not to jostle him. As I approached the staircase I heard a harsh snore come from the man, already back asleep. As I began to descend I steadied myself along the rock walls that twisted their way deeper and deeper into the earth. It seemed to go on for two, maybe three stories, dizzying me as I walked. Finally I reached the bottom, where an iron gate blocked my way into the passage beyond. Here was where I was to announce myself to the keeper, but he was nowhere to be seen. Concerned, I tentatively called out, "Hello?"

Nothing happened. My eyes slowly adjusted to the dim light. The passage ahead was cut through cells that ran along either side. Empty cells. This place didn't look anything like the map Chapman had shown me. There was no treasure hold anywhere, for one, and the shape of the chamber wasn't right at all. On the map all of the cells had been situated around the hold, but this room was laid out as a long rectangle, not a square.

I froze. This was not the place we had planned for. Had Chapman given me a false map? Maybe Kiron had been right about him all along. Should I go back? Maybe we should rework the plan, find out more details about what I might face under the city. My breathing quickened as I imagined myself trapped behind the bars of one of those cells. It was too dangerous a plan to do it with flawed information.

I was just starting to back up, to turn and head up the stairs, when I heard it.

A groan erupted from the farthest cell down the corridor on the left. It was followed by the sound of someone rummaging around, knocking things over, and then the *thwack* and accompanying cry of pain that I could only guess came from bashing a toe against something hard.

"Arrgghh!!!" came the angry voice.

And then he was out of the cell, glaring at me down the long hallway. There wasn't time. He would see me fleeing and call the guard. I had to stay.

He limped towards me, cursing as he walked. As he neared I could see that he was dressed from head to foot in gray rags. They hung off his bony frame and dragged along the dirty ground as he approached. His hair, gray and tangled, hung limply on his shoulders. His cheeks were ruddy and pockmarked, a large bruise running down one side of his face, and his nose crooked from a break that had never been set. His scent moved ahead of him and hit me before he made it to the gate; liquor and a long unwashed body.

"And who," he glared and looked me up and down, "are you?"

I opened my mouth, but no sound came out. I was so intimidated by this disgusting man that I failed to speak quickly enough for his taste. Quick as a cat his hand flashed out through the bars and grabbed the top of my left ear. He yanked it down hard, and my head followed his agonizing grip until he had brought my forehead to rest on the cold steel of the gate. I squirmed in pain and tried not to cry out. Calder hadn't been kidding. No wonder children were so frightened of this man.

"I said," he growled his breath into my face, "who…are…*you?*"

This time I spoke quickly, anxious to persuade him to release me. "My name is Deen, sir. I am here to replace Calder."

"Deen? Deen what?" he sneered. "What is your surname, boy?"

"I—" I stumbled, grasping for the right answer. "I have no surname, sir. No father."

At this he released me, seemingly satisfied with this response. This was part of the plan I had worked out with Kiron. It made my whole disguise more believable to the keeper. Of course I would have no father. I was just a poor boy from the town, forced to help feed my family by working in this place in the dead of night.

My hand rubbed the now throbbing ear he had held, but I tried not to look too pathetic. He glared at me as his hands fumbled through hidden pockets in his…were they pants? It was a sort of robe, I decided. Maybe once it had been a sleeping gown made from rough linen, but once he had put it on, it looked as if he had never taken it off again. Years of liquor and darkness down here seemed to have made things like cleanliness unnecessary to him.

At last he found what he was looking for, and his bony fingers pulled out from the depths of the gown a long, black skeleton key. He roughly jammed the key into the large hole along the side of the door and turned it with a grunt. A loud clang came from the lock as it disengaged, and he opened the gate and beckoned me inside.

"Thank you, sir," I said, taking care to be as polite as possible. I never wanted this man to have reason to touch me again. I stood at attention as he locked the gate, wary of walking on ahead, until he turned and shuffled back down the hallway. I took one last glance at what appeared to be the only escape from this place, and then I followed.

At the end of the hallway he led me into the cell he had emerged from. A pile of blankets lay on the floor, two bottles, one empty, one half full, and a chamber pot. Thankfully, the chamber pot was empty.

I was surprised when he pushed against what looked like a solid wall, but turned out to be another doorway. He ambled through it and I soon found myself in a large square room as big as a gymnasium.

This was the room we had seen on Chapman's map! Relief flooded through me as I identified one of the two doorways we had seen on the schematic; I was standing now in the second, and the other was directly opposite me. In the center of the room was an enormous cage lit on all sides with torches, the only light source in the place, and what lay inside it took my breath away.

Treasure.

But it was unlike the treasure I had seen in books or movies. In them, the treasure was always gold, shining like fire contained in metal. But here, long, thin stacks of silver coins lined the walls of the cage. I had forgotten about the strange absence of gold in the Fold, and it was strange to witness riches that cast off such cool light.

The keeper picked up a bucket of rags that sat next to the door to his cell and motioned for me to follow him. He ambled directly towards the center, towards the piles that lay locked behind those tightly meshed bars. As we walked, the dark outlines of prisoners hiding in shadow regarded us from every side. They did not speak or make a sound, but their hollow eyes followed each step we took as they watched us from the black of their cells.

It was true, then. This place was full of men. I shivered. It was like being watched by a hundred ghosts. I remembered the boy from the pub and his description of the prisoners: ghouls. I shrank back from the bars.

I was so full of adrenaline and horror as I studied the dungeons that I barely noticed when the keeper stopped at the door to the hold, and I nearly knocked into him. Catching myself mere inches from bumping him in the back, I fought down a yelp of surprise. His hands were fumbling in his pockets again, and soon emerged with a different key, this one pewter. He jiggled it into the huge lock, and it gave a loud click as it released the door. My breath grew more and more shallow, and as he opened the cage.

Silver. Everywhere silver, draping the cage in its icy glow. Silver chalices piled up in one corner of the space, silver coins in another. On the far wall hung ornate works of art in enormous carved frames. And in the center of the square cell a pile of books stacked high on the floor.

The keeper thrust the bucket into my hands and shoved me inside. Then, to my horror, he slammed the door and locked it, trapping me inside. He saw the look on my face and his mouth broke into a wide, green grin.

"What, you didn't think I'd leave you with an escape, did you, boy?" he drawled. "All this treasure and rats like you thinkin' you can come in here and nick a coin or two. The old man ain't so stupid as you little brats seem to think I am."

"But sir," I protested, "I was told that I was here to clean the—"

"You're here," he snarled, "to do what I tell ya to do. Now, the fool that came here before ya was a slob and left spots all over the cups. Cadoc," his hands absently touched the bruise on the side of his face, "weren't happy. You do it right, boy, or you'll have me to answer to. Or," he sneered, "maybe I'll just leave ya in here until it *is* done right."

"Yes, sir," I answered quickly. I desperately wanted him to go, both because I wanted to start my search and because he was so terrifying. I may be trapped again, but I was itching to start digging through that pile of books.

The smile dropped from his face and he looked at me curiously. Maybe I had been too quick to answer him, or maybe he wasn't used to getting good behavior from the boys who came down here on a normal day. But, drawn by his drink or his nest of blankets or both, he didn't care enough to linger, and he walked back through the aisle to his cell. Once he was out of sight, I turned to the books.

They were all larger than the one I had seen in my dream. Most of these were as big as an old-fashioned encyclopedia, but the book I had dreamed of would have fit inside my pocket. I tentatively touched the volume closest to me at the top of the pile. It was bound in the finest leather, and engravings carved the surface. I lifted it and was surprised by its substantial weight. Turning it over, I saw no sign of the golden ovals that I was looking for. Not deterred, there were at least fifty books here, I placed it carefully on the ground beside the pile and picked up the next.

For half an hour I dug through the pile, inspecting each tome carefully for anything that indicated it had information about Almara. But I found nothing. I had been hoping that maybe the small green book would be hidden down deeper in the pile, but as I placed the last book from the very bottom to the side I sighed with frustration. What was I supposed to do now?

"It isn't here," croaked a voice from the surrounding darkness. I gasped. I had been so immersed in my search that I had completely forgotten that this place was full of prisoners. And they had been silent until this moment. I squinted in the light of the treasure hold and looked out through the bars in the direction from which the voice had come. Moving closer to the edge of the cage, I was able to see more clearly into the dungeons beyond, and I was unnerved by what I saw. Down the row in both directions were ten or more sets of eyes, all trained on me.

"He took it," came the voice again.

"Who took it?" I whispered to the room at large, still unsure of which set of eyes belonged to the speaker.

"The man in black," said the voice, and I caught a faint movement just to my left and across the way.

"What did he take?" I whispered, looking in that direction.

"Almara's book of codes, of course," he answered.

"How—what—how did you—?" I spluttered.

"It doesn't matter how I know, what matters is that it isn't here. And if you want it, you're going to have to find *him*."

My heart sank.

"Find…who?" I asked hopefully.

"You know *who*, boy," the voice snarled.

The thought that I would have to hunt Cadoc down once I got out of here, if I ever did get out of here, almost brought me to my knees.

"I can't go after Cadoc," I whispered. "Are you mad?"

Just then a clanking noise, followed by swearing and a fit of coughing, came from down the hallway. I froze. In front of me ten pairs of eyes silently faded into blackness. Thinking fast, I grabbed a rag from the bucket, the closest piece of silver I saw, and began rubbing it with the cloth furiously.

The clanking continued and grew louder as it drew closer. I put down the first trinket and picked up a goblet, continuing my false cleaning. The keeper was singing a drunken tune as he approached.

Down here be

The prisoners three
Beneath the walks of stone

Be you fool
Or soldier cruel
You'll join them, overthrown

As he neared the hold his song was cut short.

"What're you thinking you're doin', you idiot?" he drawled, significantly more drunk now than he had been half an hour ago. Behind him dragged a long steel chain.

I looked up, but didn't meet his gaze. "I'm cleaning, sir," I said.

"You fool!" he bellowed. "You're cleaning the *books*? The books don't need cleaning you dimwit!"

I quickly stood up and started to stack the books, now strewn all over the cell, back into their orderly pile in the center. "I'm very sorry, sir," I said. "I thought I was to clean everything in the room."

The keeper paused and looked all around, his gaze losing focus as his eyes moved over the room.

"Idiots! All of ya are idiots!" he bellowed to the room at large. "It's no wonder I'm feelin' so old, stuck down here with a bunch of morons!"

I stood still as a statue, hoping he would let it go without punishing me, seeing that I had good intentions. Or that maybe he was too drunk now to care. It seemed to be taking him a lot of effort to remain upright. He turned, grumbling, and clanked his way over to one of the cells. Through the bars he hoisted the chain, wrapping it around and around the edge of one of the cell gates and then drawing across several more of the cell doors. From his pocket he drew a large padlock, and he fastened it around the two pieces of chain and clicked it shut.

"There," he mumbled. "Won't be getting' out now, will ya you dirty thieves!" he yelled. The keeper turned then, and shuffled his way back down the hall to his room, shouting, "Idiot!" as he went. His arrival back to his cell resulted in further crashing, and a tirade of curses echoed down the hall.

I let out a long, slow breath. I couldn't panic. I needed to find a way out of here. The keeper might be a drunkard, but he was still a great deal larger than I was. I would stand no chance in a fight against him without my weapons. Maybe he wouldn't hurt me right this moment, but in a few hours when he woke from his blackout with a pounding head, I had a feeling that I would be an appealing target.

I moved silently back over to the edge of the cage, carrying a silver cup and one of the rags with me in case the keeper returned. Pushing my face up against the steel I whispered into the darkness, "Who are you?"

The eyes appeared once more, but none of the prisoners spoke. Then, slowly, ten men approached the bars of their cells and held out their hands one by one. Carved into the back of each hand, were the symbols of Almara I had been searching for.

My mouth fell open. I took several steps backward and turned to look out of the bars opposite where they stood. Several more men on the other side of the dungeon held out their hands for me to see. I spun around; I was surrounded on all sides by what could only be servants of Almara, now prisoners. Above each symbol, on the soft side of their forearms, numbers were marked into their skin.

3333-135

3333-189

3333-096

And on. And on. Thick scars stuck out from where the numbers had been carved into their flesh.

"We have all been here," said the voice slowly, "for a long time."

I moved back to the side the voice had come from, and now a man stood there, clothed in rags the color of ashes, skin and bones.

"The Stone," he continued, "gives long life."

Horror came over me as I considered what he was saying. The Stone?

"How long have you been down here?" I asked.

He did not answer. I gripped my fingers tightly through the mesh of the cage.

Up until this point my reason for chasing after Almara had been simple; I wanted to go home to my own world. But while I had been hungering for the comforts of home, I had also been having quite an adventure. My time in the Fold had become increasingly difficult, but I couldn't deny that it had been amazing. Now, faced for the first time with the harsh reality of the evils that were transpiring in these worlds, right under the feet of its inhabitants, I pushed aside all thoughts of home for the first time.

I would have to help them.

"How do I get out?" I whispered through the cage. "Is there a key?"

"No, no key," said the man, raising his hands and gripping the bars, "but there is magic in that cell with you. Find it and you will find your escape."

"What am I looking for?" I asked, my eyes darting around the cage. I quietly began picking up pieces of silver, inspecting each closely.

"It's not silver you want, boy, but wood."

I stopped my searching and looked up at the man. Wood?

"What can a piece of wood do?" I asked. "Is it some sort of wand?"

"No, it is a staff. It has been many long years since I last saw it," he said, sadly. "They tried and tried to unlock its power, but could not do it without me, and I hid my associations with it well. Eventually they gave up their efforts, but they knew that they still had a mighty weapon should anyone ever determine how to wield it. It has been buried in the hold among the other treasures for a hundred years. It will be nearly as tall as yourself. Look there, underneath the pile of tapestries."

I did, and after a few sweaty minutes of peeling back the woven artwork one sheet at a time, I found the wood. The branch was entirely common and dull. It lay on the stone floor like something dead.

But as my fingers neared the staff it came alive, raising off the ground, floating, until it met my outstretched grasp. The wood was warm to the touch, and that warmth radiated through my fingers, up my arm and into my chest, where the heat lingered and swirled over my heart. I stood and held the staff out at arms length, inspecting it carefully. Never in my life had I heard of something like this happening. When Kiron had made me the backpack, I had been impressed, surely, stunned by something solid becoming invisible before my eyes. But holding the staff was different. The way it made my body feel, warm and safe and... powerful. This was something new.

I gazed at it for several long moments, turning it around and around in my hands, eagerly studying every crevice. Behind me I heard a muffled sound, but I was so entranced by the staff that I did not turn around.

"Boy!" came the sound again. I spun on the spot; the prisoner looked at me with agitation.

"Oh!" I said. "Sorry."

His eyes bored into mine, studying my face. "Am I going to be able to trust you with that, boy?" he asked.

"Trust me?"

"Yes, trust you. I haven't been waiting down here for two hundred and eleven years to give all my power away to a thief."

I gaped at him.

"But how?" I asked. I still didn't understand how the power of the Stone worked. "How can a rock bring you long life?"

"A rock?" croaked the man. "The great jade Stone of Borna is a little more than just a rock. It is a magical object more powerful than any I've ever learned of in the Fold. From the Stone an elixir can be drafted. Drinking it fills one with its power. It can heal wounds. It can bring the gift of years. A gift that becomes a curse over time. Cadoc has forced it on us since our first days here."

My mouth hung open again, and I shut it quickly for fear of looking like an idiot.

"But how did you end up down here in the first place?" I asked.

The man's eyes hardened, bitterness etched into every line of his face, and his eyes pierced into mine as he spoke.

"When Almara fought Zarich for the freedom of Stonemore," he began in a hoarse whisper, "those of us who followed his teachings fought alongside him. Almara had been carrying the stone on his quest, and while we knew not where he journeyed to, we knew we had to defend him at all costs. In that battle the Stone was wrested from Almara, causing all to despair. It was thought that the Stone would be the key to healing the land. After he fled the city, all of the remaining Almarian's found refuge in the deep mazes that snake through the alleys above.

"But our relief did not last long. *Zarich*," he spat the name, "or shall I say, *Cadoc*, had found some new magic, perhaps from the stone itself, and with it he drew us out from hiding. One by one he captured us, locking every one of us into these cages until no followers of Almara remained on the surface. We had hoped that Almara would come back for us, free us from this misery. But he never came. No one ever came."

My neck and arms were covered in tingling chills. "But there *are* followers!" I blurted out. "I met one and he helped me find the way down here."

"Now I think *you* are the mad one," he said wryly. "No followers of Almara remain in Stonemore. Cadoc's magic would have found them all long ago."

"Well, I don't know why Cadoc didn't find him," I said, "but there is one person up there who still believes, and he and his family before him have never been discovered."

"I think you must be deceived, boy," he said after considering my words. "I do not see how this is possible."

"Look, I know that this man is a follower," I protested. "He gave me the map of the dungeons, and gave us shelter from Cadoc's army on our first night here." He looked at me skeptically. "You'll just have to believe me. This man is on Almara's side."

"Us? There are more of you?" he asked.

"My...friend. We both came to Stonemore together."

"What are the names of these men of whom you speak?" asked the prisoner.

Here I paused, not willing to give up Kiron or Chapman's names, especially to someone with such a murderous look in his eyes. I stalled.

"Why are you here at all?" I asked, "Cadoc has kept you down here for...centuries? Why?"

His face fell into a harsh grimace. "In his mind, we belong to him. He keeps us here, right next to his treasure. His greed has kept us imprisoned and the city starving. We are not men to him, but trophies, a reminder of his victory over Almara. He would rather feed us just enough to keep us alive, his collection, than feed his own people up above."

It was disgusting. I tried to stay calm, but the revulsion I felt at learning of Cadoc's horrific acts was overwhelming. The chills on my neck turned to ice, and a deep, true fear about the feasibility of my task began to creep into my mind.

"Now," he said, "you may be unwilling to give up the names of your companions, but as I have already asked you once, will you show yourself to be trustworthy with that trophy? Will you release us from our torture?"

I didn't move, thinking again of Calder and his creepy warning about the prisoners. But these were just men. Seemingly magical men, yes, but they were tortured, cursed souls. Cadoc's treasures. Surely anybody imprisoned for hundreds of years by the power of one evil man would turn and fight against him once released. They were on our side.

The wood pulsed beneath my fingers, sending warmth where the chills on my skin had driven it away. And my decision was made.

"No," I said, "No, of course I won't take it. It's just that I've never—it feels so—it's amazing." I was distracted from our conversation again, and my gaze fell back upon the wood.

"Thank you," the man replied. "A full year to craft it and I should expect that it would have such an effect. Now, if you don't mind, I think the men and I here would be appreciative of a little holiday from this," he gestured around the room, "*paradise.* Enjoyable as it's been, I would be most thoughtful of you to liberate us. After you free yourself, of course." He gestured to the staff.

"Oh! Yes," I replied, breaking out of my stupor. "What do I do?"

"Touch it to the gate," he said, "and that should be enough."

Could it really be that simple? I nodded and walked over to the cell door that imprisoned me and the treasure. Feeling somewhat stupid, I clumsily tapped the lock with the staff. To my surprise it sprang open, and the gate swung free on its hinges. I cringed at the loud creaking it made, but after a few moments of frozen silence I tentatively stepped across the doorway.

I turned in the direction of the man I had been speaking with, and, making it to his cell, quickly released him from it. He stepped out of the cage, and a grim smile came across his face.

"Thank you, boy," he said. "It has been too many years since I saw the sun. I hope that this day my eyes will see the outside world once again." His face had changed noticeably. The creases in his skin were not cut so deeply as they had appeared to be just moments before.

"You're welcome," I said.

"What is your name?" he asked.

"Aster Wood," I told him. There was no reason I could think of to lie to him.

"Ahhh," he said, "Stars and Earth. That is a fitting name for a follower of Almara. And only a true follower could have used the staff in such a way. I am Owyn Gildas, follower of the sun, and of Almara." He held out his hand for me to shake. I did so, and though his bony fingers were cold, I felt the touch of friendship in the greeting. If he recognized my name, he did not show it.

"May I?" he asked.

"Oh! Yes, of course!" I said, handing him the staff.

He took it, his fingers running up and down the carved wood lovingly, as if it were an old friend he had never expected to see again. Then, turning, Owyn spoke, much louder than I thought he would dare or was wise.

"Friends!" he boomed across the dungeon. "Our day has come! The staff has been locked, lifeless and unreachable in the silver cage while we have been locked in our own jails. We have wasted down here in the earth for these centuries, waiting in vain for a follower to come give us our freedom once more. Today, finally, that wait has ended. ASTER WOOD!"

The men all shouted together, "ASTER WOOD!"

"ASTER WOOD is our savior today." Owyn lifted the staff above his head and, swinging it in a wide circle, each and every dungeon door swung open. The men ambled from the gates and shuffled over to where we stood, gathering around us.

"Today," Owyn continued, "we will be free once more. But our fight is not over, friends. We must fight for not only our own freedom, but for the freedom of every soul living in Stonemore. Are you ready?"

"AYE!" shouted all of the men together.

In the brief silence that followed their affirmation, another sound could be heard echoing through the dungeon. The keeper was hobbling his way down the aisle, shouting as he went,

"What's going on in here? What do you think you're—" He froze, seeing the horde of men, all free now, standing in the aisles. I could see his brain working furiously to understand what he was looking at, but it took him too long to process it. Before he could turn to run the men were upon him. For a moment I worried that they would kill him right there. But they simply dragged him, kicking and screaming, to the treasure hold. Two of the larger men held him while a third reached into his pockets for his keys. Then each took one arm of the keeper and threw him into the cell so forcefully that he toppled the heavy pile of books. The gate crashed shut, and a roar of cheers burst forth from the prisoners.

"Now, brothers!" bellowed Owyn. "It is time!"

With a cry of fury the men ran for the exits, half in one direction, half in the other, as if the entire event had been planned for many long years. Owyn paused and spoke to me.

"Wait in the outer hall until all of the men are gone. The Shield will be so busy trying to beat them back that they won't even notice you. You must find the man in black and take back the book. The book of codes is our only path to Almara, if he still lives. Then, together, we must find the Stone of Borna and destroy it. If we don't, Cadoc will live on, and all of Maylin will be lost."

"But," I said, confused, "if we destroy the stone won't it kill you?"

"It will, eventually, yes. But its destruction is the only way to ensure the destruction of Cadoc as well. He cannot die while the stone exists and rests in his control."

"Yeah, ok," I panted.

"Meet me on the north side of the city," he continued. "The gates will remain open for mere minutes after we have surfaced. We will flee from there, and discuss our plans once we are clear of danger."

Everything seemed to be happening at warp speed. It had not

been my original intention to release a horde of angry prisoners into the city to fight The Shield, and while I was happy to do so, I now worried about both Kiron and Chapman's safety. I decided I would have to trust Owyn to get them beyond the walls.

"Listen," I said. "You have to help my friends. Find the man named Kiron and bring him with you. He will be waiting behind the soup lady in the square. And the other, Chapman. He runs a small shop in the square with a silver spinning sculpture in the window. *You must not hurt them.* Do you understand? If you want my help finding The Stone, you have to help my friends."

He gave a curt nod of his ragged head. "Yes," he said. "You have shown your worth to myself and my men today. I will find these friends of yours. Meet us outside the wall."

Owyn turned and ran after the prisoners, and I followed. Then, in the outer passage, I waited for him to ascend the spiral staircase before I started up. I paused only to retrieve the black skeleton key, which now hung from the lock it had opened at the base of the stairs. I wrenched it from the keyhole and stuffed it into the one on the other side of the gate as I closed it, locking the keeper inside. I put the key my pocket before I crept back up the staircase to the surface, listening hard for any sign of pursuit. There was nothing.

On the last step I paused and glanced around the corner. The building that disguised the entrance to the dungeons was deserted. Morning had come at last, and outside people ran, panicked, in all directions. Men on horses galloped through the street, seeking the escaped prisoners. Townspeople screamed as they searched for cover from the chaos of the fight. I stuck my head out the door and looked in both directions, but I saw no more soldiers, just the dusty trail left by the horses. I left the safety of the doorway and started running, myself. I headed for the soup lady's stand in the square, where I knew I would find my pack and Kiron close by.

As I hurtled down the street, I looked into every doorway, every side passage, for the man I sought. The man in black. I had to find Cadoc now, before we could leave the city and join Owyn. I passed a group of soldiers that were fighting spectacularly with three of the prisoners. The men, though thin and dirty from their years underground, were quick and light on their feet. They were running circles around the guards, tripping up their horses, who were whinnying and rearing from the snarl. Their antics reminded me of clowns in a circus performance, only with a much more sinister purpose.

He hit me like a wall. I never saw if it was a building he appeared from, or an alleyway, but in any case there he stood. I had been running so fast that I slammed into him and then backward to the ground. He bent over me and grabbed my jacket with two hands, pulled me back to my feet and then off the ground entirely, and stared at me with his cold, dark glare.

The man in black had found *me*.

CHAPTER FIFTEEN

My efforts to fight him lasted only a moment. I wriggled around, trying to break the iron grasp his hands held on my arms. But, fueled by some unknown power, Cadoc's grip only tightened until I cried out in pain, certain that he would break my bones. He shook me roughly until I stopped fighting completely, and then put his face close to mine, staring into my unfocused eyes. His putrid breath filled my nostrils with its stench.

I was dizzy. His rough face floated in front of my vision, and as he spoke his voice sounded muffled to my ears, like someone speaking to me through a heavy door. I couldn't make out what he was saying, only the anger with which he spat the words at me. My heart pounded in my ears, much louder than Cadoc's voice. My blurry vision cast downward as he raged at me. He held my body up above the ground so that my face was level with his neck. A thin golden chain ran around his neck and over his solid chest, out of place on this enormous man. Something else wasn't right about this, but my brain was bound by panic, and I couldn't figure out what. The pendant that dangled from it was large and round, etched with the shape of a star.

As my eyes slowly began to focus, I met his gaze for the first time.

In an instant, his grip loosened on my coat. His face was shocked, surprised, as we looked at each other. He slowly lowered my feet back to the ground. His fingers grasped a lock of my hair, still dark from Kiron's disguise, and wiped away some of the soot, revealing its white-blond color.

"*You*," he said. His mouth remained open in disbelief.

I could feel the blood rushing back into my fingertips, his hands having all but released my arms.

"You were in the dream," he went on. "But how is that possible? How are you here now? It was only a dream!"

What?

His grimace slackened, overcome by his memory, and for a moment I stared at him, confused. Then I came to my senses and realized the opportunity his distraction gave me.

"You," he said, "you were over there." He stood upright and pointed across the road, only one hand on me now. A sliver of green winked at me from underneath his overcoat. The book!

"And I was here," he continued. "And you were running—"

Had we shared the dream?

I didn't have time to ask the question of him, or even ponder it myself. I braced my feet on the hard street.

"And you were so fast!" he said, his eyes glazing now as he looked over my head at something only he could see. Perhaps he was remembering me running away from him down that very street.

I made my move. My free hand flew up to his jacket and snatched the book from the inside pocket before he could even register my movement. I put the book, no bigger than the palm of my hand, firmly between my teeth and ripped my arms out of my jacket, pulling the sleeves inside out as I freed myself from the canvas.

As I took the first frantic steps away from him, I could feel his hands grasp for me, but his fingers barely grazed my shirt as I flew down the street. His screams of fury echoed in my ears as I was ten, then twenty paces away, the prize now clutched tightly in my hand as I ran.

The world seemed to be moving in slow motion around me as I careened towards the square. Cadoc's yells followed me as I ran, but with each step they were more difficult to hear. The city people who were left on the street stood, dumbstruck, as I ran by them. In the distance I could hear rapid hoofbeats reverberating off the walls of the streets, getting closer, closer. I ran harder and, sooner than I had thought possible, burst through the entrance to the square.

I was focused now. Somewhere in the back of my head I was aware that I was running fast, *really* fast, but it felt so natural that this thought caused me no alarm. I felt, for the first time since entering Stonemore, safe. They couldn't catch me. Nobody could.

I shot across the square like a bullet. Ten yards from the soup lady I shouted, "Reveal!" and the backpack my eyes were searching for popped back into existence, propped against the wall behind her stew pot, the ax tied to one of its straps. I barely broke stride as I leaned over to snatch it. I strapped it to my back and held the ax out and ready as I continued towards the road to the outer gates of the city.

The entire place was erupting into chaos as I ran. Shield guards were beating the townspeople bloody, as if the release of the prisoners had triggered some sort of vicious, automatic retaliation against the citizens. As I careened through the square, I suddenly saw something that nearly stopped me in my tracks.

Kiron and Chapman both stood back to back, fighting off soldiers who approached from every side. Chapman held a simple metal shield, and he used it to protect himself from the constant blows of the guards. Kiron wielded his long, silver sword, and he slashed out at the men as they bore down on the duo. For an instant he saw me, and our eyes met.

"Run!" he yelled, alarmed at my stillness amidst the battle. I had stopped dead without realizing it. The fear and fury in his eyes jarred me back to my senses and I tore myself away from the scene, running towards the street on the north end of the square.

Once I rounded the corner out of the square, I found the path almost entirely deserted. Screams and slamming doors echoed off the buildings as the people hid from the violence. Dead ahead of me I could see the gates in the distance, already starting to close. The alert must have made it to the guards, and now they would try to cut me off before I could break through. The strip of daylight between the two enormous wood and iron doors was getting thinner and thinner with each step I took towards them. I didn't let my eyes leave that ribbon of light as I ran for my freedom. The men shouted to each other as they heaved on the doors, but their voices I heard for only a moment. As the doors swung in earnest, first feet, then inches from closing, I blazed through them in a flash before they thudded shut, sealed against the world.

My feet ran on grass now, my whole body grateful for the soft turf. But I didn't make it far. Soon I slowed to a stop and melted down into the cool blades, my chest heaving with the effort of the flight. I turned back to look at the city, elated by my increasing strength and glorious escape. But what I saw there quickly dashed my joy.

Over the rooftops the fireworks of battle raged. In one corner of the city a group of buildings burned. Explosion after explosion rocked the air above the square and reverberated off the walls. They would never make it to me in time. And their escape was closed off. Was there another way out of the city? I didn't know. I contemplated scouting around the perimeter of the wall to look for another point where I might be likely to meet the men from the dungeons. But then something caught my eye on top of the city wall.

A cloud of smoke twirled on the spot, undulating back and forth. Curiously it danced and then fell twenty feet to the ground on the outside of the city, its form not breaking from the impact. I rose to my feet, alarmed, as the smoke unmistakably started in my direction. But it moved unnaturally fast. Before I could turn to run it was upon me, and then in front of me, and then it wasn't smoke anymore at all.

It was Cadoc.

The sneer on his face was triumphant as he stood on the rocks above me, his teeth shining from under his lips as if he wanted to devour me. His magic, whatever it was, we had all underestimated.

I would not be meeting my party after all.

"You have something of mine," he growled. "Little boys should learn that there is punishment when one steals."

I slowly rose to my feet as he made his way, almost casually, towards me.

"I always told that fool Owyn Gildas that I would beat him in the end. He may have escaped his cage for the afternoon, but he'll be in it again by sundown."

My left hand gripped the book of codes tightly, the right my ax. I searched around me frantically for a path to escape.

"He could have chosen to follow me instead of that old fool, Almara. But then, we are not all born to make such choices. It takes a man who has left cowardice far behind him to recognize the road to true power."

He raised up his left hand and twirled his fingers through the smoke of the miniature tornado that now spun on top of his palm.

"Had he chosen more wisely, things would be different for him now," he said as he manipulated the smoke, "but he did not choose wisely." His eyes focused on me again. "How, I wonder, will you choose, young friend?"

His lips curled up into a grimacing smile, and I took a step backwards.

"No, no," he said, taking slow paces towards me. "Don't you worry, now. I won't hurt you if you don't make the same foolish mistake as Owyn. Come with me now and we can explore together the wonders of what this place has to offer us. It's not every day, after all, that one is so lucky as to share a dream with another."

It wasn't *any* day that people shared dreams, at least not where I came from.

"You seem to have a...sense about things that I haven't seen in quite some time," he continued. "And, as you might have guessed by now, I've been around for a long while. You and I, we could do...such *wondrous* things together." The snakelike persuasion of his voice licked around the edges of my mind, but I rejected it with revulsion. His eyes lied underneath his black brows.

"Who *are* you?" I asked.

"I am the one," he murmured, distracted now by the black wind in his hand, "whom you would best not keep waiting much longer. I am of the *Corentin.*" His eyes changed as he said this word, and within the black irises red streaked across from one side to the other. He lowered his hands to his sides, palms outstretched, and black smoke began to pour from them and onto the earth below his feet. At the first touch of the smoke, the grass shriveled and crumbled. The black air reached out across the earth between where he and I stood, coming towards me.

"Tell me, Aster," his voice became slippery and smooth, "what is it that you desire? What are you searching for?"

I backed away, but found I could not shift my gaze away from his palms. The smoke was alive as it caressed the tips of each blade of grass.

"I want to go home," I said, entranced.

"Where is home?" he asked, taking silent steps towards me.

"Earth," I said automatically.

"Ahhh," he replied. "I can help you there. So little gold remains in the Triaden. And without gold, you are bound here." The thin gold chain shimmered against his chest. In the far reaches of my mind, I realized that was why the necklace had seemed so out of place before. We stood in a world without gold, except for that which hung around Cadoc's neck. "I alone have the power to send beings along the pathways of this universe."

This statement brought me up short, breaking the hold of the magic on my mind just long enough for me to use my own reason. He had not been the one to send Brendan Wood to Earth; Almara had done that. It might be a power that he also shared, but he was not my only hope. This terrifying man, a man who haunted my dreams and locked away my allies for centuries, was not my only hope.

He began to approach me again, and I did the thing that had so easily become second nature to me; I swung my ax. It flipped, blade over handle, and soared through the air directly towards his chest. I watched with satisfaction and then horror as it met its mark…and then burst right through the other side. The center of Cadoc's body split open in a giant puff of black smoke, and then closed itself again. He was completely unharmed. He looked down at his chest, a look of mild surprise on his face.

"So be it," he snarled, turning his murderous eyes to me. He advanced.

I could not wait any longer. I could not fight this magic, and I doubted I could win in a race out here in the open, even with my speed. I held up the book, decorated with thin, golden paint, thrust it into the air, and screamed, "GO!"

"NO!" Cadoc yelled as the pull of the jump enveloped me. His red eyes seemed to burst from his head and follow me into the spin, but in another moment they melted away like the smoke in his hands.

CHAPTER SIXTEEN

I landed on my back in deep, soft snow. *Snow?* I had only ever seen pictures of snow, saved from the days before the famine. I gripped bunches of it frantically in my fists as I lurched to my feet. Above, a million burning stars punctuated the blackness of space. The cold was jarring, something I had never felt, but panic overpowered my wonder at this strange landscape. I spun, searching frantically for any sign that Cadoc had somehow followed me. Nothing but low, rolling hills stretched out as far as the eye could see. Not a single tree sprouted from the frozen ground for him to hide behind. I was alone.

It wasn't until my breath started coming in thin wheezes that I realized I couldn't breathe. I opened my mouth wide and lifted my chin. I could not overpower my fear of his pursuit.

This was different than the asthma that came with my bad heart, but I recognized the sensation. When I was three or so years old, before I had gotten sick, I had been jumping on my mom's bed one night before dinner. Delighted by the heights my tiny body could reach, I bounced right off the edge of the mattress and landed on the carpeted floor, flat on my back. Every molecule of air that had been in my lungs was thrust out in a whoosh from the pressure of the impact. I lay gasping for what seemed like hours, but had only been seconds.

I was doing the same now, but each gasp seemed to only bring on more panic as I scanned the sleeping land. I moved quickly despite the reassuring emptiness of this place, not thinking as clearly as I might have if I had remained still and allowed myself to calm down. But it was too much. I had faced too much danger to do anything now but continue to escape. I ran, panicking, through the knee-deep snow into the darkness of night, but it wasn't long before I realized I couldn't get far in the state I was in. My chest felt like a deflated balloon, and no matter how hard I tried I couldn't suck in any air. I fell back down to the freezing earth.

Cadoc. He wasn't a man. Not a normal man, anyways. He had been flesh, and then smoke, and then flesh again. And his eyes, those red eyes had tried to follow me here.

I lay down, unable to flee, my body trying desperately to obtain oxygen. As my chest heaved, my eyes drifted upward to the clear night sky. Two moons, one large and white like our own on Earth, and one small and dim with a purple glow, shone full. The white snow rose up all around me, the cold flakes brushing up against my cheeks and fingertips. As air slowly returned to my flattened lungs, my gasps made large plumes of vapor in the cold air with each ragged breath.

My body gave an involuntary shiver and I crossed my arms over my chest stay warm. Slowly, so slowly, my breathing calmed.

I slowly sat up and looked around. Yes, I was alone, safe, it seemed, from Cadoc. But I was in trouble. My teeth began chattering involuntarily. I wrestled free of the pack, revealed it and ripped it open with my quickly numbing fingers. There had to be something inside that might keep me from freezing to death. I grabbed at each item, hoping for the feel of fur, fleece, anything. My panic resurfaced as I threw aside apples, jars of jam, and the last of my dried meat. He had to have packed *something*, maybe a blanket for sleeping outdoors. Did they have such things as sleeping bags in the Fold? I was starting to despair, my body shaking with cold, when, at the bottom, my fingers brushed up against something that made me exhale a long sigh of relief.

Kiron had stowed a wooly blanket at the very bottom. I pulled it out and spread it wide. The material was thin, but the piece was broad, much larger than a beach towel, and I quickly draped it around my body. Instantly I could feel warmth returning to the skin on my arms as the fabric insulated me against the biting night. I tied it at the base of my neck and got back to my feet, fumbling through the snow, picking up the items I had tossed aside.

Once I had repacked the bag, I sat down in the snow and hugged it to my chest, holding on to the one piece of Kiron that was still with me. I was on my own now, and I held the pack protectively, as though someone might snatch it from me at any moment. Though cold, the air was completely still, and the blanket brought me incredible warmth despite its thinness. He must have done some sort of magic to it, or maybe the fibers themselves possessed some rare power.

I pulled the green book from my pocket and inspected it in the moonlight. On the front cover was Almara's symbol, but when I opened the little book the pages inside were blank. It wasn't surprising, but it was disappointing. Where was I supposed to go? The other links had been maps, but this one showed no destination, no golden ring. I lay back into the snow, frustrated and exhausted.

My body began to feel weak as I calmed down, and I stowed the book in my pocket and raised my eyes to the sky again, studying the two moons. The bigger of the two was much larger than our moon on Earth, though not as bright. The surface was covered in pocked craters, as ours is, but hovering around it was a thick ring of dust. The smaller moon was half the size of ours, and very dark by comparison. Its grayish purple hue barely reflected any light at all, and its surface was smooth as a marble. Both moons were completely full. I wondered how unusual it was to see two full moons in the same sky on the same night. But then, looking around, I realized there was no one here to see the moons but me.

My eyes meandered to the stars that dotted the cosmos beyond the moons. There were so many more than I had ever seen from Earth. Living in the city, we couldn't see anything but a hazy, orange glow in the night sky. But here I was awash in the brilliance of a billion points of light. It was this, more than anything, that comforted me, though I couldn't quite pinpoint why. The stars weren't a familiar sight to me, though I did have a memory of seeing them, just one time, before.

I was maybe four. She had fought with my dad, and when he took off into the street, she took my hand and we left the apartment. We stopped at a neighbor's door; I never knew her name, but she and my mom would talk from time to time in the hallway. After several minutes of hushed conversation, and what sounded a lot like pleading on the part of my mother, the neighbor handed her a single, silver key. Before the woman could change her mind, Mom grabbed my hand and together we ran down the stairs. She giggled, of all things, and I was so excited about the smile on her face that I followed suit.

The key was to a car, a rusted monster with leather bench seats and just a single working headlight. We drove out of the city as the sun was setting, and soon I fell asleep with my head in her lap. Some time later, she woke me, tickling my feet until I was finally upright. She had driven us to the mountains, she said. She grabbed an old, smelly blanket from the trunk of the car, and together we walked up a small incline to a precipice. She bundled me into her arms and wrapped the blanket around us both. I didn't mind the musty smell so much, not with her warm arms around me.

We lay back into the dead grass, and only then did I realize that the sky was full of strange pinpricks of light. They were stars, she told me, and when she was a girl they could be seen from just about anywhere in the world. Her long fingers zigzagged above our heads as she murmured to me about dust particles and the birthing of stars, science too big for me to understand, but I didn't care. I lay my head on her shoulder and listened to her talk about how much she missed being able to walk out her back door and look up at the stars.

"Why can't we see the stars at home, Mama?" I had asked.

"Things are different now, baby," she said. I watched her eyes drink in the light from the sky, the look on her face peaceful and calm. "Do you like them?" she asked.

"Yes," I answered, and I did. If she liked them, so did I. Besides, I had never known that an entire universe lay hidden behind the veil of smog that blanketed our world.

"Me, too, baby," she said. She sighed. "To me, seeing the stars is like seeing a family member you've never met, and yet somehow knowing them just the same. They make me feel…warm."

I was happy there with her, but I was starting to wonder when we might be going home. Little sharp pricks of grass were sticking into my backside, making me long for my warm bed and soft sheets. I didn't understand quite what she meant about feeling warm, especially since the breeze was starting to blow beneath our blanket, and I shivered beneath her embrace.

But now, lying on this soft, thick bed of snow, somewhere deep in the Maylin Fold, I understood. She didn't miss seeing the stars just because they were pretty to look at. She missed them because seeing them gave her some sort of feeling of connection that our cities of millions, and my father, couldn't bring. She missed them because of the way looking at them now was making *me* feel. I was lost, hopelessly lost in a frozen expanse of snow, separated from my home and all that I understood. But deep inside me, a primal animal was calmed and brought peace where before there had been discomfort and emptiness. She missed them because for millions of years, us and every other animal that had ever been had looked upward to see their familiar sparkling each and every night, relieved by their reliable appearance. It was a privilege now lost to those who lived on Earth.

I now understood a small piece of what the famine had taken from them, and from everyone who came after, and I wished that I could package up this sky and bring it back to her. Because when we look at the stars, we are comforted, rebalanced. And we are home.

CHAPTER SEVENTEEN

I woke, my face smashed into the cold snow, the howls of an already forgotten dream following me into waking. As I rolled onto my back and covered the snowy part of my face with the blanket, I realized that the howls weren't from any dream at all. The mournful cries met my ears again and again, and I sat bolt upright, looking around.

The rolling white hills betrayed no predator I could see, but the howling continued, each cry piercing the silent night around me. I scrambled up, ready to run away, but in what direction? The noise came from the spot in the distance where the purple moon came closest to the horizon. The moons had sunk low in the sky. How long had I slept? It had felt like hours. Where was the sun?

Each howl that echoed in the night made me more and more nervous, and I quickly gathered up my pack and set off in the opposite direction of the noise, walking fast but not yet running. My boots were tough and warm, but my feet sunk several inches into the snow with each step. Progress was slow, but soon I was warm enough from the efforts of walking to lower the blanket from my head. The howls sounded, and I moved over the landscape in the opposite direction. My nerves jittered, but with no threat that I could see, all I could do was walk away. After a time I started to feel like a sheep being herded to a pen, but my experience with the faylons still sent me scurrying. I didn't want to be anywhere near whatever it was that was making that sound.

This place was strange, much stranger than the green grasses of Kiron's or the medieval stones of Stonemore, and utterly silent but for the howls in the distance and the crunching of my feet on the snow. The hills were so alike that there was no way to tell which was which, and my trail of footsteps was the only clue as to what direction I had come from. Without the moons to guide me I would have been entirely lost; at least I knew I was heading in one general direction. From time to time the howling would start up suddenly, pushing me to change course, but the longer I walked, the fainter the cries became.

I pulled out the book again and studied it as I walked, hoping for a clue about where to head next, but the pages remained stubbornly blank. I trudged on, hoping I would find somewhere to hide. The animals, if they caught my scent, would surely be faster than me in this snow.

After an hour, I came to the lip of a valley, the first change in the land I had seen. The basin was enormous and round, surrounded by the same little hills on all sides, and down in the very center stood an object I couldn't identify from this far away. All I could tell from the edge of the bowl was that it wasn't a tree or a house. Then what was it? Some enormous animal?

I stood for a time and watched it, but after a few minutes it still didn't move. I carefully started to walk down the hill. The snow here was deeper, and I found myself almost up to my waist in the stuff as I struggled to keep upright. My feet were still dry, but a thin layer of snow melted against my pants, and soon I was shivering again.

I finally made it all the way down and cautiously approached what I now saw was some sort of monument. When I realized that the statue that stood atop it was carved into an enormous wolf, I froze. The wolf stood tall, his form lifted fifteen feet off the ground by a marble base.

It's not alive.

But my hammering heart didn't hear the logic in my head. I inched towards it until I found myself face to face with the enormous stone statue.

The howling had stopped completely, and now he and I stood silently together in the moonlight. He stared off into the night, dominance carved into his face. This was *his* land.

I stared at the stone wolf for what seemed a long time. Whoever had carved this statue had possessed fantastic skill. Even from the ground I could see the details in his fur, the delicate shape of his ears. Everything about him seemed alive, everything but his eyes. Cold, flat stone looked out at the surrounding valley.

I moved around the base, looking for what, I didn't know. All around each of the square sides were inscribed these words:

> *At the place where the sun meets the land*
> *Lies escape they have surely not planned*
> *Discover the code and you'll see*
> *The way forward to win you the key*

I walked around the podium again and again, trying to make sense of the inscription. It told me to go somewhere where the sun met the land. But where? This place seemed to be in a perpetual state of darkness.

I moved on to the next line, *escape they have surely not planned.* My hand dragged along the surface of the monument, feeling the roughness of the rock as I paced around it. On one side several horizontal notches were carved out, just deep enough for me to fit my fingers into. I stopped and moved my hands back and forth over the rough grooves. Maybe this line was about my escape from Maylin, my journey back home. Who would want to keep me from escaping Maylin?

Discover the code. Of course! I stopped pacing and took the book from my pocket, When I opened it a wave of relief washed over me. The pages were full, top to bottom, with writing. This was it! It wasn't a map, that was true, but this little tome would give me what I needed, I was sure of it.

I walked around the base of the statue again, looking for a place to enter the code, but found none. I ran the last line through my head again and again. *The way forward to win you the key.*

I circled it again, searching this time with my hands. Starting at the ground the base rested upon, I worked my way up each side of the rock until my fingers were extended all the way above my head. Still nothing. I took several steps back from the base. Maybe I needed to see this whole thing differently.

I slapped myself on the forehead for my own stupidity. The horizontal notches I had been running my fingers over, they weren't just random notches cut into the stone. There were five of them extending from a foot off the ground and all the way to the flat top of the pedestal. It was a ladder.

I fitted the toes of my boot into the lowest rung. The carving was so shallow that I could barely get a hold of it with my foot. Extending my arms to the rung above my head I gripped the rock hard with my fingertips and began to climb.

My first few attempts to ascend the structure resulted in my flailing and tumbling to the snow below. But on the fourth try I was finally able hoist my weight up onto the platform. I carefully stood up on the edge of the base and came face to face with the stone wolf.

He was gigantic. Standing as tall as me, his eyes were almost perfectly level with mine. No snow stuck onto any surface of his body. I reached out to touch the stone, and was surprised when I didn't feel rock beneath my fingertips, but the soft warmth of fur. I snatched my hand back, alarmed, but he didn't move. I stretched out my hand to touch it again, entranced. My fingers could press in on the fur, but it otherwise remained entirely motionless. What was this thing?

I carefully lay my ear against its back, listening. I heard no heartbeat or other sound. I was both relieved and disappointed by this. So it wasn't alive then, but something else. In such a lonely place, part of me had been hoping to hear a sign of life beneath the marble. Though the idea of being greeted by a huge, live wolf was terrifying.

I dropped back down to my hands and knees and began to brush away the snow that covered the rest of the platform. It didn't take me long to find what I was looking for. My icy fingers moved over the four distinct notches carved into the base. Above each rectangle shaped notch, strange ciphers were written. I pulled out the book and flipped through the pages in the moonlight.

The book was split into three sections. Each one had a large set of characters decoded several times into different types of what I could only guess were alphabets. I focused on the first character of the code on the stone and searched the book for its twin.

I found it quickly enough in the third section. This part of the book only had about thirty different characters translated, and I saw with relief that several of the translations were written in letters from the alphabet that I had learned back on Earth. Was I supposed to draw the letter? It seemed a logical conclusion to write it onto the stone, but with what? I reached out a single, frozen finger and traced the first letter in the sequence onto the bare stone, which was J.

Before my finger had even begun the loop on the bottom of the letter, the path it had taken on the stone came to life. Gold shimmered beneath my hand as I completed it, and then the next. And the next. At last I found the final letter in the code, an E, and completed the word.

J-A-D-E

A loud click came from the base as an unseen lock slid into place.

I stared at the stone, waiting for something to happen, but nothing did. No secret compartment opened in the floor. No other codes or letters alighted on the stone. I rested on my hands and knees, searching for some sign that I had accomplished something. But the unforgiving stone had remained hard and lifeless.

Then I heard it. Breathing. Right above my head. I closed my eyes, willing it not to be true, but the hot breath that blew over the back of my neck was undeniable. I slowly sat back on my heels and, trying not to scream, looked up at the statue.

He looked right back at me. No longer was the wolf made of stone. His fur rippled with the movement of his breath, shining white hot in the moonlight. His eyes, now full of life, stared deep into mine.

I had little control over what happened next. In my primordial brain the alarm bells were ringing; I needed to escape this predator. My mouth hung silently open as I stood and backed away from the beast, completely forgetting that I was fifteen feet above the ground. I backed right off the edge of the platform and fell to the snow below.

You might think that landing in snow would have broken my fall, but you would be mistaken. The snow, only a foot or so deep in the center of the basin, was maybe enough to keep me from breaking my ankle, but definitely not enough to keep me from injury. The pain shot up through my leg and I yelped, clutching at it and writhing on the ground, the wolf above all but forgotten. In the background of my own cries of pain I heard whining. I looked up just in time to see the wolf jump down from the platform.

I tried to scramble upwards but I was unable to put any weight on my leg. The whining continued, and slowly the animal made his way over to me, snorting giant plumes of vapor into the frigid air. I struggled to push myself backwards in the snow, but there was nowhere for me to escape to. He approached me, snuffling the air around my neck. I lay back into the snow, breathing hard with terror and panic.

This was it. This was how I was going to die. Not from a heart attack or a bout of asthma, or even whatever it was that Cadoc had planned for me, but instead eaten alive by an impossibly alive wild animal. I tried to close my eyes, to give myself over to the inevitable, but they stayed stubbornly wide.

Suddenly I felt something entirely unexpected; a warmth was spreading from the center of my chest outward. I looked down into the face of the beast, and was surprised to find him resting his head on my rib cage. I barely breathed. He looked at me through silver eyes and a low whine came from his throat.

Could this really be happening? He didn't *seem* to want to eat me. I waited, but neither of us moved.

I tentatively lifted one hand and touched the wolf's head between his ears. He blinked at the touch and sighed. My fingers slowly dug into the fur and scratched the skin beneath it, and his eyes closed with pleasure. Was he...tame?

I slowly sat up and he raised his head as I did so, eyes following mine. When he didn't attack, I risked trying to stand again, and once more crumpled to the ground with a whimper. The wolf watched me try this again and again until I lay motionless in the snow, defeated. He moved then, nudging his head underneath my arm and sliding forward on his belly until it rested on his back. He pushed his back into me, nudging me farther and farther until his body was almost completely underneath mine.

I then did what was probably a very stupid thing. I swung my injured leg over the back of the wolf as if he were the old draft horse on Grandma's farm, and held my breath.

He positioned his legs underneath himself and rose from the ground, me hanging on to two tufts of fur between my fingers. I tried to grab big handfuls of fur instead of just a few strands, not wanting to hurt him, but he didn't seem to notice the pulling at all. I steadied myself on his back as his feet pranced underneath. Then he lifted his shining head into the night and gave a long howl. The sound echoed across the basin, bouncing back to us until a chorus of howls filled the darkness. It sounded like a hundred wolves were responding to his call. I looked around, expecting to see an army of animals descend from the surrounding hills, but the landscape remained empty.

He moved then and quickly broke into a run. I flopped myself down closer to his back, hugging my arms around his neck to keep myself from flailing around. But I soon realized that his gait was smooth and easy to balance with. I sat back up and watched the land around us zip by in a streak. My eyes watered from the cold air, and I released one of my hands to pull up my hood to protect my quickly freezing ears.

It should have been wonderful, glorious. But what I remember most about that ride was that it was freezing, icy cold. His giant head bobbed up and down in front of me with each stride, and though his fur glowed brightly in the moonlight, little heat came off him to warm me. I kept my fingers from freezing by gripping the fur close to his skin, but my face and ears were soon stinging. I bowed my head closer to the wolf as he ran, my head throbbing in protest.

As we moved through the night, a new set of howls and yips began to echo around us, different from those clear cries that had driven me to the wolf. What were they? I couldn't be sure. The few times my frozen body would let me raise my head to look around, I saw nothing pursuing us. I remembered Cadoc with a shudder, and hoped that this place didn't hide the same sorts of monsters that Stonemore did.

I don't know how long the wolf ran for. We left the expanse of rolling hills behind us and began a long climb to the top of a mountain range that blocked our path. In the back of my mind I fretted over the condition of the animal, running so hard and for so long, but I was constantly brought back to my own worries. My toes were slowly getting tingly, then numb, and my teeth started to chatter furiously. I tried to stay bent forward to keep what little heat I had left in my body from escaping into the frigid air.

When we finally reached the top of the mountain the wolf stopped. He barely panted at all from his exertion, and I followed his gaze out over the land below. In the far distance a series of lakes stretched out, vast open plains and more mountains to one side. Nothing moved, and the howling had stopped.

He turned and leaped off the peak, and we descended the mountain in a rush of wind and speed. I began to long for home, or Chapman's warm closet, or Kiron's cottage; anywhere that I could defrost my body and find warmth again. Little else mattered to me in that moment but to get out of the cold.

Finally, after dropping what must have been thousands of feet to the floor beneath the mountain, the wolf came to a stop. He stood erect, his breathing coming faster now, the breath billowing out in big plumes from his snout. He had stopped right at the base of the mountain, and in front of us was a round, silver boulder.

The stone was as tall as my waist, a perfect sphere. Five feet in front of it a rock tablet was set into the ground. The outline of two carved handprints was just visible in the shadow of the moon.

The wolf did not move. We had reached whatever destination he had intended. I slumped off his back onto the ground in front of the tablet, curling up into tiny ball, and putting my frozen hands underneath the blanket to thaw. After a few minutes the subtle magic in the blanket began to warm me, more powerful now that I was out of the wind. My teeth slowly stopped chattering, and I was able to think more clearly.

The wolf stood above me, looking between the stone and I expectantly. I got to my hands and knees and crawled over to the tablet, each movement sending a jolt of fiery pain from ankle to knee in my damaged leg.

I slid my hands over the stone and found that the small platform was warm to the touch. I eagerly welcomed the heat that spread up through my hands into my upper body. I moved my two palms across the rough surface until they fit neatly into the spaces carved into the rock, greedily searching for more heat.

Once, when I was about five, I visited the tiny city petting zoo with my mom. Keeping animals as pets was no longer a priority for people on Earth, but this one small place was built to teach the younger school kids about food production. The more people the government could interest in growing food, the better.

Mom had been distracted by the dramatic wailing of a toddler who had been knocked down by an overeager goat, and I took the opportunity to sneak away. I had really wanted to come to the zoo to see the horses, but I quickly found out that they weren't in the area where they let the kids roam around. Pigs and goats are all well and good, but I remembered the velvet touch of Grandma's draft horse's nose, and I was determined to at least find one to say hello to.

I snuck through the swinging door of an empty stall in the pen and out the other side, tiptoeing towards the little shelter where three ponies stood. They looked at me with interest, and one of them even snorted a low rumbling nicker in my direction. I eagerly approached the wooden fence that surrounded them and climbed up, not noticing or caring about the thin silver wire that ran along the edge of the top board. My hands grasped the top rung as I climbed, and then, just to get a little bit higher, I grabbed the wire itself.

Big mistake.

The jolt that went through my arms was not enough to kill me, or even to hurt me really. But it was painful, and so surprising that I leapt away from the fence, tumbled through the air and hit the ground hard. Now I was the one wailing, and I ran for my mom, never having placed a single finger on any of those fuzzy noses.

I had stayed away from anything that resembled an electrified wire ever since that day. But nothing about the rock betrayed it as dangerous as I slid my hands into the carved handprints. With a loud crack, electricity burned from my fingertips to my elbows. For a moment I was stuck there, glued to the thing, and then I was tossed backward, landing on my back in the snow.

My hands felt like fire. I shouted with pain and rolled over onto my side, cradling them into my chest protectively. The rest of the world ceased to exist for a time. I could hear very little that occurred outside my own body. Inside, my heartbeat echoed in my ears, erratic, and the nerves in my fingers screamed as the blood pulsed angrily in and out of them. Coming out of this pain took a while, and everything seemed to right itself at a slow, agonizing pace. Then a howl broke through my haze, something large knocked into me, rolling me onto my back. I sat up, still clutching my hands, but immediately most of the pain vanished, replaced by the awe of the scene in front of me.

Everything had changed. The sky, the deepest night just a moment ago, was now bright with the light of morning. On the horizon I could see planets, I counted five, seemingly very close to where I now stood. I had seen shows on TV about our solar system before, but this was more vivid than anything in my wildest fantasy. The planets were a rainbow of color, rotating slowly around a bright, but not blinding, star. My imagination made their impossibly huge movements audible in my mind. They looked as if I could reach out and touch them with my bare, throbbing hands.

The light had transformed the land as well. The cold snowy wilderness that surrounded us now reflected soft pinks and oranges of sunrise. The mountains cast cool blue shadows on the ground between the shafts of warm yellow. The water of the lakes in the distance glittered in the glow of this small sun.

I heard a low whine behind me, and I turned to see the wolf staring directly into a very different shaft of light that now rose from the round stone. Only it wasn't round anymore. The sphere had split, blooming like a flower, and through its center came a slowly swirling beam. As I approached it, a female voice spoke, deep and soft.

> *"One key for another*
> *There is only one*
> *You'll give yours away*
> *Before you're done*
>
> *Others have tried*
> *Giving what they feel wise*
> *They've only a moment*
> *To cherish the prize*
>
> *The items you bear*
> *You'd miss both most dearly*
> *And if you think hard*
> *You'll see why quite clearly*
>
> *Choose wisely, friend*
> *The item you give*
> *It must be the right one*
> *For you to live"*

* * *

The voice stopped for a moment and then repeated the rhyme, the misty light twinkling at me invitingly. Three times the voice spoke the riddle. It, or she, or the ground itself, wanted a key. I looked up at the wolf and he stood, resolutely, unmoving. I pulled the pack from my back, revealed it, and sorted through the strange trinkets, searching for a key to trade for a key.

If the voice was truthful and I didn't make the correct choice, I would die, probably in some miserable and horrifying way. My body gave another miserable shiver, and the movement made pain radiate up my leg. This was no simple offering. I had to get it right the first time. I needed to get out of here.

Other than a few pieces of food, I didn't have much with me, but I did, in fact, carry two keys. I sifted through the pack, searching for the cold hard metal that I knew was buried within. My stomach twirled as I held up the two things that might break me out of this frozen land: the book of codes and the skeleton key taken from the keeper.

It might seem that the choice in front of me was easy; the voice was requesting a key, and I had two to give. I fingered the tiny green book in my hands, flipping through the pages. What would I be giving up if I offered this book? And what, I shuddered at the thought, would happen to me if I somehow chose wrong which item to give? I inspected the skeleton key. I could not imagine needing this item again along my quest, not unless I found myself imprisoned down in the dungeons of Stonemore. While possible, that seemed unlikely. I had left Stonemore far behind when I jumped here.

I made a choice.

I put my small pile of belongings back into the pack, slipped the book of codes into my pocket, and grasped the skeleton key in my left hand. Standing shakily, I slowly hobbled over to the light, my ankle throbbing angrily.

The air all around the light shaft was warm and pulsing. The ground around the beam was unfrozen, the snow unable to stick to the patch of earth surrounding it. My body relaxed with pleasure at the touch of the hot air. I approached the beam slowly, trying to see around the edges of the rock into the depths underground, looking for the source of the light, but it was so bright I could see almost nothing below the surface. As I neared it I shielded my eyes, but soon I was protecting my face from the heat as well. I wondered if lava could be flowing beneath my feet, unknown to the snowy world above.

I tentatively held out the skeleton key and released it into the beam, grateful that my fingers didn't burn at the contact with the glow. It floated right where I let it go, hovering at eye height. Then suddenly it shot upward, twirling and flitting from side to side, and finally plunged into the depths of the earth below.

The force of the impact of that thin piece of metal was enormous. From the deep came a deafening grinding, followed by a shudder in the ground so forceful that it knocked me off my feet. I lay still, flat on my stomach, and held onto the dirt stupidly with both arms. Then, as the noise and vibrations settled, a long thin object arose from the beam, shining brilliantly in the light.

I scrambled to my feet and launched myself over to the beam. This was it! I had chosen correctly, and now I had the key! They key to what, I didn't know, but I was so relieved to still be here, alive, that I didn't care. I reached out for the object and it fell into my hand as soon as I touched it, released from the hold of the light.

I held a long, thin, green stone dagger. On the thick handle Almara's symbol was prominently carved and painted with gold. Relief flooded through my entire body. I hobbled away from the light towards the great white wolf, who stood waiting for me just on the edge of the snow.

I didn't hear the cries in the distance at first. I was so busy congratulating myself on my brilliance that the baying barely registered as noise at all. It was only when the ground started shuddering again that I came out of my reverie and looked around.

The wolf stood at attention, intensely focused on the far hills. In the distance I could make out the smallest movement, almost nothing, a shadow across the snow. With each second the shadow shifted and danced, growing closer with great speed. Then it wasn't one shadow, but two, four, fifty, all moving together, flocking like a group of birds in the sky, but racing together over the ground.

I might have run, but the booming voice of the light echoed once again. No longer quiet or soft, now it roared.

> *The choice was made*
> *Through light came your gift*
> *Tucked deep away now*
> *It won't again lift*
>
> *Your journey is over*
> *I'm sorry, my friend*
> *What's done is done*
> *Now you'll meet your end*

* * *

I couldn't believe it. The pack of shadows was quickly descending, almost close enough for me to see their legs now, and the shrieking that came from a hundred running beasts made my blood run cold.

The wolf approached me as he watched the pack. I could do nothing. Frozen with terror now instead of cold, my brain had completely jammed. A low snarl escaped his lips, and when I finally tore my eyes away from the jet black figures in the distance to glance at him I was surprised to see that he was snarling at *me*. His eyes bored into mine and I took a step backward away from him as his lips raised and he bared his teeth. Suddenly, I found myself surrounded by *three* distinct dangers. My eyes flitted from the shaft of light, to the pack of whatever new beasts were heading this way, and back to the wolf. My useless brain tried wildly to make sense out of what was happening.

Then he hit me. His great, furry body knocked me to the ground. The knife tumbled away from me and disappeared into the snow. His enormous head bowed, the wolf had run at me as a bull would a bullfighter. I lay, splayed out on my back, sure that this would be the end of me. Would he go for the jugular? Would he tear me apart? All was confusion as the world swirled around me. My impending death came at me from every side.

But instead of ravaging me, he turned. Towards the pack of shadows, his paws flew silently over the snow until he was twenty feet away, squaring off to the approaching beasts. He then lifted his nose into the air and let out a long, night-shattering howl. I clasped my hands over my ears in pain. When his head came down from the cry, an enormous force emanated from his body. The air rippled out from him like an explosion, and the wave of the blast rushed over me and pinned me to the snow as it passed.

Silence. Only the sound of my breathing made it to my ears, but nothing else. The barking from the flock of monsters had stopped. The voice from the shaft of light was silent. I got to my feet.

The wolf was still. New air filled the space around us, casting a purple glow on the snow. The pack of beasts stayed a hundred feet away, trapped behind some sort of barrier, pacing back and forth. The beam of light from the flowering sphere shone just outside the edge as well. The wolf and I stood together in a circle of protected space, unreachable by fire or demon.

I approached him, uncertain. No wind or ground moved within the circle of light, no fur rippled in the air around us. But as I rounded his head, I found that his eyes held mine. He stared at me with an incredible intensity as he watched me approach. We looked at each other for several long moments as the dangers on the outside tried to work their way in, and I suddenly understood what he had done, and at what cost. The blanket of stone started at his toes and slowly wrapped around his body, around each tiny hair of his silken white coat. Then, as my hand reached out to touch the fur under his chin, the light slowly faded from his eyes. Nothing but the vacant expression of stone remained.

The protective shield around us was fading, dissipating quickly. The beasts outside began the breach the barrier and run for me. The ground rumbled as the rocks deep below the surface ground against one another. The air filled with the noise of impending attack. The protection of the white wolf, my friend, would not last.

I stood back from him, a statue once more. Searching the ground I found the backpack and the small divot the knife had left in the snow when it landed. Then, as the pack of monsters was almost upon me, I held the dagger in the air and spoke the command that sent me spinning into space.

CHAPTER EIGHTEEN

A scream of fury followed me into the jump. I had escaped the clutches of whatever power ruled that world, and its wail echoed in my ears long after I had landed on dry, yellow grass. I lay on my back, exhausted, and looked up at the sky. Cotton ball clouds slowly drifted across the powder blue, and the grass floated back and forth on the easy breeze. Slowly the warmth of the earth crept up through my skin, until finally I was sweating in the afternoon sun.

I sat up and looked around, hot tears of frustration and sadness running down my cheeks. He had sacrificed himself for me, used his power to save me from those shadowy monsters and certain death. And now he was stone again, trapped inside that hard shell of rock that encased him. Would he spend eternity there, staring out across the snowy plains? Would he ever be freed again? Or would the beasts who had trailed us destroy even the stone memory of him?

I wiped the tears from my cheeks and my hands came away black. I realized that my head and face were still covered with Kiron's charcoal, and I angrily rubbed at my hair with my hands. I didn't want to be disguised anymore. I just wanted this to be over.

As the sun slowly sank over plains and both my tears and mouth began to dry, I finally rose to my feet and inspected my surroundings.

The golden grass stretched for many miles around me in every direction. On one side a large ridge of mountains pushed up from the earth, towering in the distance. A small group of trees stood between me and the rock. On every other side the grass simply continued on until it met the golden horizon, blurring the line between earth and sky.

I limped toward the trees. As I walked, sharp jabs of pain shot through my leg, but I didn't care. Tears sprang to my eyes once more from the pain, but it was the pain of the loss more than that of my leg that brought them. Step by excruciating step I slowly neared the shady grove.

When I finally made it underneath the canopy, the sun had just disappeared behind the mountains. I collapsed to the ground in a heap, and sobbed in earnest until exhaustion overcame me and I faded into sleep.

The entirety of the next day I spent on my back under the trees. I was too listless to bother with anything, even food. The only thing I did ingest was water from two small jugs that Kiron had insisted I pack in the bag.

I had a hole in my heart again, but of a different sort. I lay there hour after hour, watching the leaves slowly dance through the sunlight that seemed to race across the sky. I took the green stone dagger from my pocket and examined it in the hot, dry air. Almara's golden symbol glinted at me as I rotated this hard-won prize in the light. I couldn't argue with the fact that it had been worth it, worth the sacrifice in order to find escape from the snow world. But despite my victory over death, I could find no shred of happiness about it.

The knife was small and heavy. Was this the Stone of Borna? I couldn't think how I might destroy it, as Owyn had suggested, even if I had wanted to. It was a peculiar color, a lighter green than I had expected jade to be, and seemed both opaque and translucent at the same time. I spent several hours over the next few days holding it up to the light, watching the sun play with the different shades of green deep within the rock.

My energy came back to me gradually, over days, not hours. Eventually the gnawing of my empty stomach forced me to rise and eat some of the food stored in the pack. The long hours of meditation on everything that had happened in the snow slowly arranged things in my mind, and the events began to make more sense. Over time, I came to the conclusion that the wolf was not lost forever. He had returned to the form he had started in when I had arrived in the snow world. But he wasn't *dead*. Had he ever really been *alive?* The sadness remained, though I felt sure that the wolf still existed in some form back in that world.

On the fourth day I finally rose. My ankle still hurt, but the days I had spent motionless on the grass had done it a lot of good. I was able to put my full weight on it, and this progress, combined with the regular intake of food, was enough to bring me out of my funk. I began to plan. I would rest one more day, and then set off towards those mountains. This knife was like the book, not obviously a map. I would need to move before I got any hint of which direction to travel in.

That night I tried to come up with a plan. I had two things to find now, not one. I needed the next map to get closer to Almara. But I had made a promise to Owyn that I would seek the Stone of Borna, that I would destroy it if possible. The thought of my friends back in Stonemore made me double up as if I had been punched in the gut. Were they still alive? Were they imprisoned again, destined to be trapped for centuries longer beneath the stones of the city? My insides squirmed with regret as I imagined Kiron underground, his treasure of links stolen from around his neck. And what about Chapman? Poor Chapman would drive himself mad with fear over time.

I couldn't get them out if they had been captured. Not from here. But if I managed to find the Stone, and somehow destroy it, then their captor would eventually meet his end. The destruction of the Stone would result in the freedom of the Stonemorians, maybe for generations to come. Though whether it would result in freedom for my friends, I didn't know.

From here on out, I would keep to my original purpose and follow Almara's trail as long as I could. But I would also seek the stone. I vowed to destroy it, somehow, should it ever cross my path.

The morning of the fifth day dawned cool, and I rolled over, nestled inside the blanket. I kept my eyes shut, aiming for just a few more minutes of slumber before setting off on the next leg of my journey. But an unfamiliar snorting sound sent me bolt upright, scouring the area for danger.

Fifty feet away from me, under the branches of the farthest tree in the cluster, stood a herd of horses grazing in the morning sun. Horses! My heart leapt in my chest and I jumped up to see them more clearly.

There were ten, maybe fifteen of them spread out around the base of the tree. Most of them grazed, a few looked to be dozing. I stood still and watched them for a time, and then began walking carefully towards the herd. Soon, ears started pricking up in my direction, and halfway to them I had a dozen sets of eyes on me. They watched me curiously as I picked my way through the grass, crunching the dry blades underfoot. They didn't seem fearful of my approach, although I wasn't that close yet. As I neared I could see the variety of markings they each bore. Some were solid brown or black, but others had patches of white on their sides or rumps, or tan in their manes or tails.

From the center of the herd walked a deep tan horse with a midnight black mane and tail. He approached me at a brisk walk, and the rest of the herd followed behind him cautiously. As he got closer to me he whinnied a loud, clear song. The sound gave me shivers of excitement, and the echoing calls of the herd made my insides leap with joy and anticipation. It was all I could do to keep myself from sprinting towards them.

But I didn't need to run to them. Their strides closed the distance between us quickly, and I soon saw why. They were *huge*. These were not your run-of-the-mill trail horses, not your average working farm horses; these horses were as tall as elephants.

I slowed my pace, but the leader did not reduce his. He walked directly towards me, finally stopping when his face was inches from my own. His head bowed down to greet me, his giant nose snorting warm breath all over my face and hair. His eyes were as large as baseballs, and they looked at me with kindness and a strange familiarity. Soon the rest of the herd was doing the same as the leader, and from all sides their tickling noses snorted onto my neck and nibbled my shirtsleeves, sending shivers across my skin. My fear evaporated.

It was bliss. To be so small, surrounded by such giants, but to be so comfortable and feel so safe was unlike any feeling I had ever had in my life. Their huge feet, the size of serving platters, could have crushed me to bits, but these were no monsters. No anger or fear showed in their gentle eyes. They welcomed me to this place and to the herd as if I was one of them. Unable to contain my joy, I wrapped both arms around the leader's neck and buried my face in his warm fur, his dark mane covering my hair and ears. He lifted his head, pulling me up and off my feet, almost jokingly. I let go and landed at his shoulders, and he gave a low snort.

I could have stayed there, maybe not forever, but for a good long time, if it weren't for the heat that started to burn my leg. Looking down, I found the jade knife glowing bright and hot in my pants pocket. I passed it back and forth from hand to hand, and gradually it cooled until I could comfortably hold it once more. As I inspected it, the leader of the herd became agitated. His hooves danced in the grass and he lifted his head, whinnying loudly. The other horses followed suit, and soon the air rang with their song. They began to move away from me, not frightened, but on the move. They acted like little children being called by their mother, and soon they all set off away from me at a brisk pace.

I ran back to my tree and hoisted my pack onto my back, frightened that they would leave me behind. Running for the first time in days to catch up, I soon found myself alongside the giant animals. With each step I took along with the herd, they increased their speed, just slightly. Soon they were running at a full gallop, and I was dashing along beside them, laughing as I impossibly kept pace.

I felt my heart, hard and strong, as it beat in my chest. Whatever evil may be transpiring in the Fold, I couldn't deny that I felt alive here, *really* alive. The power that had come to my once sick heart didn't only heal me, it transformed me. Here I wasn't just a runty kid with defective parts. I was powerful and strong, my purpose vital and significant.

The warm wind blew across my face as we ran. Their hooves thundered over the grass, and my own feet seemed to barely touch it at all. The smell of sweat and earth filled my nose. The sound of fifteen huge beasts sucking in and pushing out air, snorting and nickering to one another, elated me, and I felt an enormous smile break across my face.

The run seemed to go on forever, and neither they nor I tired. The grass flew by in a blur, and the gigantic animals wove in and out of my path, tossing their heads and nickering to each other, to me. After a time, the ground we ran on seemed almost unnecessary; I thought surely we must be flying. As the frolic took us over miles and miles of plains, the mountains slowly rose up in front of us. The details of the great, granite cliffs came into focus, and as we neared them their peaks rose high over our heads, reaching for the skies above.

The leader slowed to a walk as we reached the outer edges of the great cliffs. Along one side, invisible from a distance, he walked purposefully down a path that cut through the mountain. His herd followed closely behind him, and I behind them. For a time we walked single file, picking our way between enormous rock faces that stretched a thousand feet above our heads. They were quiet now; only the soft sounds of breathing and the breaking of rocks under their heavy hooves made their way to my ears. The horses' massive shoulders rubbed the sides of the rock as they squeezed through the narrower parts. The jade rock burned in my hands, and I became alert, searching for the source that seemed to excite the stone. But I could see very little, sandwiched between two enormous beasts and two faces of rock. Then, quite suddenly, the path opened up, and we emerged into a long, wide gully.

The water that had cut this path through the mountain looked to have long since evaporated. The remains of the stream bed were barely visible beneath the new growth that overtook the pebbles that had once laid underwater. After the whole herd was through the opening, the leader approached me. He lowered his head and nudged my hair with his nose. Then he turned and walked farther down the gully.

I followed him deeper into the mountain, the herd resting in the rocky, shaded entrance. We walked until they were nearly out of view, and he stopped short in front of a particularly smooth face of the rock. Here the jade dagger became too hot for me to handle any longer. I fumbled with it, tossing it from hand to hand, until finally it fell, searing a welt along my forearm on the way down. It clattered to the ground, and I blew at my burning arm and fingers. I removed a cloth from my pack and wrapped the handle and blade carefully, covering every part that could potentially burn me, and stuffed it deep into my pocket. When I looked up again, the horse was watching me. He seemed to be waiting.

The granite in this part of the gully was damp. Along the sides lowest to the ground grew a thick bed of moss that crept up the face of the rock a hundred feet above our heads. The horse brushed his nose over the green blanket, like a common horse sniffing for a treat. He nuzzled the moss, working his lips from side to side, over several square feet of rock, and then took a gentle bite from the sheet and tore a swath of it away.

Up until this moment, I had considered these horses to be nothing more than what they appeared to be. The were surely magnificent and huge and beautiful, but were they of equal intelligence to a human? No, I didn't think so. They had animal minds and animal senses, not intelligence that rivaled my own.

But beneath that six inch patch of moss was something that quickly changed my mind about this. Under the curtain of green a tall, deep crevice extended into the rock. I stared at the leader of the herd in wonder, and he looked back at me with the knowing eyes of a wise old man.

The horse gave another snort and blew a breath in my face before he started off again, walking back towards his herd. I watched him go regretfully, wishing I had known before now what he really was: an intelligent soul, and a friend. I wanted to stay with him, or for him to come with me into this dark mountain. But there was no question; this would have to be where our paths split. As the echoes of his hooves across the smooth rocks began to fade away, I heard him whinny loudly to his companions on the far side of the gully, their responses ringing out towards him as he returned.

I turned and peered down the path that lay before me, my eyes searching for a sign of what was to come. And then I took my first step down the passage, alone, into the darkness.

CHAPTER NINETEEN

I was immediately blinded. The walls of the cave were chalky black and reflected almost none of the light that peeked in through the crack I had just walked through. The knife in my pocket burned, and I removed it, unwrapping it carefully. It shone brightly, and beneath the beam of light I could make out the rough path in front of my feet. I held it in front of me like a flashlight. It was constantly glowing now, and I hoped that meant I was headed in the right direction.

I picked my way down the path, moving as quietly as I possibly could. The crack went on and on through the rock. Nothing seemed to threaten me here. There was no being, human or beast, and no sound except the light tread of my own feet.

It was impossible to tell how long I had been in the throat of the mountain with no light of day to give me any clues about the passage of time. I ran my hands along the walls occasionally as I walked, searching for differences in the structure of the rock, or maybe a path that could be easily missed in the blackness. But the mountain did not divulge any of its secrets until, suddenly, the walls were gone completely.

I stopped dead in my tracks, confused by the lack of hard stone on either side of me. Holding the knife up, I saw that I was in a large chamber. I tried to see the edges of the mountain around where I stood, but the only thing I could make out was the ground for a foot around me, no further. Three paces backwards was the crevice I had just walked out from, and I went back to it, relieved when my hand met the solid, black stone. I followed along the outer edge of the cavern wall, shining the light up and down rhythmically as I walked, searching for a new path to follow, or a new danger to flee from.

The stone grew hotter with each step I took. Twenty paces away was another large crack in the rock. As I approached, I took care not to make a sound, though I was so anxious I felt certain my heartbeat must be audible. I had been in the dark for quite long enough, and was becoming increasingly eager to find my way back out again.

I had been hoping to find a path towards light, thinking that maybe on the other side of that crack I would find the comfort I was seeking in this black and lonely place. Maybe I would even see a hint of the world beyond this mountain.

As I reached the crevice and put my fingers around the corner, the stone burst with a surge of heat so great that I yelped and threw it to the ground. There it blazed, brighter and brighter, until the light coming off the thin blade was like a miniature sun. I shielded my eyes from the glare, and then looked up at the cavern I was standing in.

Five hundred feet across and ten stories high, an enormous dome of black granite rock was suspended above me. The light from the stone illuminated the entire space, obliterating all shadow. I marveled at the size of this hole in the mountain, but no other hints about why I was led here were forthcoming. No markings decorated the walls, no artifacts were anywhere to be found. The cavern was completely empty but for myself and the stone.

Then I heard it. I had been so transfixed by the behavior of the jade that the sound had not registered in my brain immediately. But now it did. Somewhere nearby somebody was singing. It was a gentle, soft tune, and the singer sounded like a child. I peered all around the dome, but found nothing that could be making the noise. Then I saw another, dimmer light coming from the crevice. As I approached the crack, the soft blue glow seemed to bounce to the rhythm of the song. I turned the corner and left the brightness of the dome behind. There, at the end of the passage, was a girl.

She lay on a bed, tucked deep underneath the covers. This cavern was smaller, the size of a child's bedroom. From under the covers her white-blond hair poured over her shoulders, and her arms were above her head as she hummed the melody. Just above her hands bobbed a dim orb of light, and she passed it back and forth from hand to hand as she hummed. She seemed to control the orb with the tone of her voice, and the light danced around above her head with each note she sang.

Across the plains of Borna
Horses run wild and free
And if you see my darling
Please bring her back to me

"Hello?" I asked softly. She did not respond.

For on the plains of Borna
My darling went to see
If magic comes to those who run

Pure-hearted to the sea

Now on the plains of Borna
My darling hides her song
Please find my darling before
She is away too long

"Hello?" I tried again. This time she heard me, and both her song and the light ceased immediately. I stood in darkness with only the glow from the jade that peeked in from the other cavern.

"Hello," I said. "I'm sorry, I didn't mean to frighten you. I'm not here to hurt you or anything. I…I'm looking for something here."

"What are you looking for?" she hissed from the shadows, her voice more menacing than I expected.

"Well, that's sort of hard to explain," I began. "I'm looking for a map…or maybe something sort of like a map…" How could I describe a map of Almara's, when I didn't even know what the next one looked like myself? "And a stone. It's a large, jade stone." I felt like a fool.

"A stone?" she asked.

"Yes, well, it's complicated," I answered. "Would you mind…I mean would it be possible…it would be easier for me to explain it to you if I could see you."

She was silent for a moment, and then the blue orb glowed to life once more, illuminating the cave around us. I took a step in her direction, "You see, I was—"

"DON'T!" she commanded. "Don't come any closer!"

I froze. "Ok, ok!" I said. "Why not?"

"You are not the first to seek the stone," she said wryly. "But its power is not drawn into being the way you all think. Who are you, and why do you seek this prize?"

"I'm Aster," I said. "I'm not looking for power. I'm looking for the stone so that I can destroy it." I left out the fact that I seriously doubted I would be able to do the job myself.

The sound of her laughter laced with sarcasm suddenly filled the chamber. It irritated me, being laughed by this little girl after all I had been through to get here.

"What's so funny?" I snapped at her. But my irritation seemed to make her laugh even harder.

She slowly started to compose herself as she spoke again. "What's funny," she said through a giggle, "is that you think you're looking for a *stone*. An actual stone. The others were dull, to be sure, but they at least understood *what* it was they sought." And then she lost her grip again and was howling with laughter.

I didn't know what to say. I *was* looking for a stone. And who were these "others" she was talking about? Had travelers come before me seeking the stone? Were they also trying to find Almara?

But this girl not only thought that my plan was wrong, but that it was so pathetic as to be hysterical. I lost my temper and bellowed, "WHAT IS SO FUNNY?"

Her eyes widened in the dim light with surprise at my yell, but she continued to laugh. Then a deep cough echoed through her chest and she dissolved into a fit of hacking. She rolled over onto her side in the bed and coughed, a sad, empty sound. It went on for several minutes, and I began to worry that she would choke from the violence of it. When the coughing finally quieted and she caught her breath, all traces of her smile were gone.

"Boy," she whispered hoarsely. "You are not looking for a stone. Those who have sent you here after a simple rock have either misled you or been misled themselves. What you have failed to learn before now, along all of your traveling, is that you are looking, in fact, for *me*." Then she lay back on her bed, her eyes trained on the low ceiling of the cave. "But you can't have me to either use or destroy," she continued quietly. "There is no way out of this place."

"Looking for you?" I said. "I don't understand."

"I hold the power. The story of the stone serves only to hide me."

I took another step.

"STOP!" she bellowed, coughing hollowly once again. "Stop. If you come any closer, you will be trapped in here with me. And, forgive me, but I don't think I could handle another two hundred years here with someone as simple as you."

"I am NOT simple!" I protested immediately. Two hundred years? "You don't know me. You don't know what I've been through or where I've come from to get here. Now why—"

"If you take one more step in this direction," she said angrily, glaring at me now, "then you will be trapped in here, a prisoner like me, forever. Is that what you want?"

"But what do you mean?" I asked, stopping. "There are no bars holding you in. There's nothing keeping you here. If you want to go, then *go*."

"You understand *nothing!*" she bellowed. "Do you think I would stay here if there were a way, any way, to break free? You are a fool."

"I am NOT—" I began.

"Try it then," she said menacingly. "If you are so wise, go ahead. Try to throw me something from where you stand."

"Throw you something?" I asked, confused. I had been about to launch a tirade of my own.

"*So I can show you,*" she said, her voice grating with irritation.

I glared at her for a moment, and then relented. I removed the pack from my back and dug out an apple, my last. Standing, I threw it directly at her head. But as it flew through the air it made a ripping sound halfway between the two of us. It seemed to pause a little bit midair, as if it was tearing through a thin sheet of paper. Then it broke through to the other side; she caught it in one hand and held it up for me to see.

"Ok," she said. "Now watch." She tossed the apple back towards me. I lifted my hands, ready to catch it, but it did not meet my grasp. Instead, it bounced off an invisible barrier, and landed on the floor next to her bed. There was a wall between us, though I could see nothing.

"You see," she said, finally, "if you come through the wall, you will never, ever be able to get out again. There is no escape." She pulled her covers up to her chin and rolled over, facing away from me.

"Is there..." I began, then I paused, unsure of what to say. "Is there anything to be done? Is there *any* way out?" It was a stupid question, I knew, but I could think of no other.

"No," her back spoke. "There is no way out."

No way out.

I backed up against the wall and slid down to the floor. I tried to make it all fit together right in my head. I could not destroy the Stone of Borna because, according to her, there was no Stone of Borna, only this slight little girl. I wouldn't hurt her, even if I could reach her. But could I leave her here? Should I continue on to search for the next link?

What I knew for certain was that Almara had led me *here* to find the next link. Owyn had wanted me to destroy the Stone, but it was

Almara I needed to follow. Whether he had meant for me to find this girl, I didn't know, but here, somewhere, would be an answer to where that link was hidden.

I looked up at her again and, realizing she really couldn't get to me, decided to tell her why I was really here.

"It's not just the Stone I'm looking for," I said. "I'm looking for a link to lead me to Almara."

"You are looking," she said, rolling over in her tiny bed, "for Almara?" She studied me closely, her eyebrows furrowed together.

I scrambled over to the edge of the invisible wall so that she could see me.

"Yes, I have been looking for him all this time. I've been following his links for the past few weeks and the last one led me to here. To you."

Her eyes grew wide with disbelief.

"But you are not Brendan," she said, shaking her head slightly.

"No, I am Aster. Aster Wood," I said.

"But where is Brendan?" she asked.

Did she not know?

"Brendan is dead," I said. "He died on Earth, my planet, ages ago."

At this her eyes grew even wider, and then slowly filled with tears.

"He is dead," she said quietly.

"Yes," I said. "So I am trying to get to Almara instead. I am Brendan's descendant, his great great grandson."

She ignored me.

"He is dead," she said again, and rolled over to face the wall again. The light moved across the room to her and hovered over her head.

After several long moments I broke the silence.

"Do you know where I can find the link?" I asked.

"Of course I knew he must be dead," she said quietly. "No other explanation exists for why he would not come for me."

"You knew Brendan?" I asked.

She did not respond to this question, but to the other one.

"Yes," she said. "I know where the link hides. But it is not a secret I can tell. I must be with you to find it."

"But why?" I asked. "Why do you need to be with me? I've had help to find the other links, but I'm sure if you just tell me where to look I'll be able to get to it."

She chuckled softly. "No. The link is entwined with my own wild magic. Without me, you will never, ever find it. Almara made it so."

"Ok," I said, scrambling. "Then we're going to have to get you out of here."

There had to be a way.

"You and I," I said, "we'll figure it out."

"The lock is too complicated, too difficult for even someone with my talents to force open. A secret word must be entered into it. He does it every time he comes to torture me, but I have never seen the letters he enters. There are many languages, and even if we knew which one we would need the correct word. One must possess the key."

"A key?" I said. I didn't have a key. The skeleton key from the dungeons had been lost to the snow lands. But it wasn't a normal lock she was talking about, it was a code.

"I have a book of codes. Will that work?"

Her head moved slightly as she tilted her face a fraction towards me. "You have a book? Of codes?" she asked.

"Almara's book," I said. I dug through the pack and pulled it out.

She rolled over again and held herself up on one elbow, looking over at me with interest. I opened the book and showed her the codes inside.

"How did you get *that?*" she asked, amazed. A look of longing crossed her face.

"It was one of the links," I said. "I stole it from Cadoc."

"You *stole* it from *Cadoc?*" she asked incredulously. "How are you still alive?"

Good question.

"Nevermind that," I said. "What sort of word should I look for?"

"How do you know of Cadoc?" she asked, interrupting me again. Her eyes narrowed now with suspicion.

"I'm trying to tell you," I said. "I took it from him. He was chasing me in Stonemore, and then I set the prisoners free, and then—"

"Cadoc," she said, "is my captor."

I stopped blubbering and stared at her. On her face she wore a grimace of distaste and pain.

"Cadoc put you here?" I asked. She nodded. I felt I had known this all along. Who else would do such a thing?

"Don't you understand?" she said. "Even if you could free me, he will know. As soon as this enchantment is broken he will come for us both."

This statement froze me in place. Cadoc would know? The last thing I wanted to experience ever again in my life was to come face to face with the man in black. But a tiny voice in the back of my head reminded me of what he had said the last time we met: that he had the power to send me back to Earth. Could it be that if I faced Cadoc now, this whole thing might be over and I could go home? Or might I be better off leaving her here and avoiding him altogether? Maybe I could find the link on my own if I searched this land for long enough. Maybe the magic that gave me the power to run in these lands, maybe it would be enough to break the link free. Then I could get to Almara and avoid Cadoc altogether. Once I found Almara, he could come back for the girl. I looked up and found her watching me.

"You see," she said quietly as our eyes met, "you cannot free me. This is not your battle. You are best to go on your way. Go now, before he returns." The tears that filled her eyes did not fall to her cheeks. The strength of two hundred years kept her sorrow controlled just enough to prevent her crying.

What horrible things Cadoc had done. Not just to her, but to everyone he had ever come across. He had tortured, killed, or kidnapped anyone who had stood in his way. Or who possessed something he wanted. I realized that I, too, had something Cadoc wanted. I didn't know what it was, but why else would he offer to help me get back to Earth? This girl had something he wanted, too, and look how he had treated her. For *two hundred years*.

I couldn't leave her.

"We need to move," I said. "How do I apply the key? Is there a dial somewhere or what?"

"You are a fool," she said. "You are making the wrong choice."

I sighed with frustration. "Look, kid, I don't have any more time to deal with your attitude. You need me to get out of here. And I need you to get me to the next link so I can get home. Are you going to help me or not?"

She glared at me, offended by my tone. But then, with some effort, she extended her arm past the edge of the bed and pointed at the floor a few feet away from where I stood. I hadn't seen it before, but on the floor, carved into the rock, were four large squares.

"You put the code there," she said, "He always blinds me when he comes for me, so I can never see which characters he enters. I've never seen a single one."

I knelt in front of the squares. "Never seen a single one," I mumbled as my hands traced along the borders. So many markings and symbols lined every page of Almara's book; surely there were millions of different options to fill in these four pieces of code.

Without asking her, I tried the first word that came to my mind. It was the same code I had entered at the stone wolf: J-A-D-E. This time, instead of golden light following my finger as I traced the letter, thick, black smoke trailed it.

No dice.

"What should we try?" I asked, flipping through the book.

"Cadoc speaks in a strange tongue when he breaks through the wall," she said. "It is the language of *Sabellioc*, or the language of the dead."

I held the book up so she could see the pages began flipping through, hoping she would recognize one of them as this Sabellioc. The last few pages of the book caught her interest, and I moved it as close to her as I dared.

"That must be it," she said, wheezing a bit. "It is the only one I do not recognize."

"What word?" I asked.

"Try wood," she said.

"Why wood?" I asked. What did this have to do with me? But she did not answer. I flipped to the right page and deciphered the word from the alphabet I knew into the Sabellioc characters. I carefully drew the squiggly shapes into each square with my finger. Nothing happened.

"No, that's not it," I said.

"Try czar," she said.

I did. It didn't work.

"King," she said.

And on and on it went. For at least an hour she would spit out words to me, anything she could think of with four letters, and I would translate them into Sabellioc and enter them onto the stones. Nothing worked.

Finally I stood up from the cold rock and threw the book at the far wall in frustration. How was I supposed to get her out of here? I sank down to the ground and put my head into my hands. She seemed to give up, too, and rolled over again.

"I told you," she said quietly. "There is no way out. Flee while you still can."

Maybe we had the wrong language, I thought. Maybe I should try all the words again with different symbols. But the more I thought about that the more unlikely that seemed, and the longer I spent buried deep in this mountain the less time I felt we had. She was right. If Cadoc spoke the language when he was here, the very language we had been trying for the past hour, then I was almost certain that it was the right one. What was I missing?

I thrust my fist against my forehead, tapping it again and again, trying to crack a code that this girl, herself, could not crack after two centuries of effort. The last time I had tried to free Cadoc's prisoners, the key to opening the cells had been right there, hidden in the treasure hold. It was so powerful that not even Cadoc could figure out what to do with it. But the prisoners knew. They had just been waiting for someone to come along who was willing to help them. But this girl had no such hidden power. She had no idea how to get herself out.

The prisoners. I thought about them in their rags, their bony faces looking at me from behind their cages. Them all approaching the bars of their cells in unison, holding out their arms...

Suddenly I was on my feet. I had been so stupid! How could I not have realized it before now?

"Who says," I said, approaching the edge, "that the code is made up of letters?"

I knelt down at the base and quickly entered in the only set of numbers that came to mind. The only numbers that Cadoc tattooed every single one of his prisoners with, branding them like cattle. 3-3-3-3.

The effect was immediate. I stood up and took several steps backwards as the rumbling started. The barrier between she and I began to glow brightly, like a pane of glass filled with light from the inside out, and the invisible sheet made little tinks and cracking sounds. Then, with a burst of force, the surface blew apart with a loud crash, the remaining shards of the barrier falling to my feet in a shower of a thousand pieces.

The girl stared at me with wonder, completely amazed. "How did you—" she began.

But it was my turn to interrupt. "We don't have time," I said. I moved across the space to her bedside and extended my hand to her. "Can you walk?" I asked.

"No," she said helplessly.

"No worry," I said. I bent over the bed and picked up her frail body, bony and too light. I walked with her in my arms through the narrow tunnel back out into the cavern, and I got a good look at her in the light for the first time.

Her eyes were fixed on the light coming from the dagger in the center of the room. At first they were simply wide, her mouth moving silently as if she were trying to work out an impossible equation. And then a smile, a real smile, broke across her face for the first time. Soon she was laughing with delight, tears breaking the hard barrier of her resolve and streaming down her face.

"Who are you?" she said finally, her enormous green eyes meeting mine for the first time.

"I told you," I said, "my name is Aster. Aster Wood."

Her pale, delicate finger reached up to her face and brushed away a tear.

"It is a great pleasure to make your acquaintance, Aster Wood," she said through hoarse breaths. "I am Jade Aednat Enda Wood, Princess of Borna."

CHAPTER TWENTY

I gawked at her for a moment, trying to make sense of what she was saying.

"You're a Wood, too?" I finally asked.

She laughed breathlessly, wheezing a little.

"Yes, of course," she said. "But please, young Aster, let's stop talking for now. You have brought with you a jadestone. Please hand it to me." She motioned to the dagger on the floor, which was now spitting sparks and hissing with brilliance.

How did she know that? I shook my head. "I can't hand it to you," I said. "It's not safe. It's hotter than anything I've ever touched. Look, I've already burned myself." I held out my arm and showed her the red welt on the base of my wrist.

She smiled weakly. "Alright, then, please take me to it."

I hesitated, then walked over towards it, still carrying her, and turned my head to shield my eyes as we neared the intense rays of light.

"Closer," she said. "You need to get me closer to it."

"Are you sure?" I asked.

"Closer," she replied.

My eyes clamped almost completely shut now, I moved to within a few feet of the stone.

"Closer."

I knelt down to the floor, and rested her body next to the stone. She reached out her hand towards it, clearly intending to grasp it.

"Jade, no!" I cried, pulling her back from the light.

She looked up at me, her big green eyes pleading. "Trust me," she said.

I hesitated, but then relented, pushing her close to the stone so that her hand could reach out and take it. Her fingers stretched out and clasped firmly around the golden handle of the dagger. A small cry rose from her, but she did not drop it. Then, with what seemed to be enormous effort, she picked up the heavy knife and brought it to her chest, holding it there with both hands.

The light was too bright and the heat too intense for me to hold her. I released her onto the floor and stepped back several paces. I raised my hands up to shield my face, and caught occasional glimpses through my interlaced fingers.

She lay on the rock, both hands covering the blade that rested its heavy weight on her chest. Slowly her arms raised above her head, lifting the stone as they moved. Soon the glow from the stone extended to her hands, then her arms, and then her whole body was enveloped with the glowing light. She shook slightly as the radiation pulsed all through her body. Then, slowly, the light receded, and her arms relaxed to her sides. The dagger rested on her chest, and its light slowly drained away to a dim glow.

I approached her cautiously.

"Princess?" I asked. Her eyes were closed. "Jade?" She did not reply, and I dared not touch her. Slowly her lips curved up into a smile.

"Are you alright? I asked. "How did you hold the stone like that? I tried to touch it before and it was so hot; I couldn't hold it at all."

Her eyes remained shut as she softly spoke. "My story is long, young Aster," she said, and her voice was noticeably stronger than it had been in her cavern, "but the short of it is that I am a master of stone. Jade, the stone for which I was named, is the most powerful to me. All these years I was kept alive by other stones, granites and common rocks are enough for one as me to survive."

She removed the knife from her chest and placed it on the floor next to where she lay. Then, bracing herself with both arms, she moved up into a sitting position. The change in her appearance was dramatic. She seemed, somehow, fuller now, her skin less transparent. There was life in her movements where before there had only been weakness, and a low pink tint colored her cheeks.

"Within each stone lies a different power," she continued. "Some can heal, some can kill. But the only stone with the power to free me from the spell Cadoc cast upon me is jadestone. He has carefully kept it from me all these years, knowing that I so much as touched a piece of jade he would be no match for me. His enchantment held me to the bed, too weak to move or fight." Her eyes opened now and held mine in their emerald gaze. "You saved my life," she said. "For that I am most grateful."

"It was no trouble," I said awkwardly. "I mean, what else could I have done?"

"Ah, many other choices lay before you," she said. "It gladdens me that my rescuer is so pure he did not see them. But now we must go. He will be here at any time." She started to push up to her feet.

The blush that had momentarily raised on my cheeks was immediately extinguished by the thought of our pursuer.

"Wait," I said. "Where are we going?"

"We must escape this mountain and the Corentin. If we can find the tools I need to use my powers, then we can find the link and follow Father."

There was that word again. *Corentin.* And who was her father?

"What is a Corentin?" I asked. "And I thought we were following Almara, not your father."

"There is not time, my friend," she said. "Can you ask your questions as we walk? You said before that you know the way."

"Yes," I said, a little irritated. She was one to be calling me young. "Let me get my things." I walked back through to her chamber and collected my backpack in the dim light. When I came back out I obscured the pack as I approached her.

She was smiling at me, eyes wide. "That's a nice trick," she said.

I knelt down and she put her arm around my neck. She gripped the jade stone, and I helped her to her feet. Her legs wobbled beneath her, but with my help she was able to walk slowly forward. When we reached the narrow passageway that led back out into the gully, I couldn't hold her any longer; the space was too confined.

"It's ok," she said. "I'm getting a little stronger. I can hold onto the sides." She stretched out her arms and gripped the stone walls. The knife was awkward in her hand as she tried to hold onto both it and the wall.

"Do you want me to take it?" I asked her.

"No," she said. "It's better if I keep hold of it."

I took the lead.

"So," she began as she walked, "if memory serves me, we will have some time in this passage, even if we make haste. We can share our stories now. We do not know what will await us on the outside."

"Ok," I said. "But where are we going to go when we get out of here?"

"The link lies on the other side of the grasslands. This land is not large, and Father gave me many details about how to get there. It lies in a cave where the rock meets the water. Father told me the signs to look for along the edge of the sea."

"That doesn't sound very exact," I said. "It's *the sea*. That could be anywhere."

"Yes, I know," she said. "But what other choice have we? We are hunted now. It is the only way I know to escape him."

"But—" I stopped walking and turned again.

"What do you propose?" she interrupted. "The jadestone brought you to me, but I am not a paper map or an amulet imbued with the power of travel. Do you think such things would have survived with me back there for all these years? If you want to go back, or anywhere other than here, then this is the only way I know." She folded her arms across her chest resolutely. "And every time you stop, you allow the Corentin to come closer to us. We must *move*."

How could such a little girl already have this type of attitude? And then I remembered, she was a little girl in body only. Her mind was that of a woman, over two hundred years old.

I turned and continued down the passageway. She was right. We couldn't spend more time arguing, or if we did, it would have to be while we walked. Cadoc was coming. Jade might be able to fight him with her powers, but I had nothing like that to defend myself with. Besides, I had no better plan.

"Your father left you the link?" I asked. "But I thought Almara was the one who hid it."

"They are one and the same," she said.

"Almara is your *father?*" I asked, surprised.

"Yes, of course he is," she said dismissively, as if I should have guessed this. "Brendan was to find me, and hopefully free me with whatever primitive magic he gained from his travels. But he did not return for me, and neither did my father. Brendan," her voice caught in her throat, "was my brother."

This brought me up short and I turned and stared at her again. She stopped walking abruptly, almost running into me, and her eyes fell to the floor. This little girl standing before me was my great, great grandfather's little sister. Just a moment ago she had been bossing me around. But now...

I opened my mouth to speak, but then I realized I had no idea what to say. What a mess I was in. What kind of family was I from, anyways? Finally I asked the question.

"If your father is Almara, why didn't he come back for you?"

"He tried," she said, a lonely tear sliding down her cheek. "He could not break my bonds."

"So he just left you there?"

"I don't know. I don't know," she almost shouted. "I don't know why Father didn't come back. I don't know why Brendan didn't come back." Tears began pouring in earnest from her downcast eyes.

"I'm sorry," I said. "I'm sorry. I just don't understand."

She began to move again, her quiet sobs echoing in the narrow tunnel. But I didn't let her pass.

I had never had a sister or brother, or even a friend, no one my age to care about before now. But she was so sad that I opened my arms and wrapped them around her tiny frame. She stiffened at the contact at first, but then her misery overcame her and she wailed into my shoulder.

"Father and Brendan fought," she said, her voice muffled through the fabric of my shirt. "Father didn't want Brendan to go, but he was determined that answers would be found on Earth. After he left, and I was taken, Father realized that he could not free me from Cadoc's prison. He told me Brendan would come for me, that he would follow the links and come for me. But nobody ever came. And I—and I—"

"It's ok," I said to the top of her head. "Everything is going to be ok now." How many times had my mother held me and said the same thing? "You're free now. And you are never going back in there. Do you understand me?" I pried her arms from around my middle and put my hands on her shoulders, forcing her to look me in the eye. "Never."

Her watery eyes doubted my words, but gradually they began to change from fear and misery into something different.

Resolve.

She nodded.

"Now let's get out of here," I said. I turned and continued our escape. Following me I could just make out the sound of her soft footfalls.

We walked for some time in silence. I didn't want to make her cry again, especially considering our current danger. But after several minutes she spoke.

"Tell me," she said. "How did you come to be here?"

I began telling my story. I told her about the attic, the details about each land I had been to, about how I could run now, here in this world, but not in my own. I told her about how Kiron's tale had reflected so perfectly the ills that had befallen Earth in the past hundred years. The distasteful tale of the prisoners in Stonemore and my brush with Cadoc came next. And finally, I sadly relayed the story of the wolf.

"You have experienced much of the Fold," she said when I was finally done, "but I fear you have been led astray. Certainly there is much you do not understand."

I didn't respond, unsure of whether or not she was taking a jab at me for my ignorance about Maylin and Almara.

"The wolf is not dead, you know," she said. "Do not let his departure trouble you."

I thought about these words, took them in and swirled them around inside me, trying to determine if they were really true.

"How do you know?" I finally asked.

"He is a member of the White Guard. Your seeing him is impressive. It means that you must be very important, indeed. To have a member of the White Guard reach out to help a human is very, very rare. I misjudged you. Perhaps there is more to you than what is apparent."

We walked for a few minutes in silence while I mulled this all over. I certainly did seem to be good at this questing stuff, if you considered all I had accomplished. Freeing the prisoners in Stonemore and releasing the princess from her cave were pretty big feats, things that had been attempted for hundreds of years before now. And here I was, just a sick kid from another world, and I had managed both in a matter of weeks.

"What do you know about people coming to the Fold from other places?" I asked.

"Not much," she admitted. Her breathing was less ragged the

longer we walked. "There was a story I heard long ago from Father, about travelers making enormous jumps like you have, but I was very young. And then, of course, Brendan left us."

"Why did he go?" I asked.

She sighed. "He had to, really. He and my father quarreled frequently, so I do not think he was sad to go, but he certainly expected to return back shortly after. He was the one of the eight chosen to seek help in other worlds, but Father felt that Earth was too far, too unstable, for him to make the leap. I was too young to join the quest, but my power was undeniable, even to my father. With him I crafted the link that sent Brendan to your world."

"You know how to make links?" I asked. "Why don't you just make one to send us to Almara right now?"

"It doesn't work like that," she said. "One must know where he wishes to arrive before crafting a link. We know not where my father landed after he left this place. Our only choice is to make haste to the location of the link he left for me."

"But," I continued, "if you know how to make a link then can't you send me back to Earth?"

"I cannot," she said. "My knowledge of stones did help Father with Brendan's link, but I could not do such a thing on my own. I am no cartographer. Besides, Earth is not stable."

Perfect.

"What do you mean?" I asked.

"Earth lies within the boundaries of the Fold, but on the far edges. The Fold moves, vibrates, and Earth being so far away from the center vibrates more than the planets closer in. Imagine a rose held up in the wind. The air would flutter the edges of the outer petals, but barely

227

touch those in the center. It is like this with Earth, perched on the very tip of the outermost petal of the rose. It is not stable, and nearly impossible to plot. One must be a master."

I remembered the argument between Kiron and Larissa, about whether the Fold had a center at all. It seemed that everyone had differing opinions on the matter.

"What is a Corentin?" I asked. "I heard that word before, and you said earlier that we had to escape the Corentin."

"You know not the Corentin?" she asked. "It is strange to me that you have come so far, and know so much, and yet the most basic knowledge seems to elude you. The Corentin is the force that has taken over Cadoc's mind. It means *hurricane of death*. Cadoc was once not Cadoc at all, but Zarich of Stonemore. I knew him as a young girl, and I was playmates with his little daughter, Amelia. He led Stonemore and was loved by his people. When Almara first came to the city, Zarich helped him. They worked together for a time, trying to find the answers to the evils that plagued Maylin.

"Then, one day Amelia fell ill. She lay in her chambers for weeks as she wasted away from sickness. They tried my elixir on her, but it did not help. Zarich spent every moment tending to her, his work with Father forgotten. How could he have seen it as having any importance at all, with his baby's needs so great? Father let me visit her only once, but she could not hear me. Her eyes stared into the air, glazed and unmoving. She died a few days later."

Jade fell silent. We walked on in silence. She continued several moments later, a hoarse tone to her voice.

"After Amelia's death, my father and Zarich began arguing. Over time it became apparent that they could no longer work with one another.

Zarich was acting with increasing strangeness, and my father had forbidden me to speak with him. Then, one night Zarich attempted to murder my father while he slept. A great battle ensued, and the whole of Stonemore's army was directed to fight against my father and his followers."

Her breathing grew heavy for a time with either emotion or fatigue. I waited for her to catch her breath.

"I was lost. The battle was so chaotic, and I was unable to locate Father again to flee with him. His followers were dying. The fate of the Fold rested with him. He had to go. Zarich turned aside, though, and didn't chase him further. I was the prize he had sought all along."

I couldn't believe it. She had been left alone in the middle of a battle by her own father? But then I thought, *sounds familiar.*

It felt strange to be having such a dark conversation with a young girl. Really, she looked only eight or nine years old. But her mind had grown, even if her body had never followed suit. Really, it was amazing that she wasn't completely mad.

I turned to her. "How is it that you are still alive? I mean, that battle was centuries ago, and you—and the prisoners in Stonemore—I don't understand how all of this is possible."

She leaned against the wall, too tired from the walking, or maybe from the misery that radiated from within and outlined her face now.

"It is my power," she said. "When I was born it was obvious from my first breath of life that I had a gift. My mother had gifts of her own, and normally she would have been my guide, but she died when I was very little. Over time my gift was developed with the help of both my father and brother. What we didn't know was that Zarich was watching from the shadows, the Corentin gradually overtaking him. Our every move was noted by him until, as his hidden dark power began to take control, he made his move."

"That still doesn't explain how you're still alive," I pointed out.

"No, I suppose not. You know it as the power of the Stone of Borna. I told you that I can use various stones in my craft. Well, when one mixes my power with that of granite," she gestured to the walls around us, "I can create a healing draft. We developed it with the help of Zarich, with the intention to use it to heal the people of Stonemore from illness. We hoped that someday, maybe, the lands of all Maylin, everywhere in the Fold, could also benefit from its use. But the magic had more to it than we knew, and after my capture, Zarich, who renamed himself Cadoc, proved that extended use of the brew would bring the drinker an extension of life. This is the reason he brought me to this particular mountain." She grimaced harshly, a look that did not suit her young face. "From time to time he comes, forcing me to produce the elixir for his own purposes, but offering me little sustenance to keep my own body alive but for that very same drink. This is how I became so weak." She touched the jadestone lovingly. "Without jadestone I can live. I can drink the elixir and survive in the most basic way, as you saw. But with it," she held the light above her head and the intensity of its glow increased tenfold. "With it I am more alive than most any other in the Fold."

The jadestone pulsed and hummed from the connection with Jade. Her eyes took in the brightness eagerly, starved for light for centuries.

"So for all that time he was able to keep you trapped," I stated.

"Yes," she replied, lowering the stone. She pushed off the wall, and we began walking again. "Once, in the very early days of my imprisonment, one of the guards wore a small jadestone around his neck, carved with the crest of his family. They didn't know then about my connection to that particular stone, but they knew soon after. I broke free with the use of the jadestone, just that tiny piece from his necklace, though I was caught soon after. I am small, after all," she gestured to her petite body. "They never made that mistake again. I was soon locked behind the curtain, and I never escaped again. Until now."

"How did you stand it?" I asked. "I mean, how could you, anyone, survive underground for hundreds of years without losing their mind?" I wondered about the prisoners in Stonemore, too, and how many other hidden underground prisons there were in the Triaden, full of Cadoc's innocent victims, slowly being driven mad over centuries.

"I did go mad," she answered. "After the first year or so, the rest is a blur; a long, unending nightmare of misery and loneliness. I have been mad all this time. Only now that I can hold the jadestone close to me do I feel some of my old self stirring inside. Only now can I even remember what life was like for the nine-year-old girl he took."

We both fell silent. The sadness and desperation in each of our stories had finally proved to be too much to continue discussing. I realized that we shared a sort of bond, different as we were. Both of us were being hunted by a monster. Both of us were abandoned by our fathers. And both of us were focused on a return home.

After another half hour of picking our way back out through the mountain, we at last came to the edge of the crack that led into the gully. We stopped at the mouth of the opening and listened for any sign pursuit, but there was no sound. The horses had left the gully the night before, and now not even the croak of a cricket could be heard. We cautiously left the protection of the mountain.

Jade was silent as she crept out onto the loose stones, but her face shone with delight and relief in the moonlight. She stopped ten feet from the opening. She stood quite still, her neck craned upwards, basking in the glow of the heavens, breathing in the cold night air in long, deep breaths. Her thin nightgown clung to her body in the slight breeze and she shivered, but she didn't seem to notice or care.

I dropped my pack and dug out the blanket from the snow lands. I draped it around her tiny frame, and only at the touch of my hands on her shoulders did she look away from the sky and at me.

"Thank you," she said. Any air of superiority had vanished. She looked at me with true appreciation.

I smiled, hoisting the pack onto my back again, and we both set off into the gully, led only by the moon.

CHAPTER TWENTY-ONE

Jade walked over the gully floor in silence. Her little feet may have not even touched the ground, but every time I looked behind me she was still there. It wasn't until we were through the great crack that led to the grassy plains, and the sun began to rise, that she spoke again.

"Here," she said. We had rounded the first corner after making it through the walls of rock that led from the gully to the plains, and the golden grass was laid out before us like a warm blanket over the earth.

I stopped and looked back to her. She was standing with both palms outstretched, and hovering in the air above them twirled the jade knife. It rotated slowly, and she closed her eyes and mumbled words I could not hear. The knife slowly came to a stop and pointed clearly in a single direction, as a compass would point due north. She opened her eyes and grasped it by the handle, tucking it into the folds of the blanket she wore. Then she held out her arm and gestured for me to head in the direction the knife had pointed.

"This way," she said.

I gaped at her.

"How did you do *that*?"

She just smiled and started walking in the direction the knife had pointed.

We set out in the early morning sun, skirting around the edges of the grass. The grasslands that surrounded our right side were now deserted. The horses were gone, and not a single bird hovered overhead. Aside from the waving of the tall blades in the breeze, the place was almost lifeless. It reminded me of the feeling I would get back on the farm when a summer storm was brewing. The grass would blow in the gusts of wind, and the critters that remained would retreat to their shelters to wait out the storm. Far away on the horizon, I saw storm clouds gathering. We would have to find shelter before the rains came.

As we walked, Jade hummed merrily, like a little girl with an unexpected day off school. Her long, white-blond hair bounced behind her as she skipped over the rocks. She was strange. She had lived for hundreds of years, and yet so many of her childlike qualities remained. She let the blanket fall from her shoulders and the breeze ruffled through her nightgown. I hadn't realized it until now, but all these hours she had been walking with no shoes.

"Jade," I said, "aren't your feet hurting?" She had walked over all variety of rocks, sharp and jagged, smooth and round, without a single complaint.

She laughed. "No," she said. "Among stones I am safe. We exist alongside one another. It is not possible for us to bring pain to the other."

"But rocks can't feel pain," I protested. "They're rocks."

She chuckled. "As I said, you know very little about this place."

She bent over and scooped up a handful of pebbles. Then, blowing on the little mound in her hands, the rocks began to swirl in the air above her head. It wasn't like the way Cadoc manipulated smoke; that was ominous and frightening. What Jade did with the rocks was more like a dance. As she moved, the stones moved, flocking together like a group of birds flying across the sky. She twirled them up, up, up, until she finally held out her hand again and they all plinked delicately into it.

I had to make a real effort to close my open mouth. We continued walking.

"If you can move rocks like that, why didn't you just move the mountain right off you?" I asked.

Her face fell. I immediately felt ashamed for having brought up that place now that she was finally free of it, and clearly enjoying herself so much.

"I'm sorry," I began. " I didn't think."

"It's alright," she said quietly. "You have questions. I understand that. The answer is that not even I can move a mountain."

We walked for the entire afternoon, skirting around the exterior edge of the mountain. The wind that had started off as a gentle breeze had gradually grown into a full gale. Finally, as the sun disappeared behind the wall of clouds, we stopped for the night. I found a tiny cave to use as shelter. The food was completely gone except for just a couple bites of meat for each of us and some old, stale bread.

"I'm sorry I can't offer you something better," I said to Jade.

"No matter," she replied. "Food is only a bare necessity to sustain me. I have what I need to continue on." She clutched the jade dagger close to her body.

Outside, raindrops began pelting the rocky soil.

"Rain!" she said, and jumped to her feet and out of the protection of the narrow overhang.

"Wait!" I yelled. "What are you doing? Don't go out—" My

words were cut short by the broad smile on her face. She stood with her face raised to the charcoal-gray clouds, the raindrops landing harmlessly on her skin.

"Ah," she said. "It has been so long since I felt the rain on my cheeks."

I didn't understand. "Doesn't it hurt?" I asked.

"Hurt?" She looked back at me, perplexed. "Why would rain hurt?"

Then I understood. Carefully, I stretched out my palm and allowed a single drop of rain to fall into it before snatching it back into the safety of the cave. It didn't burn. It didn't irritate the flesh. It merely sat in my hand, an innocent drop. I got to my feet and cautiously stepped out into the downpour.

On Earth, when the rains did come, they fell first through the layer of pollution that blanketed the planet. But here, here the air was still clean.

The first few drops made me cringe and flinch, but a moment later I realized that the rain was just water. A lifetime of fear evaporated in the span of only a few moments.

I smiled and joined her, the cool shower washing away the heat of the day from my hair. She surprised me when her tiny hand slipped into mine.

"Thank you so much," she said. "I never thought I would ever feel anything but darkness again."

I shrugged, still grinning despite myself, amazed at the simple joy of standing in the rain. "Anytime."

Later, once we were both fully soaked and had had our fill, we both retreated into the small cave. Jade gathered an armful of baseball-sized stones and placed them in a pile at our feet. She held her hands above the rocks, humming a strange tune, and they began glowing a bright orange. In minutes the little space was as warm as we ever could have hoped for.

"What's it like?" she asked me, gnawing on the last small bit of chicken. "On Earth?"

I stared at the rocks, which glowed like hot embers from a wood fire.

"It's…different. Really different than here," I said. "The rain is poison and not much grows. And there's no magic."

She sat up. "No magic?"

I laughed. "No. On Earth, we do everything the hard way." I didn't hold her gaze, dropping my eyes back to the rocks.

"Is it sick?" she asked. "Father said it was. He said that's why Brendan shouldn't go. He said it was hopeless. Too late."

I thought about Grandma's barren fields. About the growing towers in the big cities, the only place our food could grow protected from the stinging rain. And about my father. My poor, mad father.

"Yes."

"Then why do you want to go back?" she asked.

"It's my home," I said. "It being ruined doesn't change that."

She nodded. "I don't know what awaits me. But I want to go, anyways. It can't be worse than that cave."

No, it couldn't.

When the rain finally died, she crawled back out of the cave and sat on the rocks just outside the entrance.

"Aren't you sleeping inside?" I asked her.

"No," she said dreamily as she lay back onto the dirt. "I think I've spent enough time in caves to last me…a lifetime."

As we both lay back, a nearly full moon rose over the grass. I watched her gazing up at the sky. Then slowly her eyes closed and she drifted off into sleep.

My eyes did not close. I lay awake for what felt like hours listening to the gusts of the wind on the other side of the shallow cave. Jade was outside, but somewhat sheltered behind the little hill that was formed where cave was dug into, so her hair fluttered only occasionally in the wisps of air that curled around the sides of the rock. The sound of the wind as it increased from a gust to a howl did not rouse her. But I could hear what was going on out there, and sleep didn't find me.

This was no good. I needed to sleep. It had been nearly two full days since I had rested. But with each whistle of the wind, I found myself more and more awake.

The stars above twinkled as brightly, though the wind continued. Something about this wind didn't sit right with me. As the night wore on, it gradually changed, its tone speaking to me in a language I couldn't understand. The more I listened, the more garbled the message became. But the brief joy I had shared with this weird little girl was soon gone, replaced by a dread I didn't yet have a name for.

Eventually I, too, succumbed to sleep. When I finally awoke, it was not due to the sound of more wind, but instead the total silence. Sometime while I slept, the powerful gusts had vanished completely. I stood up from the sheltered mouth of the cave and took in the landscape. Not a single blade of grass seemed to move in the still air.

At first I was worried by Jade's absence from the campsite, but I quickly found her once I climbed up on the mound atop my shelter. She was standing on the edge of where the grasslands met the rocks, staring out across the motionless plains.

I walked up behind her, looking over her shoulder at the view.

"This quiet concerns me," she said, unsurprised by my approach.

"Yeah," I agreed.

"For a land to abandon all of its natural ways, and with such suddenness..." she turned, facing me, and then started to walk back to the camp. "We must use extreme caution from here."

I turned and followed her. "What do you think it is?"

She looked at her feet as she walked.

"Nothing good," she replied.

Jade did the trick with the knife again, and soon we were on our way, this time veering slightly to the left and back into the low hills that surrounded the mountains. After no more than an hour or two of walking this way, we caught our first glimpse of the ocean. The slight scent of salt was in the air, though no wind could be felt here, either. The stillness made me uneasy after such howling winds the night before. Usually the world, even Earth, is full of sounds, birds chirping, bugs creeping, but here there was absolutely nothing. Still, the sight of the ocean buoyed my hopes. At least we were headed in the right direction.

The overwhelming quiet changed the closer we go to the ocean, until finally I could recognize an actual sound that wasn't the stomping of my boots on the ground. When we reached the cliff that separated the land from the sea, the dull roar of the waves far below was audible, though still quieter than I expected. The lack of wind had an effect on the waves as well, and they were muted as they softly licked the shores of the beach.

The closer we got to the ocean, the brighter the knife became. Jade would stop every hour or so and redirect our route. Soon we were climbing over the jagged rocks that lined the cliff, eventually descending on a narrow path down the face of the granite that carved the barrier between island and air.

Jade, in the lead now, soon halted our progress. Over the past twenty four hours or so she had become quite agile compared to the weakened state I had found her in, and her excitement over finding the link was palpable. She turned back to me.

"I think this is it," she whispered. "We must be incredibly quiet. If the cave is not deserted, then we will surely be roasted."

I stared at her blankly. "What do you mean, *roasted*?" I asked.

Her eyes shifted away from mine, looking suspicious.

"Jade, where are we?"

"We are in a place where beasts once dwelled," she said softly, "but it is my belief, and hope, that they no longer do so."

I felt a familiar twinge of nerves in my stomach, and a hot knot of anger rose up in my throat. "What sort of beasts are you talking about?" I asked through gritted teeth.

She looked out over the ocean as she spoke the words that brought terror into my heart. "This was once the lair of a dragon."

"*What?*" I exclaimed, more loudly than I had meant to.

"Be quiet!" she hissed, looking back at me sharply. Then she peered around the edge of the cave entrance, looking for signs of trouble. She turned back to me. "It is almost certainly deserted," she said.

"If it's deserted, then why do we need to be so careful?" I challenged.

"Because dragons can live hundreds, sometimes thousands of

years. The legend was that he was long gone, but it would be prudent to still exercise a little caution. Don't you agree?"

"I do agree," I snarled, "but it would have been nice to know what I was getting into before you led me to the edge of a giant cliff before telling me!"

"You would have never come," she mumbled, her eyes casting downward. "People who are older than children, or who *think* they are older than children, seldom listen to their advice."

She had me there. How many times had I tried to explain to my own mother that I was healthy enough to lead a normal life? Even here in the Fold, where I had powers beyond the average person, I was still thought of and treated like a young child.

"Look," I said, "I'm a kid, too, in case you haven't noticed. And if we're going to be doing dangerous stuff you need to tell me ahead of time, alright?"

She nodded.

"So what's the plan?" I asked.

Looking a little more hopeful now at the change in my tone, she breathed, "We will go in as quietly as possible. You will watch the mouth of the cave, and I will go to where the rocks are piled. Father told me that the dragon who lived in this mountain was rumored to be a hoarder of minerals as well as treasure, so it is believed that a wealth of Maylin history is buried in this chamber. I will find the rocks I need, there are only two, and when I come back out we will flee to find a safe place where I can work with them."

"What will the rocks do?" I asked.

"They will break free the link, and then we can leave this place."

"Sounds simple enough," I said.

She smiled. "It may or may not be simple, but if things go as planned then we will escape this strange change in the weather tonight."

The real possibility of returning home struck me at that moment, and I felt hopeful that she was right. Maybe, with Jade at my side, Almara was just a jump or two away. Maybe he hadn't gone far at all, not wanting to leave his daughter too far behind.

"Let's go," I said, feeling renewed energy. I was ready to go home.

We crept around the edge of the cave opening. Jade stopped, peering inside, a look of dread on her face as she inspected the enclosed space. I could hardly blame her. She took a deep breath and stepped over the threshold.

We found ourselves inside an wide, tall cave. The walls on all sides were burnt black from the fire of the beast that had once called this place home, and vicious cracks ran down the stone. The light of the sun, dropping low in the sky, opposite the cave combined with the light that emanated from the dagger was enough for us to make our way inside without disturbing anything. Silently we crept farther in.

Suddenly, a gust of smoky wind blew at us from deep inside the cave; it was so unexpected that it made the hairs on the back of my neck stand on end. I spun around searching for the threat, certain that my worst fears would be realized, but no danger revealed itself.

"I think we should change the plan. Let's stay together," I said in her ear in my lowest whisper. She nodded silently.

As we moved deeper into the cave the wind coming from within it increased until we were both squinting our eyes to protect them from getting filled with dust.

"What's happening?" I hissed to her.

"I don't know," she cried.

We pressed on and finally reached the far wall of the cave. Through the strange interior gale we saw giant mounds of silver treasure, and to one side a large pile of every sort of rock imaginable. I quickly knelt by the pile and began digging through the rocks.

"What do they look like?" I shouted to her over the noise of the wind.

"Stand back!" she yelled.

She raised her arms and I moved away from the rocks just in time. The entire pile of stones lifted into the air and slowly began swirling around like a debris field around a young planet. Two stones moved toward Jade amidst the chaos of the others. One was a ruby, the size of an apple, and it landed firmly in her right hand. The other, a small, shiny stone as black as coal, landed in her left. Slowly she released her hold on the cloud of rocks, and it gently came to rest again on the cave floor.

Jade's face was exhilarated. A sheen of sweat covered her forehead, and a deep flush of effort colored her cheeks. She smiled an big, satisfied smile.

"This place is amazing!" she exclaimed. She held out the two stones for me to see, and I moved closer.

But her precious rocks were soon forgotten. Hovering in midair where the swirl of stone had been a moment before, was an ancient piece of folded parchment.

"Look!" I pushed past her and took the page from the air. As I unfolded it, Almara's symbol shined up into both our faces. "It's a letter!" We peered over the page and read.

"Oh! Father!" Jade whispered at the sight of the familiar script.

* * *

Dear Brendan,

If you have found this letter it can only mean that you have succeeded in freeing your dear sister. For this I thank you, truly. She is the key to everything.

I do hope you have fared better than we on your journey, for the party here has been decimated by the dangers of our quest. Foramar was lost to the wild cats of Rohana, Jamisor to the beast in the bit of Borastar, and Yirsa and Tristan to the dragon that called this cave where you now stand home. Samael, Seto and Sazar have fallen to the darkness.

I am the only one left.

So soon on our journey and already such hardship and loss. I fear that we will fail, but I will not quit. The book is out there, we just have to find it. My trust in the ancients is unwavering.

I move on now, alone. Follow me with this link. I will search the caves of Lilit next, as we decided, and then move on to explore Daromir. After that I will return home and await you and Jade. My strength, it is not what it was a year ago. I feel my heart falling with so much death and despair. I return home to fight the loss of hope. Perhaps, once we are together again, we will prevail.

Be safe.

Father

As we both studied the letter, something scratched at the back of my brain. I couldn't figure it out, but something was different. Was it Jade? Had she changed somehow with the proximity of so many powerful stones? Or was it this letter? It was an undeniable link to her past, as well as to her future. Maybe it was her breathing, which was coming hard and strong. Or maybe it was another sound I was responding to, or a lack of sound. I suddenly realized that all the wind that had been howling through the cave had totally ceased.

It was then that he spoke.

"You are fools…" his deep voice drawled, enjoying the pronouncement.

We both pivoted on the spot.

There, smoke swirling around him, stood Cadoc, the man of our nightmares, both in waking and in sleep.

CHAPTER TWENTY-TWO

He sprang upon us so quickly that we wouldn't have had time to run even if we had thought to. In a flash Jade's arms were encased in his enormous hands, and he raised her off the ground and shook her back and forth. The stones in her hands fell to the floor under the force of his grip. Her eyes were wide with horror, glazed with the terror of facing her captor. I stuffed the letter into my pocket.

"HA!" he roared at her, flecks of spit showering her face. "You thought you could run from me?" He shook and shook her, and her head bobbed back and forth violently. "You are mine, girl." He pulled her body close to his, sliding his finger down the side of her face from ear to chin. He gazed at her possessively, almost lovingly, and then he relaxed his grip.

The jade knife, the last thing she had managed to hold onto, glowed brightly with a pulse of power. But too late. Finally overwhelmed, she dropped it to the floor and lay lifeless in his arms.

"What did you do to her?" I bellowed at him.

He dropped her to the ground like a bundle of rags, turning on me next.

"And *you*," he spat, approaching me in the fading light.

I stood helpless, searching everywhere for an escape. But I was completely trapped. He stood in front of the only exit from the lair.

"What do you want with me?" I asked, much more bravely than I felt. My eyes darted back and forth from him to Jade's form on the cave floor.

He reached me in three long strides, towering over me and bending at the waist until his eyes were level with mine. I could smell his rotting breath and see the tiny droplets of sweat on his face and neck as he addressed me.

"What do I want with *you*?" he breathed into my face.

He smirked, his eyes full of madness. I flinched with each syllable he spoke.

"You thought you were so clever, didn't you? You thought that releasing my captives would, what, somehow defeat me? Well, your friends are all mine again, locked up below my city where they belong. And what I want with you *now* is simple, boy." His lips curled upward in a snarling smile.

I stared at him in shock, trying to make sense of his words.

And then he hit me. Pain like nothing I could remember feeling suddenly blazed across the left side of my face and echoed off the insides of my skull. He had backhanded me, his fingers covered with jagged rings that cut my skin as his fist met my cheek. Wet with blood, I fell to the ground, hitting my head against the stone. The world became a blur as Cadoc flipped me on my back and hovered over me. His lips moved and I could hear muffled sounds coming from him, but I couldn't rouse myself from the force of the blow. He was yelling at me now, his face so close to my own, but I couldn't concentrate on him, on the imminent threat of him, surely preparing to kill me.

I thought only of my friends. Owyn. Kiron. Chapman. All his again. Locked up forever. And now Jade, crumpled on the floor.

NO.

He couldn't have them back. They were free now. I had made them so. Anger filled my entire being as I searched through my haze for a way to hurt him, to lash out.

My eyes caught a glint of gold hanging below his neck. Dangling over his chest, the trinket twisted on its chain, catching the little remaining light that came through the cave opening. As he raged on, his words still muffled to my ears, I realized I had seen it before, in Stonemore when I had last been in his clutches. Only now I understood its immense value. The tiny amount of gold contained in that single piece of jewelry would be enough to make a hundred men rich beyond their wildest dreams in this place.

The pendant was the size of a walnut and round, and on the face of it was carved a six-sided star. As he shouted at me it twisted with his movements, and I saw, undeniably, Almara's symbol scratched into the other side.

NO.

Nothing with Almara's symbol belonged to this man, if he even was still a man. And no one who followed Almara belonged to him either. That symbol represented *me*. *My* family. *My* people.

I focused my blurry brain as hard as I could on the necklace, and right as he began to stand, I shot out my hand and grasped the pendant. As he moved upright the chain snapped and fell into my palm.

Shock and fury outlined every inch of his face. He came down hard on me, but I rolled out from his under his massive weight, crawling towards Jade. If I could just get to her, maybe if I gripped her as I gave the command then we would be able make the jump together. Hadn't it almost happened once with Cadoc? And he hadn't even been touching me. It was the only chance we had to escape.

I was fighting, hard, to live. My attention was entirely focused on reaching Jade. But when I felt his iron fingers close around my ankle I became wild. He squeezed my ankle so hard I thought it would break, and then dragged me backwards across the floor to him, my hands hopelessly reaching out for the broken girl in front of me. I thrashed around, trying to escape, but his grip held me fast, trapping me. He flipped me onto my back with his enormous hands, and when I dared glance up at him an unmistakable look of joy shadowed his face. Raising his foot high into the air above, he brought down his boot with the full force of his body and struck me on the chest.

I both felt and heard my ribs crack, and for a moment my insides seemed to be mixed up; ribs jostled with my heart and lungs, each searching for their proper place in my chest. Then I found my voice and let out a wail of agony. Suddenly everything was perfectly, vividly clear. Each tiny sound in the cave registered clearly in my ears; Cadoc's panting, Jade's quiet, ragged breathing, my own gurgling attempts to keep air coming into my lungs. After the first shock of the blow, the pain faded, feeling far away now as the rest of the cave came back into focus.

Cadoc grimaced at me, a knowing look on his face. His work with me was done. I was dead, or would be soon. He moved away, back over to Jade, releasing me, not even bothering to collect the gold chain that was still in my fist. I was free of his grip, but the damage to my body kept me pinned down to the floor.

As he walked away from me, my brain urged my body to act, to help her. I remembered her face, smiling as it lifted to the falling rain. She deserved to live, to be free of the misery he had laid on her. But I lay there, broken. He murmured to her in a sickening hiss as he approached her limp form. I watched helplessly through the gasps of my blood-filled lungs.

"Princess," he cooed, "why did you do this? You know you belong to me. Your power keeps us both alive and strong. Were you meaning to kill me, little darling?"

"Don't do this," I croaked. "She was Amelia's friend. Don't do this."

He turned and stared at me. Perhaps it had been two hundred years since he had heard her name.

"You're sick," I choked. "That's all this is. You're sick and we can make you better. You can come back and be the man you were, Zarich." It was a lie. If Jade's elixir hadn't helped Amelia, I doubted it could help someone as far gone as Cadoc. But I was determined to keep him away from her.

My heartbeat was erratic. From moment to moment the pounding of it changed in my ears, sometimes too many beats at once, sometimes several seconds between each one. My fingers and toes became cold, and tears rolled down my face. I could feel warm blood trickling out of the side of my mouth. Slowly, painfully, I lifted my knees off the floor and pushed myself closer to Jade with the heels of my boots.

Cadoc's face changed from shock to hatred.

"You dare speak to me of Amelia," he spat. "Precious Amelia. It was *his* fault. *He* killed her. *Almara.*"

"She wouldn't have wanted this for her friend," I said. "You *know* that. You must release her."

Cadoc looked down at Jade, and carefully picked her up from the floor.

"No," he hissed, possessed by the sickness that held him. He breathed into her ear. "She is...*mine*." His body shuddered involuntarily as a strange spasm shook his muscles.

Jade's arms hung limply at her sides. She began to whimper in fear or pain, her eyes still closed, like a child in the clutches of a nightmare.

My breathing came in gasps as he held her, as if I were under a heavy weight and was having the air squeezed out of me. As I watched the scene playing out in front of me, my heartbeat quickened with fear for her, and then quieted and slowed as my blood drained away. I pushed against my heels again and was two feet closer to them. My hand reached out and grabbed the burning, glowing dagger. Cadoc didn't see the light, he only saw his prize, now secured firmly in his clutches.

"Your friend, I fear, is dead," he said in her ear, a wicked smile playing on his lips. All of his attention was on her, as if she and he were the only two people in the universe. I scooted closer as his large hands fastened around her neck.

I *was* dead. He was right about that. I didn't think that even a fine hospital back on Earth would have been able to save me now. But I wasn't going to let him kill her, too. I didn't need him anymore. I wasn't going home, not ever. I wasn't going to make it five more minutes, not on any planet.

But she still had a chance.

I stopped breathing, giving up on my own life and concentrating every piece of my being on saving hers. I didn't have enough strength left to raise my body off the floor, but that didn't mean I was done fighting. I hoisted my torso up on my elbow and drew back the knife. The heat from the handle seared into my palm, but I didn't care. I had my target in sight. For a flash I remembered the tree trunks back at Kiron's farm, and I focused now, as I had then, with everything I had left. I released the knife, hurling it with every last bit of energy I possessed.

Time slowed to almost a stop. As the blade turned through the air, each rotation brought a new revelation to my mind.

Almara is lost.

One way or another, to despair or to death. His letter, so full of misery, and the violence of his story, told me no hope remained that we would find him alive. He could not help us.

The knife spun along its trajectory.

There goes my chance.

I would never see home again. I would not survive my injuries. Even if I could, by some miracle, Cadoc would never send me back.

The blade caught a glint of the setting sun.

I am a hero.

How unlikely it was that I, just a sick kid from a place that had long since stopped believing in magic, would do something to change the lives of the people in these worlds. And yet I had. My whole life the odds had been stacked against me, but deep in the Fold I had managed to defy them.

The point of the knife split the fabric of Cadoc's shirt.

Goodbye.

Goodbye. Goodbye. The word echoed soundlessly in my brain.

Goodbye Jade.

Goodbye Mom.

The dagger stuck firm in Cadoc's side.

At first he looked at me with surprise, then mere irritation. He yanked the blade easily from his side and tossed it to the floor. I fell backwards to the ground again, knowing my life was over. My arms and legs were cold and more difficult to move with each passing moment, and my throat was choked shut with blood. I moved my head upward, trying to open my airway, to move the air in and out. I was sure now that my heart had been punctured by a rib, and I felt its beating sputter beneath my skin.

"You little piece of vermin," he spat as he approached me. He raised his foot over my skull and I braced for the final blow.

But it didn't come.

A tiny trail of thin, black smoke was seeping from the hole the knife had left. The smoke slowly reached up to his face, and when he finally became aware of it his eyes grew wide and he stumbled backward. His head jerked down, and he scrutinized his side, poking his fingers furiously at the pit the dagger had left. Not a drop of blood fell from his body, only smoke poured from the hole. Jade got to her feet, suddenly awake, and stepped aside, avoiding the smoke that hung in the air in front of Cadoc now.

Cadoc's fingers continued to work over the wound, and his face wore expressions of increasing panic, but there was no stopping the flow of evil that poured from his body. He fell backwards and slammed into the wall of the cave. Smoke now seeped from his nose, mouth and hands, giving him the appearance of being on fire without any flame.

"You have not won," he shouted to the cave, blinded by the smoke that flowed from his eye sockets. "Four brothers are we, joined by the Corentin. You have not won!"

Then he fell silent, unable to make any further sound through the inferno raging inside his body. His jaw hung open in a mute scream as the smoke left his body, which crumpled without it to hold him upright. His lips moved inaudibly, speaking a name only he could hear. He form was eaten away by the vacating vapor, just as a sandcastle might blow away in a strong wind. He melted against the cave floor, and then he was gone entirely, only a pile of black clothing remained where he had fallen.

I became aware of a jostling, and in the far reaches of my mind I could hear Jade's frantic voice as she shook my body. Her face hovered directly above mine as she spoke words that no longer held any logic or form to me, and the deep green eyes for which she was named pierced into my own. How pretty they were; wisps of green and black and the occasional fleck of orange entwined together in her irises, so deeply woven that they hinted at something much, much greater than this life.

I moved my own eyes back upwards and watched the ceiling of the cave. Nothing moved there, but a lightshow danced in front of my vision as my body approached death. First the colors were muted, flowing across my field of view as a fog would roll across a mountaintop. Then the hues changed, brightening as the wisps of light danced together. Pinpricks of white were born from the masses of color until I was staring at an expanse of twinkling lights, each not more than a pinprick in size.

My eyes met Jade's again. All around her the tiny white suns dazzled my eyes. Her gaze held mine as my heartbeat slowed. Beat after agonizing beat pumped the last bits of life into my body. I stared at those wide green eyes floating in a field of twinkling lights. Then the green began to fade, growing darker, disappearing. Finally those deep jade eyes dissolved completely into a sea of black, leaving me, alone, in a never-ending wilderness of stars.

CHAPTER TWENTY-THREE

I don't know how long I was truly gone for. Had I been dead? Asleep? These were answers I never received, not then or in the many years since. But I was gone, really gone. I floated in that cosmos of stars for what must have been years, decades, comforted in knowing my place among them, at home in the heavens. I did not think or speak or move, I just observed. I did not interact, I just *was*; a peaceful entity floating for centuries, millennia, on the fiery plains of the universe.

I came back to life, back to this place of awareness where one feels and breathes and stirs, slowly. First, before I experienced any other sensation, I became aware of gravity. Gradually my floating being became pinned down, wrestled into the submission that a body must tolerate in order to exist. I didn't like the weight of being held to a place, and at first I fought against it. But as time moved on I became aware of something else; myself. Specific memories did not float around in my brain, nor could I remember who or what I was. But a feeling of urgency began to creep in upon my peaceful existence, and I suddenly had a desire to move, to find consciousness.

When I first began to feel sensation on my skin I started to awake in earnest. Below me a soft, gravelly, warm substance nestled around my fingertips. Above, a gentle breeze stroked my cheek. I could feel air moving in and out of my lungs, though it was a movement I had no control over.

Next came sound. It began not from a muffled place, like I had experienced when Cadoc had crushed me into death, but simply a quiet one. The beating sounds of water and earth mingled with that of my beating heart, and soon joined together as one deafening roar in my ears.

And then my eyes. On another day, in another place, I would have been sad to see the stars around me disappear, extinguishing themselves in little pops until there was nothing left but black emptiness. But there was that sense of urgency I was feeling, and as I followed it, desperate to determine why it existed, I barely noticed the vanishing of the cosmos. Strange blotches of dark and then bright red swam beneath my eyelids. Then, finally, a white so bright that its sting pierced my eyes. Soon I could feel my own arm, shielding my face from a blinding sun overhead.

I was gasping. I rolled over onto my side and took in enormous gulps of air as if I had never tasted it before. My hands gripped the ground underneath me as I fought to fill my body with oxygen, and I found that the ground slipped right through my fingertips. I had been lying on sand.

As my breathing slowed I became aware of a pressure on my back, and when I looked up the first thing I saw was those green eyes, the ones that had faded from view so long ago, looking down at me with concern. Jade knelt on the beach next to me, her hand resting on my shirt, supporting my weight when I couldn't. As I slowly caught my breath, her face relaxed into a smile.

"I thought you were gone there for a while," she said.

I tried to speak. I *had* been gone. But when I opened my mouth I found it so dry that only a hoarse croak passed my lips.

"Don't try to talk yet," she said. "Here, have some of this." She held out a small stone cup filled with water.

Nothing in the world had ever tasted so good. The water soothed my throat and I quickly gulped the entire cup, wanting more. I sat up, determined to support my own weight, but I fell back to the soft sand.

"How—how long—" I tried to say, but she cut me off.

"Don't," she said. "You've been through a lot in the past few days. Best to let me tell you the story."

I gave a slight nod.

"After Cadoc...well...after he left, I thought you were going to die," she began. "In fact, I thought you *were* dead for a little while. He had all but broken you in two." I nodded, remembering the blazing pain of my cracked ribs tearing apart my insides.

"Well," she went on, "I panicked for a while. And after you stopped breathing I really thought there would be no hope. But as I began to accept that you were dead I sort of came back to myself. We were in a cave; a cave made of *granite.*"

I didn't understand what she meant, though she was surely talking about something that I should find significant.

"Granite is the stone that I've used for centuries to make the elixir of life," she said. "So, once I came to my senses again, I got to work. It wasn't easy, mind you. There was no light in the cave by that point, so I could only see by what little light I was able to conjure myself. But I made do, and eventually I was able to make the draft."

She paused here, and her eyes became glazed and unfocused as she looked over me and off into the distance. "It wasn't supposed to work. I knew that it wouldn't, in my heart. I had failed with it before. The elixir has only ever given life back to those on the brink of death, not to those who have already crossed over. And even then, not always. But I poured it down your throat anyways. Then I took up the pendant, grabbed tightly onto you, and brought us here."

"How did you get us—" I began.

"I told you to shush!" she retorted with a smile. "Here, drink more," and rolled me back onto my side and pushed another cup towards my face.

"When we landed here you were still as dead as any man I've ever seen," she said. "But I didn't give up hope. How could I? I determined to give you two weeks to respond before moving on. But after just two days and three nights you began breathing again. This brought me enormous joy, and I've been waiting close by your side ever since."

"How long since?" I croaked out, and she glanced at me with mild irritation.

"Three more days," she answered. "Today is the morning of our sixth day on the beach. I couldn't—" she hesitated. "I couldn't stay there in that place."

"No problem," I said hoarsely. I, myself, had seen enough of caves to last me a while.

She smiled at me, and a warm feeling of gratitude filled my chest. I lay back down on the sand, but my eyes still held hers. I stared into the eyes of a friend.

"Thank you," I said.

"You are quite welcome."

I slept then, but in an entirely different way from before. Images flashed across my vision now, and the strange dreams of a normal slumber filled my mind.

When I awoke it was late in the day, and I felt stronger than I had before meeting Cadoc in the cave. I sat up abruptly and looked around, my eyes finding Jade in the distance walking among the rocks on the far side of the beach. I got to my feet and set out along the soft sand in her direction.

I inspected the beach as I walked. Up above the rocky cliffs hung over us. Somewhere up there was the lair, the place of Cadoc's, and my, death. I guess that, technically, I was now a murderer. But it didn't feel that way. I had been defending Jade, for one thing, and was Cadoc even human anymore at the end? He had once been Zarich, but I doubted that any humanity could have survived inside that body, sharing the space with all that smoke. I looked down at my hand as I walked. Only the faintest outline of a long-healed burn mark was visible on my palm, the mark left by the jade dagger before it had left my grip.

The sand pushed up between my bare toes as I crossed the beach towards her. I had questions, but I didn't know if she, or anyone, would ever be able to answer them.

"Hi," I said when I was twenty feet from her. She was collecting stones into a small pile between a little grove of trees. She spun and smiled.

"Hello," she said. "You are up."

"Yes," I said. "I feel pretty good."

"That's not surprising," she replied. "The elixir of life is extremely powerful." She fell into step with me as I continued walking on the sand.

"Will I live for centuries now? Like you?" I asked.

"No, I doubt it," she laughed. "I only lived for centuries because I took the elixir for centuries. I suspect that now I will have a somewhat normal lifespan. Though I can tell you that people can sometimes continue on in their lives with slightly more vigor than before. You may find health where you once lacked it. And perhaps a few extra years may favor you."

We continued to walk in silence for a time. Jade fiddled with the long golden chain I had broken from Cadoc's neck, passing it back and forth between her hands. We slowed and found a place to stop.

"I don't understand something," I said as we both sat down in the sand. "Why did he die?"

She didn't answer me right away. We both looked out at the ocean as she thought.

"I do not know," she finally said. "Maybe the jadestone was able to destroy him because I was so close to it. Maybe you have a power I do not know of. It has puzzled me over these days of waiting for you."

I reached out and took the chain from her hands. Holding up the pendant, I flipped it over to see the carved symbol of Almara.

"What a treasure, don't you think?" she said.

"I guess," I said.

"You guess?" she said. "I never dreamed I would see so much gold in one place. The power in this pendant is enormous."

I looked at her, surprised. Was she messing with me? But her eyes met mine earnestly. I smiled.

"Jade, Cadoc said something while you were passed out, something that I didn't understand," I said. "He said Almara killed Amelia. What was he talking about?"

She tore her eyes away from the pendant and looked at me, and her brows knitted with confusion.

"I don't know," she said slowly. "Father didn't kill Amelia, she just died. And why would he? He is no murderer." She gazed out at the water as she said this, shaking her head slowly from side to side.

My eyes followed hers, and I stared at the glittering water.

"Well, he *was* insane," I said. "But I wonder why he said it." I glanced quickly over at her.

Suddenly, I realized that she had tears streaming down her face.

"What's wrong?" I asked, alarmed.

A sort of choking sound came from her throat and she buried her face in her hands.

"Jade? What's going on? Why are you crying?"

"I failed you," she wailed when she finally raised her head.

"What? What are you talking about?"

"I could not do it! I could not face him! It should have been I to kill Cadoc, not you! And you! You *died* because of my failure! It is only luck that has restored you to life. I am weak and undeserving of a friendship such as yours. I have disgraced myself, and in so doing both I and my family have failed you."

This was crazy! I laughed. I couldn't help it.

"Jade," I said, snickering, "you *are* my family."

She stopped for a moment, surprised by what I had said, and then she, too began to laugh. A few teary chuckles passed her lips and then she descended back into sobbing.

I didn't know what to do. I went for a stern, older-brother sort of tone.

"Look kid," I said, "I saved your life. And you saved mine.

We're square."

"I just couldn't—" she was hiccupping now, "I just couldn't face him. I am a coward."

I laughed at this, too.

"That is the single stupidest thing I've ever heard you say. And that's saying a lot, considering the list keeps on growing." She didn't stop crying. I let her carry on for a few minutes, and I put my arm around her shoulder until she settled down.

When both the sobbing and the hiccuping had finally ceased, I tried again, this time a little gentler.

"Nobody, not in a thousand years, could ever blame you for clamming up in front of someone like Cadoc. After what he did to you —" I broke off, not wanting to make her cry again. "Anybody would have been scared out of their wits, Jade. Anybody. In fact, I think you just might be the bravest person I've ever met."

She didn't look up at me, but her breathing slowed as she seemed to consider my words. Several long minutes later I spoke again.

"What will happen now?" I asked. Cadoc was dead. Almara was probably dead. And Kiron and the others, trapped in Stonemore.

"We will continue on," she said, lifting her head. A hard glint shined in her eyes. She had almost composed herself. "My father is out there. Somewhere."

"Jade, you know he might be—" I broke off, not having the heart to finish the sentence.

"I know," she said quietly. "That letter. There are many new questions. What did he mean by saying I was the key?" She shook her head. "We have to try to find him. Don't we?"

I nodded. Yes, of course we did. We had to try to find Almara, or at least to find out what happened to him. And what he had written in that letter was on my mind, too. What, exactly, had happened with my great great grandfather that resulted in him coming to Earth? I might never find out, but unless I tried I would wonder forever.

Then there was the issue of Kiron. Was he down in the dungeons, too? I told her what Cadoc had said about Stonemore and the prisoners.

Jade thought for a moment. "We try for Father first," she said. "Cadoc is gone. Perhaps the prisoners will be freed without him there to rule. But if not, and if we can find Father..."

Yes. If any chance really did exist that Almara was still alive, surely we would have much more success in a rescue mission to Stonemore with him than without him.

"Cadoc," I said. "When he was dying he spoke of others like him."

"Yes."

"Do you think they know about us? Do they know what has happened to their 'brother'?"

"I know not," she said. "Some types of magic are connected, as I am connected to the rocks and the earth. Some are independent, not attached to one another. Perhaps they do not yet know."

My skin was getting that tingly feeling again, the feeling of pent up energy. I stood up and stretched my arms above my head. Considering I had recently been dead, I was feeling pretty amazing. She stood, too, and together we started walking back to the makeshift camp she had arranged while I slept.

"Well," I said, "we'd better be off then, don't you think?"

"Let's wait," she said softly, "just long enough for the sun to set. I've really missed seeing the sun."

When we arrived back at the camp, she handed me the gold chain and then sat down in the sand, watching the sun slip beneath the ocean. Jade's face was warm with the last light of the day, and she dried the last of her tears with the sleeve of her ragged nightgown.

"We need to get you some better clothes," I said. This brought the first smile since the crying had started.

"Ok," she said, standing. "Are you ready?"

I slung the pack around my back and stood facing her.

"Ready," I smiled.

The little, impossibly old, impossibly young girl looked up into my eyes. She pulled Almara's letter from her sleeve, now uncrumpled and flat from days of her reading and rereading it. The link.

It struck me that we might not find Almara, or any trace of him, at all. The truth about what happened to him could be anywhere, lost in the maze of the Maylin Fold. We could be jumping into another snarled mess as we tried to find him.

But no matter. Whether here or on Earth, this was the only life I had. And every cell in my body was screaming at me to get moving.

"Time to go, *princess*," I said, lacing the last word with sarcasm.

She glared at me. There she was, finally back again.

"Aster Wood, you are a fool," she said coolly.

I laughed. "Ready for another adventure?" I asked.

In answer, she held out the letter again. I took it, and her hand, and held both up high above our heads.

The rocks around us burst away from the force of the link. Our insides were pulled and stretched as we leapt into the jump, our hands cemented together. I wondered where this jump would take us. Would we land in the center of a raging battle? Or find peace on an empty stretch of earth? Would the Corentin know where to look for us? Which planet lay on the other side of this link?

I looked over at Jade. My friend. My blood. Her eyes were shut tight, not seeing the whirl of color and light that spun us like a corkscrew through time and space. But I didn't close my own this time.

My eyes were open now.

Mother of two, horse enthusiast, and serial entrepreneur, J. B. Cantwell calls the San Francisco Bay Area home. In the Aster Wood series, she explores coming of age in an imperfect world, the effects of greed and violence on all, and the miraculous power that hope can have over the human spirit.

Aster Wood and the Book of Leveling is the next installment of the Aster Wood series, which follows the saga of a young man fighting to save the universe from the evil of the Corentin.

After failing to locate the celebrated sorcerer, Almara, Aster Wood has done the next best thing; he has found, and rescued, Almara's daughter, Jade. Now, the two are traveling through Maylin Fold together, still searching for the lost wizard. He is the one man who can answer their questions about why the planets within the Fold are dying, what it means for Earth, and how the evil can be stopped.

But when they finally find Almara, he's in no state to be of help to anyone. They must push on with him in tow and hope to find the little known Book of Leveling, an ancient tome said to hold the key to balancing the planets in the Fold. Little by little, tiny fragments of information leak from Almara's fractured mind, pushing them closer to their goal. Aster hopes that the discovery of the book will lead to not just the healing of worlds, but the healing of the people who inhabit them. Including the one person Aster has barely dared think of for the past eight years: his own father.

But a new enemy is waiting for them, watching every step that they take. The Corentin, a force of evil so great that few dare to pass along their knowledge of him, is examining their every move, playing with them like puppets on strings.

And Jade. Aster thought he had saved her for good, that the release from her mountain prison would be enough to bring her back from the misery she had experienced for so many years. But her happiness is fading, and in her eyes Aster sees flashes of a malice so deep that it chills him to his core.

Aster must make it to the book and wrench it from the cultches of the Corentin before it's too late. Before his friend, and her old, mad father, are lost to the Corentin's strange hold over them. And before he, himself, falls to the dark bed of madness the Corentin has waiting.

Turn the page to read an excerpt from *Aster Wood and the Book of Leveling.*

Excerpt from

Aster Wood and the Book of Leveling

by J. B. Cantwell

This was the worst idea Jade had had yet.

I was crumpled into a tight ball on the cabin bed, willing what was left of my dinner to stay in my acid-filled stomach, while the creaking, groaning ship swayed around me. With each cresting wave the wooden vessel rose up, tilting me dangerously close to the edge of the mattress, and then fell with a rush, crashing the boat down with sickening force.

Couldn't we have just walked?

The ship gave another jolt, and I buried my head in the pillow. Ugh! When would this rocking nightmare stop? I wished desperately for the end of the sea voyage, but I knew it was hopeless. It would be two more days before my feet would touch land again. Or so the sailors had told us.

The door to the tiny cabin creaked loudly on sea-salt rusted hinges. And then she was tugging at my arm, trying to peel me from the bed.

"Come on, Aster," Jade's voice reached for me through my foggy consciousness. "Don't be such a child. It will be better on deck."

"No," I moaned into the musty mattress. "Leave me alone."

"You need air, you fool," she said with a particularly sharp pull on my arm.

I snatched my hand away from her grip and rolled over. I wasn't ready to believe that relief lay anywhere but in the depths of this pillow.

"You're being an idiot," she said to my back. I had spent enough time with Jade over the past few months that I could easily imagine her face without looking around. She was the type of kid who wore a look or superiority to express almost every type of emotion. She shoved my shoulder. "Aster, get *up*."

I flung her tiny hands away and folded my body in half, warding her off, refusing to play.

She finally gave up, and her little feet stomped with all the ferocity she could manage against the wooden floor of the cabin. She banged the door on her way out and I clapped my hands to my ears miserably. The door missed its latch, and it squeaked back and forth on its hinges as it opened and closed with the rolling of the sea.

Jade had become, for all intents and purposes, like a little sister to me. I was driven to protect her, my companion and friend, from the evils that lurked in the worlds we traveled through. She looked at me for safety and stability, and I to her for experience and knowledge. She meant well, I was sure of that. And we had been through so, so much together, our battles fought side by side joining us in spirit. But along with our friendship came the rivalries and irritations all brothers and sisters have. Most days, she just made me nuts.

I had come to meet Jade after I discovered a long-hidden link that joined my home, Earth, to the planet Aerit. It seemed like years ago now since I had landed on the grassy knoll after my first jump, unexpectedly wrenched from my Grandmother's farmhouse attic and transplanted to another world. Suddenly arriving on a strange planet without any prior warning of the journey is enough to put gray hairs on anybody's head, even the head of a twelve-year-old, which I was. I had experienced many years' worth of terror and excitement since that first rainy afternoon.

But it had only been four months that I had been gone. Missing from Earth. Maybe presumed dead by now. At the thought, my stomach gave a lurch that had nothing to do with the moving ship.

When I arrived on Aerit I had learned that it was a planet within the Maylin Fold, a crease in the fabric of space that allowed travel between planets that would otherwise be too far apart to traverse. Earth lay on the outer reaches of the Fold, and it was due to its great distance from the others that I was unable to return to it. Yet.

I opened my eyes and glanced up at the small, thick glass set in the window frame above my bed. A handful of stars twinkled down at me for a moment before the movement of the ship swept them from my sight.

Somewhere out there was Almara.

Ever since I had left Earth I had spent most of my efforts trying to get back. The only way I would ever be able to see my family again was to find the lost sorcerer, the leader of the seers in the Triaden of planets within the Maylin Fold. It was Almara who had left a trail of links for me to follow. His son, Brendan, who also happened to be my great great grandfather, had left me the first link, the one I had found in the attic. But Almara had left all the rest, and I chased him through the cosmos, bouncing from planet to planet like a rubber ball, each time hoping that it was *this* time I would find the man who could send me home.

Unfortunately, my journey to find Almara had been frequently sidetracked by a variety of terrifying events, not the least of which was facing Cadoc, the twisted ruler of the city of Stonemore. Cadoc had been holding Jade prisoner for more than two hundred years, corrupted by an evil I still struggled to understand. On Earth, the thought of living that long would be seen as fantasy. But here, deep in the Fold, sorcerers and seers walked the lands, their magical powers keeping them alive long past the limits of the human life I knew. So while my great great grandfather had long since died, trapped on Earth, his three-hundred-year-old father was likely still alive.

And Jade, Almara's other child, was still alive, too. Jade, trapped in the body of a nine-year-old for the past two hundred years by a sadistic madman, was my distant relative.

It was three months past our brush with Cadoc, and since that time Jade's demeanor had changed. A lot. No longer was she the broken young girl Cadoc had buried deep in his mountain, torturing for centuries, using her own powers against her. Now, finally truly free of him, a spirit of adventure had taken hold of her, and her energy seemed boundless. She was focused, as a beam through a magnifying glass on a glaring day, on finding her father. And the bossiness that had been hinted at during our time in her cave dungeon had now reached full force. Honestly, it was quite a challenge keeping her in line.

But we wanted the same things. To find Almara. To find our individual paths home. If we were successful at discovering his whereabouts, I would have my ticket. And Jade would have her father. Though, her pace was so hurried, I frequently found myself forgetting all about home and simply trying to keep up with her.

But right now she was safely trapped on this wretched boat with me, and visions of home surfaced freely in my head. I tried to stifle the longing I felt for comfort, but all things comfortable came to mind in this cramped, smelly cabin. There were simply too many things I had to complain about, all of which were made worse by the boiling forces in my angry stomach.

This mattress for one thing. It carried the smell of a hundred sailors before me and was hard as a block of sidewalk pavement. The rough canvas cover of the pillow scratched at my sunburned cheeks as I rolled over and over, searching in vain for relief from my seasickness.

The food. I didn't know what, exactly, it was that I had been fed for dinner. All I knew was that it didn't taste so good going down, and was even worse upon its immediate reappearance. The men in the mess hall had definitely not appreciated my commentary on the meal. They sprang away from our table, disgusted and grumbling, their own appetites ruined by my presence. I doubted I would be welcomed to take meals with them again.

The stifling heat, still hanging in the air of this miserable, wooden cell, had been trapped down here since we had left the port of Kazalow on the planet Aria. What wouldn't I have given for the cool touch of my mother's hand against my hot cheek? For the comforting sound of Grandma's sitcoms on the TV set downstairs? Maybe even for the familiar feeling of tightness I so often felt in my chest back on Earth?

No, I take that back. That was something I definitely didn't miss about Earth. The heart defect I had been born with, the one that had haunted me my entire life, had seemingly vanished since I had arrived on Aerit. No matter how much I missed Earth, missed the broken, dying world I knew, I couldn't deny that the miraculous health I had enjoyed on these planets deeper in the Fold was something I did not want to give up.

I wondered, not for the first time, what would happen to my health if I ever managed to return home. Would I go back to being an invalid like before? Or would my now-strong heart stay with me wherever I went?

As the ship bucked, I pushed my mind to thoughts of green grass. And the crisp smell that came from a fresh, clean rain. On Earth, such things no longer existed, not really. Our planet had become barren and toxic, nothing like the wild lands of these other worlds I had traveled between. Now, the only green we saw back home was inside the vast growing towers that lined the perimeters of the cities most people lived in. It was the best, the easiest, way to survive. Tainted water was processed and food grown just blocks from where we slept in the glass sheathed monoliths that stretched up to the murky sky.

Those who chose to brave life farther out, like my grandmother, risked starvation and dehydration, just because they wanted a little room to breathe. But I understood why some took that risk. Now that I had spent some time walking these lands, still vibrant with life, I wasn't sure how I would handle life back on Earth.

Jade and I had last jumped to the planet Aria, her home planet, and on the other end of this sea lay the castle of her youth, Riverstone. She had bounced up and down like a five-year-old when we had finally made the hill and could see the marina below. It was all I could do to hold her back from running full-out to the nearest ship. Her caution had completely evaporated at the sight of the familiar port.

But she had been forgetting that her status here might not be what it once was. Jade had been a princess in these lands, daughter to the queen Morna. Morna ruled over Aria not for the joy of conquest, but as last in the royal line of magical blood. It had been many long years since the royalty here waged war or ruled in the traditional ways we from Earth might imagine. Instead she and the members of her court pledged their lives to helping the citizens of Aria, and those beyond. When the planets in the Fold had begun to deteriorate, Almara had stepped forward to aid in the search for a reason why the lands were dying, and why strange madness and incurable disease were ravaging the inhabitants.

Almara, a common, yet powerful, wizard, had come to love the beautiful queen, her formidable powers rivaling his own. They wed, and he moved himself and his tribe of seers to Riverstone. Soon, a son was born, Brendan Elgin Sawyer Wood, my own direct ancestor. Later, Jade Aednat Enda Wood joined the three. For a time, the family lived happily in Riverstone, working together as the children grew to find answers to the troubles that plagued the planets in the Fold.

Until, one day, Morna, herself, fell ill. Almara, Brendan, and Jade, each with their individual powers, tried in vain to save her. But their efforts were wasted, and it wasn't long before she succumbed to the foreign, unnatural sickness that had taken the lives of so many on Aria already.

It was then that Almara, heart broken and children motherless, had developed the plan to take the wizards who remained on his council and quest across the planets to find a way to end the destruction once and for all.

They disappeared. Stories of their travels were few, and all that anyone knew was that conditions had improved a few years after the quest had left Riverstone.

But all of that was a long, long time ago. We had no idea what life was like on Aria now, or what may have happened during the time since.

So I had insisted on caution as we made our way down that hill and into the port village. After a day of watching the ships from a distance, quietly asking around about their destinations, Jade chose one to take our chances on. I had decided to let her take the lead, here on her home planet, sure that she would recognize the best ways to get what we needed. Upon seeing the sailors of the chosen ship up close, however, I was somewhat alarmed.

"Jade," I hissed behind her as she approached the men on the dock, "I don't think this is a good idea. Can't we just, I don't know, find our own boat? I don't like the looks of these men." Up ahead a group of enormous brutes shuffled goods onto the ship.

"It's this one that will be going by Riverstone," she said. She gazed up at the hull and a shadow of concern crossed her face. "I was surprised that none of the others were going in that direction, actually. Riverstone was a center of trade when I was a child." Her eyes remained unfocused for another moment, but then fell from the ship and met mine. "Besides, any boat that you and I could handle alone would be swallowed up by the sea on our first night out. We need to travel by ship." She walked away towards the men.

I watched her go, so confident now compared to the child I had first met. Her worn nightgown from the caves had long since been replaced with rugged traveling clothes, pants and long sleeves. On her belt her powerful jade knife stuck into its sheath. Her fingers rested on her upper thigh as she walked, ready to grasp the handle of the blade with the slightest provocation. If it weren't for her long, white-blond hair she would have looked just like a teenage boy, too small to be mistaken for a man, but too bold to be treated as a child.

I looked up at the wooden craft doubtfully as Jade strode away. From the bow that towered over our heads, a skull carved into the wood stared menacingly down.

"Does it have to be the one with the skull?" I mumbled under my breath. I glanced around. Other ships lined the port, and none of them had skulls. Smartly outfitted and with slim young men working on their docks, they seemed like much friendlier options.

Jade returned, impatient at my delay, and grabbed my arm, dragging me along towards the death ship. As I peered back and forth over our shoulders, on the lookout for attack, she struck a deal with the largest of the men on the dock. She slid him a neat handful of silver coins and hopped onto the mounting plank without bothering to wait for his permission. I eyeballed him, and as he glared down at me from his towering height, his head slowly nodded once. I dashed up the plank after her.

It hadn't taken long for me to realize that I was not the seafaring type. Within ten minutes I was feeling dizzy from the tiny ripples of water that skirted under the boat in the harbor. By the time we set sail I was fully green. After the dinner fiasco I made my way down to our tiny room to ride out the rest of the trip in isolation.

But it was so hot. The sun had set many hours ago, but the heat from the day was still trapped down below. I considered that the men I had embarrassed myself in front of at dinner might have mostly retired for the night. A soft waft of salty air, just slightly less stifling than that in the cabin, came through the swinging door and teased my nose. Finally, I forced myself to sit up. When walking didn't seem possible, I settled for crawling from the bed to the door and out into the narrow hallway.

The ship knocked me from side to side as I scurried down the tiny corridor like a mouse. Then, from an opening above my head, cool night air gently blew down over me. I raised my head and closed my eyes, relieved at the fresh, sweet smell. A slim set of stairs, more a ladder than a proper staircase, snaked down the wall beneath the opening. I eagerly climbed out of the wooden tomb I had been holed up in.

I hated to admit it, but Jade had been right. The instant I heaved my miserable body out from the depths of the ship I began to feel better. The deck was all but deserted. One man sat at the controls of the ship, bare feet propped up on the wheel, tankard propped up on his stomach. He grinned a toothless grin at me and raised his ale in a drunken salute.

"Where's Jade?" I asked. He raised the mug in the direction of the bow and I nodded. Then he tilted his head back at a sharp angle and poured the remainder of the beer down his throat. His head remained back, his glassy eyes fixed on the stars above.

The night sky was moonless, and the heavens sparkled down on the ocean like glittering rain. Not wanting to lose face again, even in front of the nearly unconscious sailor, I stood upright, supporting myself on the edge of the ship, and began to walk unsteadily towards the front. Up ahead Jade's dim outline was cut against the dark sea beyond, her mane of hair flying out behind her. As I came closer I heard her humming, but the words I couldn't make out over the roar of the waves.

She turned at the sound of my footsteps, and her face broke into a wide smile.

"Ah! I told you you would feel better!" she said. "You do feel better, don't you?"

I smirked at her and nodded.

"Mmm, hmm," she said, and turned her gaze back out to the ocean.

"How much longer?" I asked.

"Two days. They've agreed to let us out on one of the lifeboats when we're near."

"You mean they're not even stopping at Riverstone?" I asked.

"No, it appears not," she said. If she tried to hide the worry on her face, it didn't work. Suddenly I understood her desire for speed, to get to Riverstone as quickly as possible. As I had been searching for Almara so that I could return home, she was returning home now, and hoping to find him already there. Maybe, with our arrival at Riverstone, our search for Almara would be over. And she would finally have her father back.

"How do you know these guys will take us where they say?" I asked.

"Because I know the way. Part of my education, before the rock lore became such an important piece of the puzzle, was navigation. Well, Aria navigation at least. I can read the stars from here as well as any map. I know where we are going."

I looked up at the blazing night sky. Where I saw an impenetrable mass of twinkling lights, Jade saw roadmaps, street signs. We were in her neighborhood, and it was the first time she had seen it in two hundred years.

"Does it still look the same?" I asked. I remembered visiting our old neighborhood back home once, the apartment block we had lived in before my dad left. Things had changed. Paint colors and traffic signals were different than I had remembered, and everything looked smaller than it once had.

"The stars don't change so much," she said. "Though here on the ground things are certainly different."

"We're not on the ground," I teased. Land was no longer visible at all from this far out in the ocean. Though I was having an easier time now up on deck, I still deeply regretted ever letting my feet leave its solid, stable footing.

"Oh, be quiet," she said. She stared blankly at the horizon before us. "The harbor wasn't the same. Things seemed different from how I remember. When I was a child, the town was friendly, lively even. It concerns me greatly, the lack of options we had to reach Riverstone."

Yes, I was concerned about that, too.

Months ago, when I first met Jade, I had been searching for the links Almara had left behind. Each time I found one I would use it to jump to the next location, and each jump would bring me closer to finding him. Together, Jade and I traveled for a time, and we had succeeded in finding several more of Almara's links.

But then our trail suddenly evaporated. The last link we found, which brought us from the forests on Aegis to the plains of Aria, had failed to give us any further guidance. Unlike the other links, no map had appeared, no driving heat or howl had shown us where to go. It had simply deposited us here on Aria, and no further instruction was revealed.

Not knowing where, exactly, to journey to find the next link, we chose to move on to the only place on Aeso we could think of where we might find it: Riverstone. It was a guess and a gamble. Almara had originally left these links for Brendan. Had he hoped that his son would know to find the next link in Riverstone, his home?

As the ship jerked up and down with the swells of the ocean, I let the spray mist across my face. In the distance the faintest glow of sunrise was beginning to light the horizon. It was hard to feel fearful about what awaited us in Riverstone just at the moment. I was too caught up in the relief I felt in this delicious, cool air. I leaned slightly over the railing, lifted my chin skyward and breathed long, slow breaths.

But my respite was short-lived. Before Jade could say another word, a shrill whistle pierced through the night. I guess that the few men up on deck weren't all so drunk as the driver of this great, lumbering boat. The lookouts high up in the sails had seen something, and several alarmed shouts echoed against the surface of the water.

I turned, staring around for the cause of the disturbance. No other ships revealed themselves. Land was still out of sight. I couldn't see any threat at all. What was the commotion about?

Someone next to me wasn't moving, and was, in fact, being much more silent than I usually found her. Jade's hands gripped the edge of the railing, her eyes wide and fixed on a point in the distance I could not see.

"What is it?" I asked, squinting in the same direction. She stayed silent, her mouth hanging slightly open. I searched and searched, but the darkness, still hanging on to the last hour of night, revealed little.

So dark, darker than before, I thought to myself. A moment ago, the moonless sky had still been bright with stars, the promise of sunrise teasing the horizon. But now it was as if half of those lights had gone out. Where had the stars gone? What had happened to the early morning light?

Then, with a sickening twist of my stomach, I suddenly understood. The stars hadn't gone out or moved or changed in any way at all. The sun hadn't sunk back down below the waves. The light was being obscured by something, something massive and black.

Water.

A great, enormous wave rose up ahead of the ship, much larger than anything we had voyaged over since coming aboard. Much larger, in fact, than any wave I had ever seen. And it was headed, fast, in our direction.

Please visit
www.jbcantwell.com
to learn about upcoming books in the Aster Wood series.

Made in the USA
Monee, IL
17 March 2020